MR - - '74

w 1/15

Welcome Back to Apple Grove

C.H. ADMIRAND

sourcebooks
casablanca

Published by Sourcebooks Casablanca, an imprint of Sourcebooks, Inc.
P.O. Box 4410, Naperville, Illinois 60567-4410
(630) 961-3900
FAX: (630) 961-2168
www.sourcebooks.com

Printed and bound in the United States of America
VP 10 9 8 7 6 5 4 3 2 1

This book is dedicated to two dear friends: Kimberly Rocha, founder of Book Obsessed Chicks Book Club and Colleen's Celtic Mavens; and to my author friend Tara Nina—thanks for saving me! Where would I be without you ladies?

Apple Grove, Ohio:
Population 597

Apple Grove has always boasted that it's a small town with big-town amenities. Some of the local hot spots are:

Honey's Hair Salon—Owned by Honey B. Harrington, who has weekly specials from cuts to coloring and likes to advertise the weekly special by changing her hair color every week.

The Apple Grove Diner—Owned by Peggy and Katie McCormack, featuring Peggy's pastries.

Bob's Gas and Gears—Owned by Robert Stuart, former stock car driver who doubles as the mechanic.

Murphy's Market—Owned by the lovely widow Mary Murphy (who has her eye on Joseph Mulcahy—and he has his on her), where you can buy anything from soup to nuts—the metal kind—but it's her free-range chickens that lay the best eggs in Licking County and have people driving for miles to buy them.

Trudi's Garden Center—Owned by eighty-year-old Trudi Philo, who likes to wear khaki jodhpurs and Wellingtons everywhere; she specializes in perennials and heirloom vegetables and flowers, and has been planting and caring for the flowers in the town square since she was in grade school, taking the job over from her grandmother Phoebe Philo when she passed the business on to her fifty years ago.

The Apple Grove Public Library—Run by Beatrice Wallace, the sheriff's sister—open three days a week!

The Knitting Room—A thriving Internet business run by Apple Grove resident Melanie Culpepper, who had to close up her shop when she became pregnant with twins.

Slater's Mill—Built circa 1850, this converted mill and historic site is a favorite among locals both young and old. Famous for its charcoal-broiled burgers and crispy fries served in the first-floor family restaurant, it's also been a favorite place for the younger set to congregate at the mile-long bar on the second floor.

A Taste of Home-Cooking from Apple Grove

Firehouse Chili

Serves 11 firefighters

This recipe is a huge time-saver! Using the store-bought salsa cuts down on the cooking time and lends a fabulous flavor to your chili. Garnish with sour cream and cheddar cheese and serve with a mixed green salad and corn muffins fresh out of the oven, and you'll satisfy even the hungriest of firefighters! ~ C.H.

> *8 pounds of chop meat (I always use 80% ground chuck...more fat = more flavor!)*
> *canola oil (for browning)*
> *4 large containers (48 oz. each.) of chunky salsa medium or hot (don't forget: as it cooks, the heat index of the salsa rises)*
> *2–3 cans pinto beans (great source of protein)*
> *toppings: sour cream and shredded cheddar cheese*
> *salad: mixed greens (your favorite)*
> *tomatoes (cherry if available)*
> *corn muffins (your favorite type)*

In a large nonstick Dutch oven, brown the chop meat in the canola oil over medium heat, stirring constantly to evenly brown the meat. *Note: Depending on how much fat there is, I may or may not drain the meat. If you do, you lose the flavor.

Add the chunky salsa, keeping an eye on the consistency,

careful not to add too much; there's nothing worse than a pot of thin chili, and you're going for robust here. Stir until blended throughout. Add the pinto beans, stirring constantly while heating to the boiling point. Once there, cover the pot and lower the heat to simmer for about 30 minutes, checking every 10 to 15 minutes to avoid burning. Speaking from experience, it is possible to burn food in a nonstick pan. LOL!

Serve topped with cheddar cheese and sour cream and serve with a mixed green salad and corn muffins warm from the oven.

Chapter 1

"GRACIE, PLEASE TELL ME YOU DIDN'T HAVE A GLASS OF wine before you picked up those scissors."

Grace Mulcahy stared down at her reflection. Why hadn't she just set the scissors down and stopped fiddling with what was left of her hair?

"How does it look?" Her phone was on speaker—good thing her friend Kate McCormack was back in Apple Grove, Ohio, and couldn't see her right now. When Grace didn't answer right away, Kate asked, "Well?"

Grace sighed. "I can always let it grow out."

Her friend groaned out loud. "Is it fixable or too short?"

Grace turned her head to the left and then back. "Fixable...probably...maybe—heck, I don't know!"

"Text Honey B. that you have a hair emergency."

"Not gonna happen. You know she's too busy juggling her kids and her business."

"True, but you know she'd want to help."

Grace sighed. Honey B. was her sister Meg's best friend—since forever. "It's not quite a disaster."

Kate laughed. "Honey B. makes her living fixing hair disasters. Remember that time we decided to go red?"

Grace chuckled. "Lord we shouldn't have used that Kool-Aid instead of real hair dye."

"Hey," Kate said. "It was way cheaper."

"True...but the results—"

"Were fixed by Honey B."

"I guess she did fix the Thompson twins when they

snuck away from the school gym and cut each other's hair for their school pictures."

"Mrs. Thompson was seriously PO'd."

Grace agreed. "I'll think about texting Honey B."

"Don't worry about it," Kate said. "I'll text her. You know she has a soft spot for all of the Mulcahy sisters."

"But I don't live in Apple Grove anymore—"

"What in the world does that have to do with anything?" Kate wanted to know. "We take care of our own. No matter how far away you travel, Gracie, you're still an Apple Grover."

Grace had another gulp of wine to cover the snort of laughter.

"Hah!" Kate said. "Made you laugh."

She admitted defeat. "OK, but seriously no one who lives back home calls themselves that."

"That's because they didn't think of it," Kate reminded her. "We did in second grade."

Grace wished she'd been able to convince Kate to move with her to Columbus. Maybe she should try to tempt her again. "We could get a two-bedroom apartment like we had when we roomed together at college, Kate. It'd be like old times."

"Except that I'd have to get up at three o'clock in the morning to get to the diner in time for work. You're not going to get me to move out there, Grace. Besides, there's too much work for Peggy to be opening by herself."

"You could find work here," Grace began, although she knew it was a moot point. Kate and her sister, Peggy, ran the Apple Grove Diner and had ever since their mom decided she was tired of getting up before dawn to make breakfast for the town and handed the reins of the business over to them.

Instead of arguing with her, as Grace expected, Kate said, "I'll text you the time for your appointment."

"Wait!" Grace began. Too late, her friend had already disconnected. "Great. Now the whole town is going to think I'm depressed...drinking wine while cutting my hair off."

But that wasn't the case. She was donating her hair to Love Locks. The shortest she'd ever gone was shoulder length—but chin length? It was drastic, but she'd wanted to make sure she had enough to donate and only had a yardstick to measure with.

"Yardsticks aren't flexible." That was one of the first lessons she'd had in measuring from her father—who ran Mulcahys, the family's handyman business, for years before finally retiring and letting Grace and her sisters take over. "Can't get an accurate measurement with one," her father had insisted.

Although she didn't have the talent to fix things the way her older sisters did, she was still a hands-on type of girl—hands on the computer, accounting software, filing cabinet, supply shelves. She did her part for the family business for years until she simply couldn't contain the need to follow her dream in the direction it pulled her... away from Apple Grove, Ohio, with its tiny population and close-knit community.

Grace dreamed of the bright lights and the big city. Well, not as big as New York City, but compared to her tiny hometown, Columbus was the big city—the largest in Ohio. She loved going to museums, fancy restaurants, and having coffee at the outdoor café by her office building—seriously upscale compared to the bench on the sidewalk outside of the Apple Grove Diner.

She longed for something different, to meet *someone*

different. *Suave and debonair.* But that reminded her of her ex, so she might have to rethink the suave part. Maybe she should think about a man with working-man's hands—broad and strong, able to fix anything—like her dad.

Of all the memories she'd stored up to take with her when she left, Grace wished she hadn't seen that split-second look of shock on her father's face when she'd finally told him she didn't want to live in Apple Grove. He'd been quick to cover it with a knowing smile, telling her she should go after her dreams, reminding her that she'd always be welcome to come back and visit. That look on his face now resided in the tiny corner of her mind alongside the last image she'd had of her mom in that hospital bed, battered, bruised, and broken from the accident.

Pushing those images aside, she focused on the positive changes she'd made in her life. In the year since she'd left her hometown, she'd landed a great job as an administrative assistant, working in a gorgeous office with all the latest technology. But the best part was that she wasn't the only one responsible for holding down the fort—she was one of over a hundred employees.

She liked living in Columbus, but sometimes, at night when she was lying there listening to the sounds of traffic instead of hoot owls, she felt the distance—depending on how long it had been between visits home, it was either a thank-God-I-left-town kind of way or a what-the-heck-was-I-thinking-to-leave kind of way. She'd hoped to cement her relationship with Ted by moving to Columbus—he wouldn't dream of living in a town without streetlights or traffic lights. Too bad she hadn't realized their disagreements went much deeper than that—a whole lot deeper. He was now her ex.

Grace didn't want to end her evening thinking of what might have been with Ted. So, she looked in the mirror and held up the ponytail she'd snipped off. "My hair is going to a great cause." She'd done her research.

Setting the bathroom to rights and putting the scissors back in the kitchen drawer—so she wouldn't be tempted to fiddle with the slightly uneven ends—Grace sat down at the kitchen table and fired up her laptop. She sent an email to Stacy at Love Locks and received an enthusiastic response almost immediately. Knowing that her donation would make such a difference in a little girl's life lifted her spirits. Helping someone in need always did—she'd learned that lesson as a kid growing up in the Mulcahy household.

Not everyone who needed repairs or fixer-upper jobs had the money to pay. That never stopped her dad from continuing the tradition her great-great-grandparents had begun of working for trade. Mr. Weatherbee made gorgeous wind chimes. Mrs. Winter baked the most delicious cherry pies. Sometimes when business at her garden center was slow, Miss Trudi Philo would send Cait or Meg home with a few pots overflowing with heavy blooms.

Cutting off her hair had been a bit drastic because she'd worn it long for years, but it was still in that time-honored tradition of helping others. After she sent off the email to Stacy, she decided to clean out her inbox. It took longer than she thought. By the time she finished, she felt the quiet surround her. She poured a second glass of wine and took it over to her favorite spot by the window: a comfy, overstuffed easy chair blooming with pink, cream, and green cabbage roses and ribbons. Setting her glass on the end table, she sank into the chair and relaxed. Curling her legs beneath her, she stared out the window and her thoughts drifted toward home. "I wonder what Cait's doing right now?"

The middle Mulcahy sister was probably sitting on the sofa with her feet up and a little black dog in her lap, while she leaned against her handsome husband—a second-generation small-town doctor taking care of the good people back home. Her last email from Cait had Grace worrying about her older sister's health, suspecting she was overdoing it to keep Meg and her father from arguing over hiring someone from outside the family—again.

She'd been there for the first argument and had been on the receiving end of her father's formidable Irish temper when they had been going at it over who to hire as Grace's replacement. It hadn't gone as she'd planned—at all. Pushing those thoughts aside, she let her mind drift back to Doc and Caitlin the last time she'd seen them, sitting on a bench in the Mulcahys' backyard, gazing into each other's eyes, so obviously in love that their happiness spilled over onto everyone around them.

Wonder when Cait and Doc will start a family...

Will I ever marry and have children?

She'd never really given marriage a thought until her oldest sister, Meg, got married. When Cait and Jack were falling in love, Grace had been focused on getting out of Apple Grove and pursuing a career in Columbus. There hadn't been a man in her own life since she'd broken it off with Ted, after catching him in a lip-lock with some-one else had ended their relationship. Some things could be worked through, but fidelity was not one of them.

There was an upside to breaking up with him; she

had plenty of time to work late and had earned a coveted promotion at work. Her phone chimed, bringing her back to the present. She picked it up and grinned. Kate's text read: Fri 8pm @ Honey B.'s. Be there!

She sipped her wine and thought about whether or not to answer. She decided she'd just let Kate assume she'd show up. Grace wondered what her friends would think when they saw her again. She'd gained fifteen pounds from sitting behind a desk at her dream job.

She got up and moved to her closet. Flipping through her clothes, she realized most of the clothes that fit her now were only for work—a boring assortment of black, beige, and gray. Add in a pair of black pumps and she might as well add a sign that said: *Grace Mulcahy—the invisible woman.*

When had she decided to remove color from her wardrobe? A tiny voice inside reminded her that it was after she'd gained the weight. It was past time to make some much-needed changes to her wardrobe, beginning with a pair of jeans. She'd have to make time to pick up a pair on her lunch hour. She hated the fact that she'd have to buy them two sizes larger than she was used to wearing, but she needed something for casual wear when she went home. "Damn, I should have rented the cheaper apartment. I could have afforded a gym membership." *Maybe it's time to reevaluate my priorities.*

She had to be ready to leave tomorrow right after work. Knowing Honey B. would be keeping the shop open after hours just for her, she didn't want to be late. She grabbed her overnight bag from the back of her closet and tossed in her spare pair of black heels, black wrap dress, and the clothes she'd set on the bed.

Her nephews, Danny and Joey, were bound to want

to play outside with a soccer ball—just like their daddy, Apple Grove's varsity soccer coach. "Maybe I should tell them I can't and stay inside and play with baby Deidre."

Their sad faces staring up at her filled her mind's eye. She sighed aloud. Her darling nephews were three and a half years old and a handful; it would probably be better to help tire them out outside and then play with their baby sister. *Definitely getting those jeans tomorrow.*

Once she was packed, she moved to the bathroom, where she'd lined up everything she'd need toiletry-wise for the next two days beside her large cosmetic bag. Satisfied that she'd thought of everything, she rifled through her TBR pile and packed three novels—just in case she couldn't convince Kate to go out with her—an eclectic choice to go with whatever mood she was in: inspirational romance, Western romance, or romantic suspense. On a whim, she tossed in a historical romance. "Never could resist a man in a kilt."

By the time she'd finished, she was exhausted and had nearly forgotten about her hair, until she moved to push it over her shoulders to braid it for the night—part of her nightly ritual for years. "Well, damn," she said. "Maybe I'll be used to it by tomorrow."

—∿∿—

Back in Apple Grove, her sister Meg was on a conference call with Honey B. and Kate. "So she just cut her hair off?" Meg couldn't believe it. "Does she sound depressed to you?"

Kate could hear Honey B. shushing her toddler, so she waited a moment before answering, "Yes, but I'm not sure if she's tired from working overtime or maybe homesick."

Honey B. spoke up. "When was the last time that girl went out on a date?"

Meg chuckled, and Kate huffed, "Not everything can be solved by having a man in your life."

Honey B.'s delighted laughter had Meg chiming in. "Spoken like someone who does *not* have a man in her life right now. I could talk to Mitch and ask him to talk to Deputy Jones. Maybe he could smooth things over between you two."

"I'm not speaking to Deputy Jones right now," Kate grumbled.

"Um, Honey B.," Meg said, "maybe you should ask that darling husband of yours first, before you go volunteering him for relationship duties. As the sheriff, he has enough to do, keeping the peace—and teenagers out of trouble—in Apple Grove."

"Don't you worry about Mitch," Honey B. drawled. "He'll do whatever I ask him to."

Meg chuckled and told her friend to quit bragging.

"Would you two quit kibitzing?" Kate hissed.

"So what really happened between you and that handsome deputy?" Honey B. wanted to know.

"I don't want to talk about him right now," Kate told her. "Besides, we need to focus on Grace right now."

"Kate's right," Meg said. "I think I'll send her a text, letting her know that we're having a barbecue on Saturday."

"Good idea," Kate said.

"Honey B., what do you think of Pat Garahan?"

"Great guy, broad shoulders, big hands, and a bigger heart."

"Soooo," Meg said, "what do you think, Kate?"

Kate was having a hard time following Meg's thought process. "About what?"

"Fixing him up with Grace."

"Oh." Kate tried to picture the former FDNY fire-fighter dating her friend. An image of the auburn-haired giant with the crooked smile and great personality seemed like a good fit. "Isn't he too busy now that his firehouse has had to cut back and lay off firefighters?"

"There are still enough guys on shift that everyone gets time off," Meg told her.

Kate wasn't sure about his job though. "Why him?"

Honey B. and Meg paused as if considering Kate's question. "As a friend of the family, he's usually at our family functions. He and Grace always seek one another out to talk to if they're thrown together. I think with a push in the right direction, they might discover that there are sparks there," Meg said. "Besides," she added, "we like him."

"But what about his job?"

"At least he has a job," Meg bit out.

"But it's dangerous!" Kate said.

"So is Mitch's, but I try not to let it keep me up nights." Honey B.'s voice was calm and soothing.

"OK, well then, what about Grace? Do you think she'll suspect that we're trying to set her up?"

"Not if we're sneaky enough," Meg replied. "I'll have Dan invite Pat to the barbecue on Saturday."

"What about getting your dad to invite him to Sunday dinner?" Honey B. asked.

"We don't want them to suspect anything by having Pop invite them Saturday and Sunday," Meg said. "We should probably maneuver them together a few week-ends in a row if we can swing it—spread it out a little."

"Hey," Honey B. said, "don't forget the guys play pickup soccer at least once a month."

"Perfect," Meg said. "I'll find out when the next game is and let you know. Maybe we can move the game to Dad's."

"Let me see if I have this straight," Kate said. "You're inviting Patrick to a barbecue this Saturday?"

"Yes," Meg and Honey B. said at the same time.

"Then a game and family dinner over the next few weekends?" Kate asked. "What makes you think Grace will want to come back so soon?"

Honey B.'s delighted laughter caught Kate off guard. "What's so funny?"

"Have you ever really looked at Patrick Garahan?" Meg answered. "The man is to-die-for handsome, and those shoulders of his…" Meg's voice trailed off.

"We're counting on his Irish charm to smooth the way," Honey B. said, "and get Grace to come home for a couple of weekends."

"What excuse will you use to get her home for the third weekend?" Kate wanted to know.

"I don't know yet. Hopefully, we won't need to think of anything. She'll be smitten with the man."

Kate laughed. "Smitten?"

"Grace fell in lust with Ted," Meg said softly. "My baby sister needs something deeper, something to look forward to. A man like Patrick is just what she needs."

"I hope you two know what you're doing," Kate mumbled. "I think Grace just needs time at home—not a man."

"Everybody needs a man, Kate," Honey B. drawled.

Meg and Honey B. were still laughing when Kate added, "We'd better hope that Grace doesn't find out."

"Did she say anything else?" Meg asked.

"Just that she was donating her hair to a charity that

makes human-hair wigs for little girls and teenagers who are fighting cancer and can't afford to purchase a wig."

"My baby sister always manages to surprise me," Meg whispered. "Honey B., I can't believe that I've never really thought about donating my hair. It's a great idea."

"Well, you've been busy raising your sisters and working for your father, and then Dan Eagan moved to town."

Meg laughed. "And that's when my life turned completely upside down, but I do love that man."

Kate interrupted, "So you're going to donate your hair too?"

"Absolutely," Meg said. "I braid it to keep it out of my way."

"You have for years," Honey B. added. "I like wearing mine just long enough to brush my shoulders. Gives your hair more bounce, more life."

"I'm going to call Cait and tell her about our new plans for Grace and let her know that I'm donating my hair too."

"I've always wanted to try a new hairstyle," Kate said.

"You mean other than a ponytail?" Honey B. asked.

Kate chuckled. "Yes, do you think I have enough hair to donate it?"

"Tell you what," Honey B. said. "Why don't you meet us at my shop tomorrow night at eight o'clock and we'll measure it then."

"Sounds great," Kate told her.

"Oh," Honey B. whispered. "I just had this amazing idea."

"What?" Kate asked.

"Honey B.," Meg said, "are you thinking what I'm thinking?"

Honey B. and Meg had been saying stuff like that to each other for as long as Kate could remember.

"I believe I am," Honey B. told her. "We'd better get busy spreading the word; I expect I'll have a long line of customers at the shop tomorrow."

"What are you two talking about?" Kate demanded.

"We're going to get as many people in town to donate hair as we can and make one large donation and let them know Grace gave us the idea."

"Honey B.," Meg said softly, "she'll be so surprised...and touched. Thank you."

Honey B. laughed. "Don't thank me yet. So far we have you, Kate, and possibly Caitlin donating hair—we need a lot more people!"

"OK," Meg said. "Let's divide and conquer. I'll call Miss Trudi—"

"I'll call Mrs. Winter," Honey B. said.

"And I'll tell my sister Peggy," Kate volunteered. "Between those three, the entire town will hear about Apple Grove's Love Locks cut-a-thon in an hour—tops!"

"God, I love this town." Meg sniffled. "Our neighbors and friends are always ready to lend a hand—or in this case their hair!"

"Me too," Honey B. and Kate said at the same time.

"I've got to call Grace," Kate said.

"Wait," Meg said. "I think it should be our surprise. It'll make Grace feel as if she's still a part of Apple Grove, and I have a feeling that might be just what she needs."

"Good call," Honey B. said.

"All right," Kate agreed. "I won't spill the beans. Do you think we should ask Rhonda to run a special edition of the *Apple Grove Gazette* online tonight?"

"I'm not sure," Meg said. "Grace might read it."

"All right then. I'll see you ladies tomorrow," Honey
B. reminded them.

"Night," Meg said.

"Talk to you later." Kate couldn't wait to see Grace
tomorrow night, but she didn't have time to think about
that now. She ran downstairs to tell her sister the news.

Chapter 2

PATRICK GARAHAN LOVED HIS FAMILY, BUT RIGHT NOW the oldest Garahan brother was giving him a headache. "Give it a rest, Tommy. I'm not interested in coming back to New York City to fight fires. I live in Newark, Ohio, now."

"Yeah," his brother said, "but you're a New Yorker at heart. You miss the city."

Pat sighed. It was true, he did, but that wasn't the only issue. "I like living out here." He thought of the friends he'd made and the great group of guys he fought fires with. "It's not New York, but it's home."

"Not buying it, Bro." After a long pause, his brother asked, "You coming for Ma's birthday?"

"Is Moira making the cake again?"

His brother laughed. "Not if Mike can sweet-talk her out of it."

Pat chuckled. Their brother Mike's fiancée was the light of his life and had passed the Garahan sticking test, but she couldn't boil water. The cake she'd baked for their mom's birthday last year was hard to forget—hard as a rock with super-sweet icing. "All right then," Pat told him. "I'll be there."

"Great! I'll tell everybody." His brother hesitated before adding, "You've got to stop blaming yourself for what happened—"

Not going there. "Gotta go. Talk to you soon." Pat disconnected and rubbed his temples. If he didn't take something for the pain now, it'd be a migraine in a few hours. He tossed his cell phone on the long kitchen table, poured a glass of water, and took a couple of pain relievers.

His phone vibrated across the table. Out of habit, he answered without checking the number. "Garahan."

"You up for a game of soccer in two weeks?"

Pat grinned. "I'm not sure how many guys I can round up, but we'll be there to whup your sorry ass. Next Saturday or Sunday work for you?"

"Yep," Dan said. "Not sure what day yet. I'm writing it on the kitchen calendar now, blocking out the weekend."

His friend paused and Pat could hear a muffled voice talking in the background. "Meg wanted me to remind you about the barbecue Saturday."

"At your house?"

He heard a muffled voice again and waited for Dan to get back on the line. "No, Meg said we're grilling at her dad's house."

He wondered why but would find out soon enough. "What time for the barbecue?" Pat asked.

"Come early. The boys can't wait to see you."

"So you're planning on feeding me two weekends in a row?" Pat joked.

"Not me. I'm leaving that up to Meg and Cait. And hey, if you don't feel like driving back and forth— because there will be beer—you can bunk on our sofa."

Pat laughed, remembering the last time he'd stayed overnight at the Eagans' house. He'd been the victim of a predawn surprise attack when Dan and Meg's twin boys jumped on top of him. "Let me think about it. If I do stay, tell and Danny and Joey if they promise not to wake me up before sunrise, I'll make pancakes for breakfast Sunday morning."

"They'll love it," Dan said. "Do you need to switch shifts with anyone to make it work?"

"No," Patrick said. "It's actually perfect timing. I'm just finishing a twenty-four at the firehouse and traded shifts with one of the guys who needed off next week, so I'll be free this weekend. See you Saturday."

"Cool. Oh, hey, Pat?"

"Yeah?"

"Mitch said to be prepared to lose."

Pat was laughing when he disconnected.

"Hey, Red!" his lieutenant called out, sticking his head in the kitchen. "What's for dinner?"

Pat grinned. It was hard not to when Big Jim Muldoon was in a good mood. "Firehouse chili."

"Oh man. Extra hot with corn bread?"

Pat shook his head. "Too many complaints about my chili from the guys last time, so I'm trying a new recipe. Don't worry—I've got a big bottle of hot sauce so you can add as much heat as you want."

His lieutenant seemed to be considering that option, and asked, "What about the corn bread?"

"Making corn muffins this time." He looked around the kitchen and shrugged. "I was supposed to have prep help, but Mike Snelling's MIA."

Big Jim straightened away from the door. "He's checking equipment. I'll send him up."

"Thanks." When the older man hesitated, staring at the big empty pot Pat was going to brown the meat in, Pat swallowed the chuckle, reassuring him, "Don't worry. You're gonna love it."

"Who gave you the recipe?"

"My brother Tommy."

"Family is the glue, Garahan," Muldoon told him. "Don't forget that."

Pat thought about it and slowly nodded. He didn't want to get into a lengthy conversation with his lieutenant about the family he'd left behind in New York. The brothers were tight, no matter the miles spreading between them. If there had been any way—*no*. He shook his head. *Don't think about New York or the Projects.* He hadn't had the nightmare in a few months, and he was handling things just fine without drinking.

"I'll spread the word," Muldoon said. "How soon till it's ready?"

Pat looked at the packages of meat he'd started to unwrap before his brother called. "Give me an hour."

"You've got a bunch of hungry guys waiting. Can you make it faster?"

"Sure." Patrick grinned. "Let me just scoop some raw chop meat on a platter and we'll be good to go."

"Smart-ass." His lieutenant was chuckling as he walked away.

Pat scrubbed his hands. While he added a little oil to the huge cast-iron Dutch oven, he let his mind wander. He loved his job—it was in his blood. His great-great-grandfather had started the family tradition just a few days off the boat from Ireland. Thomas Garahan had wanted to do something for the new country he'd adopted and fighting fires seemed like the perfect way to give back to his new home. Years later, the New York City Garahans were firefighters, cops, or carpenters.

While the meat browned, he stirred slowly, thinking of what his great-great-grandfather's life must have been like in those days. When the meat was cooked through, he opened a couple of jugs of salsa and dumped them into the pot.

He was stirring the mixture when a deep voice called out, "Oh yeah, Garahan's making chili!"

"'Bout time you showed up to help, Snelling."

His friend laughed. "I'm supposed to be setup, not cooking."

"Yeah, but you missed setup."

His friend shrugged. "The lieutenant needed me to do something for him. Not my fault. Put me on cleanup."

Pat shook his head. "Here." He handed Mike a bowl. "You make the muffins and I'll make the apple crisp."

"You know, Garahan," Mike said slowly, "if you move in with me, you can cook and I'd do all the cleaning—we could save money on rent."

Patrick laughed as he set out the ingredients and started measuring. "But you live like a slob."

"I can change."

Pat shook his head. "I doubt it. Hey, want to play soccer next weekend?"

"What time and where?"

"Not sure which day yet. But definitely noon in Apple Grove."

Mike nodded. "I'm there. Any chance one of the McCormack sisters showing up?"

"Which one?"

Mike shrugged. "Doesn't matter. They're both lookers and can cook."

They laughed and talked about the last game in Apple Grove.

"What do I set the timer for?"

"Fifteen minutes," Pat told him.

Snelling eyed the baking dishes filled with apples

and crumbly topping. "Do you have ice cream or heavy cream for the apple crisp?"

"That's what I like about you, Snelling," Pat said, "always thinking with your stomach."

The table was set and Mike was tossing the salad when the rest of the guys on their shift started to trickle in. Patrick loved the camaraderie and being in the heart of the firehouse—as with any home—its kitchen.

The guys were a rowdy bunch, but Pat loved the noise and the good-natured ribbing while everyone settled down to eat.

"Pass the hot sauce." Big Jim held out his hand, catching the bottle shoved down the length of the table in his direction.

Pat shuddered at the amount of hot sauce his lieutenant poured in his bowl of chili. "Did you at least taste it first?"

Muldoon shook his head and dug into his bowl. Blowing across the spoon, he grinned. "I am now." He chewed, swallowed, and took a big bite of corn muffin while his eyes teared up and his face turned red.

Pat and Mike laughed as Pat asked, "Hot enough?"

Big Jim wiped his eyes with the back of his sleeve, scooped up another mouthful, and agreed, "Uh-huh."

Static from the two-way radio on the table had everyone bracing. Muldoon grabbed the one he'd brought with him and answered. Before he finished speaking, the men were making a beeline for the stairs while the overhead alarm sounded. Pat double-checked that everything was turned off in the kitchen before following along behind.

He was the last one to the lockers, but it took only seconds to step into his boots and pull up his fireproof pants. He grabbed his hat off the top shelf and put it on his head as he ripped his turnout coat off the hook and ran toward the ladder truck that had the lights flashing, engine revving, and the men motioning for him to hurry.

Mike had grabbed Pat's oxygen mask and tanks, knowing that Pat, as the designated cook, needed to secure the kitchen and wouldn't have the time.

Pat nodded to Mike and asked, "What's up?"

Mike looked grim. "Fire in the apartments over on Third Avenue."

"Second one this week." Pat shook his head. "Arson?"

His friend shrugged. "I'm sure they'll investigate."

Pat stared out the window, wishing his mind would blur like the scenery. It would be easier to keep thoughts of the Projects and the last fire he'd fought in New York City—or the recurring nightmare he dreaded—from resurfacing. "It might be a coincidence." *Was there really such a thing?*

Ladder Three and Engine Three arrived on the scene together. There was one window on the top floor that had flames shooting out of it, while the others were belching black smoke. "The roof isn't engaged."

"Listen up," Big Jim shouted. "We've got time to do a sweep, looking for a grandmother and two little kids. Garahan, you're the can man. Snelling, you back him up. I've got the irons. Feeney, you're with me."

Pat reacted as he'd been trained. Carrying the can of water—and the six-foot hook he used to bring ceilings down—up eight floors with one hundred and fifteen pounds of equipment on his back was a piece of cake compared to what he'd done in New York. Being stationed at the firehouse that received calls from the Projects— the North Bronx—had been hard work—double the calls received in any other five boroughs. A bark from his lieutenant was all he needed to focus. Searching for victims and putting the fire out was a priority and all that mattered right now.

They followed Lieutenant Muldoon up the flight of stairs. Patrick was totally in the zone, racing up the stairs, the others right behind him. Visibility was nonexistent the closer they got to the top floor. Smoke inhalation was a silent killer.

Pat set the can and ceiling hook down and Muldoon handed him the Halligan Hooks (a.k.a. *irons*) hanging on to the crowbar and ax, so he was ready to take the door by force if necessary. Side by side, Pat waited for Muldoon to touch the door, checking for heat. "Minimal," he shouted.

Pat nodded. Muldoon waited while Pat did what he was famous for, taking the door. He inserted the hooks and swung the ax, hammer side down, against them. The door splintered apart with one blow. He and Snelling would take the left; Big Jim Muldoon and Feeney would take the right.

Feeling their way along the wall, they searched for door openings and windows, mentally counting them along the way, estimating the number of feet in between. The first door he came to, he reached back and alerted Mike. They dropped to their hands and knees, hoping to find the two little kids and their grandmother.

Time was running out. They needed to find the victims before the smoke inhalation was irreversible. Finally he found the opening—a doorway—he'd been looking for and hit the floor so he would have a better chance of locating the little ones—children were often hiding in closets and under beds when fire struck.

Ignoring the weight of his gear and the heat of the fire licking through the building, he searched with his hands, praying that he or one of his team reached them before the black smoke claimed a life.

Now that they were inside the apartment, the minutes passed like hours, every tick of the clock in his head counting down the possibility of surviving the smoke inhalation. Pat was sweating bullets, half due to the heat and half due to the adrenaline rush as their search of the first room came up empty. Undaunted, they repeated the process in the next room—another bedroom.

His breathing unit chimed, indicating he was now on borrowed time, as his gloved hand connected with a tiny sneaker. Seconds later, he was pulling a child into his arms and retracing his steps.

Conserving his air, he kept it short and sweet. "Got one," he called out as the little one in his arms coughed. Seconds later, Mike echoed the call. With their precious burdens in their arms, they made their way back to the stairway—their escape route. Help was waiting. The EMTs were on the scene, ready to take the children and administer first aid.

Thanks. His silent, one-word prayer was acknowledged as the little girls started to cry. "Takes a lot of lung power to cry like that," Mike said, following Pat back inside.

"Amen," Pat said aloud.

"We've got the grandmother," Muldoon's voice sounded in Pat's ear. "She's unconscious. Feeney's bringing her down. Let's finish the sweep of this floor and get this fire put out."

Hours later, the men were back at the firehouse, shuffling into the kitchen. Pat reheated the chili and the men were able to finish the meal this time. When he pulled out the ice cream and served the apple crisp, the men erupted into cheers.

"You guys could be bought with a gallon of ice cream," he grumbled.

"I'm not a cheap date," Snelling quipped. "I'm holding out for heavy cream."

Pat chuckled and nodded toward the fridge. "I put a quart in the fridge this morning."

Snelling tilted his head to one side and stared at Pat. "So you want to move in with me?"

The good-natured ribbing that followed was just one way that the men released some of the adrenaline they'd stored up fighting the fire. Pat grinned and shook his head. "Despite what you've heard, I'm not that easy."

Muldoon reached for the bottle of Red Hots and poured the cinnamon candy over the top of his ice cream-covered dessert.

"I'd hate to be your stomach," Pat said.

"Never get sick though," Muldoon told him. "Hard for germs to live in all that heat."

He and Snelling were on autopilot cleaning up. Three hours later, the alarm sounded again and Pat knew this shift was going to stretch right into the next one. "Get a move on, Snelling."

"Right behind ya, buddy boy."

Chapter 3

ENERGIZED, GRACE WAS ON THE ROAD AND HEADED toward home. The Pistol Annies came on the radio and she cranked it up to sing along.

With the window rolled down and her favorite music testing the limits of her speakers, she was smiling as the breeze ruffled her newly cropped hair. She felt lighter in spirit. Was it because she had the whole weekend to play with her nieces and nephews? The prospect of catching up with her best friend? Maybe it was because she'd been working nine-hour days and needed a break. Or maybe it was just because she was headed home.

Even though she loved her apartment, *home* would always be the Mulcahy farm on Peat Moss Road. She saw the sign for Route 40 and took the exit. She was making good time, singing along with Taylor Swift, nearly on autopilot the closer she got to Newark, Ohio, because from there, it would only be forty-five minutes more to Apple Grove.

She turned off Route 13 onto Eden Church Road and crossed the railroad tracks watching for Goose Pond—there! On her left. She passed by Goose Pond Road, the first street that could take her to her family's home, and slowed down so she could see the ship's mast standing tall in the middle of the McCormack's field.

God, she really missed spending time with Kate. The excitement of seeing Kate and Honey B. began to build as she turned left onto Dog Hollow Road and slowed down approaching Main Street. She signaled to turn right. The street was quiet, but it was normal at eight o'clock at night in Apple Grove. She pulled up in front of Honey B.'s as door to the shop flung open and Kate and Honey B. stepped outside.

"It's about time you got here," Kate said.

Grace got out and slammed the door shut, hurrying over to hug her friend. "Oh, I've missed you."

"Let me look at you," Kate insisted, easing out of their hug to study her friend's haircut.

"Not bad for an amateur." It was Honey B.'s turn to hug her. "I can fix you up in about an hour."

Grace eased out of the hug. "An hour? I didn't think it was that uneven."

Honey B. smiled, taking Grace by the hand. "It's not, but we have some catching up to do. Come on." She opened the door to her shop and tugged Grace inside.

"Surprise!"

Grace stopped short. "Meg? Cait? What are you doing here?" Before they could answer, Grace was surrounded and being hugged.

"What a wonderful idea, Gracie." Miss Trudi Philo patted Grace's hand. "You Mulcahy girls have always been generous to a fault."

"I've baked you a cherry pie to take home with you," Mrs. Winter said. "Such a clever girl."

Grace looked from two of Apple Grove's movers and shakers for the last sixty years and wondered what the heck they were talking about. She stared at her sisters, who shrugged. Finally the shock of the moment started to wear off and she was able to focus on the smiling faces standing in a circle around her.

"Somebody better start talking," she said, looking right at Kate.

But it was her sister Meg who answered. "Apple Grove's first annual Love Locks cut-a-thon."

Grace felt her jaw go slack as her sister's words sank in.

"Right after you talked to Kate," Meg said, "Kate called Honey B. and me—"

"A conference call," Honey B. interrupted. "So much easier than talking to one person, hanging up, and repeating the same conversation all over again with someone else."

"But I didn't—" Grace began, only to be interrupted by her other sister, Cait.

"Meg and I have been braiding our hair forever to keep it out of the way. What's the point of having long hair if you always keep it tied up?" Cait wanted to know.

"And then sometimes, a woman just needs a change," Honey B. added, fluffing the ends of her hair.

That's when Grace noticed a number of the faces crowding around her were girls ranging in age from ten to twenty years old. They all had their hair pulled back in a ponytail, ready for the cut-a-thon. Humbled by their generosity, she felt her eyes well up with tears.

"You ladies are amazing. I know Stacy at Love Locks will be delighted to accept your donation."

"Good," Kate said, "because it is all going under your name."

"My name?" Grace had no idea what was going on in her friend's mind. "Why?"

"Because you had the foresight to see the need and fill it. You told me," Kate began.

"And Kate told two friends," Honey B. added.

"Who told two friends," Meg continued.

"And word spread," Cait said.

"And here we are," little Christina Doyle finished. Her smile was catching.

Grace bent down and tugged on Christina's ponytail. "Then let's get this show started!"

"Wait!" Kate called out as excited voices filled Honey's Hair Salon. "Rhonda's not here yet."

"Is she getting her hair cut too?" Grace asked.

Kate shook her head. "She's taking pics and doing the write-up and putting it on Apple Grove's website. We're hoping to encourage other towns in Licking County to join the fun and help out a very worthy cause."

Grace was humbled by the overwhelming support of the ladies in her hometown. Kate hugged her tight and told her to smile. The clicking sound of someone taking a picture had her looking up in time to see Rhonda Beaudine from the *Apple Grove Gazette* grinning at them.

"This is going to get the ball rolling and people for miles around wanting to join in the fun."

"Did you know that Honey B. is donating her time tonight?" Meg asked.

Grace grinned. "You totally rock, Honey B."

Laughter filled Honey B.'s shop. Time flew by as the ladies chatted while Honey B. snipped off ponytails in every color imaginable: flame-bright red, strawberry blonde, auburn, brunette, light brown, and dark brown.

While Honey B. finished styling the new haircuts, Rhonda snapped pics and kept tapping away on her tablet. "I'm going to do a few pieces," Rhonda told Grace, "and send them off to Stacy. She can decide which ones to use on her website and which she wants for future press releases."

"Thank you," Grace said.

"I already have short hair," Rhonda explained. "This is my contribution."

A half hour later, the group was ready for their photo. "Honey B.," Rhonda called out, "you stand in the middle. Everyone hold up your ponytails and smile!"

When the ladies started cleaning up, Rhonda turned to Grace. "Please make sure you get everyone's name. I don't want to take a chance that I'll be working on this at midnight and forget to mention anyone."

"Anyone have a piece of paper?"

Rhonda shook her head at Grace. "Join the new millennium and invest in the latest technology. You'll never need another pencil."

"But I don't want to lose any more skills," Grace explained. "I already let the computer balance my checkbook and send my checks electronically."

Rhonda shrugged. "Makes life easier if you ask me."

"I'm of a mind to agree with Grace," Mrs. Winter chimed in. "I had to learn how to keep a checkbook when my husband passed. It's not a skill I intend to give up."

"I've been arguing with my grandnephew about updating my accounting and inventory." Miss Trudi frowned over at Meg. "Why he thinks I need to do all of that folderol when I get by just fine with the system my grandmother used is beyond me."

Grace struggled not to smile; it wasn't wise to get on the wrong side of Miss Trudi when the octogenarian was on a roll about something. "It works well for some people."

Ms. Trudi merely harrumphed and shook her head. *Well*, Grace thought. *That's that.*

By the time she'd finished the list, her sisters had already helped Honey B. set the shop to rights.

"Do you and Peggy need help over at the diner?" she asked Kate.

"Peggy and I closed up."

"All set up for the morning shift," Peggy added.

Everyone said their good-byes, leaving Kate and Grace to walk over to Grace's car. "How do you do it, Kate? Getting up that early every day—it'd drive me crazy."

Kate's smile seemed sad. "Grandma took over the diner from her mother-in-law years ago. Then it was Mom's turn. It burns you out if you let it. Deep down we love the cooking and the baking, so it's hard to let it go."

"Have you ever thought of doing something else with your life?" Grace asked. "Like moving away from Apple Grove?"

Kate laughed. "Admit it, you miss spending time with the old biddies and gossips you grew up with."

Before Grace could open her mouth to deny it, Kate continued. "You miss your grumpy Gus of a father. Where else can you get pot roast like here at the diner? And how the heck can you sleep in a place that's never quiet?"

Grace was tired and didn't want talk about her reasons for leaving—again—with Kate right now. "We agreed to disagree when I moved to Columbus. Remember?"

Kate waved her hand in the air, dismissing Grace's words, but Grace decided to let that slide, saying, "Night, Kate."

Driving past Goose Pond, Grace drew in a deep breath of summer air. She could detect the scent of water, fresh-mown grass, and the heady scent of the lilacs that grew by the south end of the pond.

She smiled, remembering the midnight escapades she and Kate had shared—climbing out of their bedroom windows and meeting at the pond. They never got caught, but she had a feeling Kate's parents and Grace's dad knew what they'd been up to. They'd left buckets of tadpoles behind the barn at Kate's farm and over at Grace's house, they'd left a bullfrog that had escaped from where they'd stashed him in the old horse trough by the corral.

Memories of childhood always had her wishing she'd had more time with her mom, but there were plenty of memories with her sisters and their father to fill in the hole left behind after the drunk driver had taken Maureen Mulcahy from them.

Shoving that thought aside, Grace focused on the here and the now as she turned left onto Cherry Valley. She didn't need to see the stand of weeping hemlocks to know that Peat Moss Road was on her right; their distinctive scent blew in through her open window. By night, that stand of trees resembled immense monsters, hunched over just waiting to pounce on her and Kate when they were kids. Now they were simply sentinels guarding the street that led to her family's home.

Grace pulled into the driveway and parked before realizing she wasn't alone. Her car door was yanked open and she was pulled into a fierce hug.

"Why did you stay away so long?"

Her words were muffled against her father's chest. He pulled back from her and asked, "What?"

She laughed and reached up to kiss his cheek. "Gotta pay the rent—and it was only two months."

"How's life in the big city?"

"Noisy at night."

"Hah!" His booming voice always reassured her as a child, and it did so now. "You need the harmony of peepers and a hoot owl to serenade you to sleep."

"I really missed you, Pop."

He bent to kiss the top of her head before easing her out of his arms so he could point to the trunk. "I'll carry your bags."

When she popped the trunk, he frowned at her overnight bag until she reminded him, "I've got to be at work bright and early Monday morning."

"Can I talk you into playing hooky?"

She stopped dead in her tracks and looked up at him. "Are you sick?"

He chuckled. "No."

"Is Meg or Cait sick? Not that I noticed when I saw them over at Honey B.'s, but—"

"Just missing my baby girl," he told her.

"Aww, Pop." Grace sniffed.

"Oh now, don't do that, Gracie," he said. "You know I can't handle a woman's tears."

She sniffled louder. "Then don't say stuff that'll make me get all weepy."

"A father should be able to tell his youngest daughter that he missed her."

Grace agreed. "Just as long as he accepts that his daughter is female and prone to get emotional."

This time his laugh boomed out, just as she'd hoped it would.

"Hell's bells, I survived three daughters, two of them hitting puberty within ten months of each other. I think I deserve some slack—or at least a medal."

She'd heard this all before and knew better than to disagree. "Yes, Pop."

WELCOME BACK TO APPLE GROVE   33

They walked up the back steps and into the kitchen, and Grace felt the house welcome her. Her grandmother's copper-topped cookie jar still stood on the counter. "With Cait and Meg so busy with their own lives, that cookie jar is probably empty these days."

"Don't worry, I've got someone who takes care of my sweet tooth." The faraway look and subtle lift of his lips lightened her heart. Her dad had finally found someone to love after years spent grieving.

"How is Mary?"

"Fine, busy as always with the store. She dropped cookies off this morning—peanut butter ones with Hershey's Kisses on top—your favorite."

"I'll have to stop by Murphy's Market tomorrow and thank her."

"She'd like that."

He was quiet for a few minutes before saying, "I like your hair short. It suits you."

She grinned up at him and patted his arm. "Maybe I can fit in one or two of Mary's cookies. Want to have some tea with me?"

He opened the cabinet by the sink and took out two heavy ceramic mugs. "I think I'd like a dash of the Irish in my tea."

"Does Doc know that you still put whiskey in your tea?"

He ignored her question. "I'll get the cookies."

She was about to fill the teakettle when he stopped her. "It'll heat up faster if you nuke it."

She sighed. "True, but it doesn't taste quite the same."

He laughed. "That's because you don't put a nip of whiskey in yours, me girl." He was smiling when he pulled out the first mug of hot water, added a tea bag and a dash of milk, and pushed the jar of honey toward her. When she added a dollop, he grinned and added a splash of alcohol. "Try it."

"How could I refuse?"

They sat down at the oak table where she'd spent so many years doing homework and sharing meals with her family, and could swear she heard her mother's voice even after all these years. *Home*, she thought, *had memories that haunted you, and ones that you treasured.* Late night talks with her father were some of the ones she held closest to her heart.

He ate two cookies before asking, "How did the cut-a-thon go?"

She leveled her gaze at him. "You knew about it?"

"Your sisters told me about Kate's idea. It was a good one and all because of your generosity."

"But I didn't have anything to do with tonight."

"Didn't you?" He paused to sip from his mug before cradling it in his work-roughened hands. "You're the one who made the donation and told Kate about it, so it all started with you."

"But I don't deserve the credit for organizing tonight."

"Ah," he said, "that's different, and you can thank Kate, Meg, and Honey B. for that."

She sipped her tea, savoring the flavor and heat soothing her throat and leaving her feeling warm and fuzzy inside. "This tastes pretty good."

"Not quite like having a shot at night, but as close as Doc lets me get these days."

"I'll clean up if you're tired," Grace offered as she finished her tea.

He shook his head. "I'm not ready to turn in yet. You need to get a good night's sleep if you're going to keep up with your nephews and niece tomorrow."

She kissed his cheek, grabbed her bag, and wished him sweet dreams.

"It's good to have you home, Grace."

"It's nice to be here, Pop."

The third step from the bottom still creaked if you stepped in the middle, but tonight she wasn't worried about waking anyone up. It was just the two of them in the big old house. Somehow it seemed sad. The house needed voices, laughter, and kids—the Mulcahy house seemed alive when they were kids.

She opened the door to the room she used to share with Cait and smiled. Same yellow gingham bedspread and curtains—and Great-Great-Aunt Adelaide's four-poster bed.

The evening breeze blew past her, enticing her senses with the tantalizing scent of sweet peas and roses from Grandma's garden. The heady scent soothed her as she unpacked and got ready for bed.

Snuggled beneath the covers, she let the author sweep her away to the wilds of the Scottish Highlands. *I wish I could meet a man like that*, she thought before exhaustion claimed her.

The pages fluttered as her grip went slack. She'd barely read two pages of the romance novel she'd brought before sleep claimed her.

She didn't hear her father enter her room or feel the slight tug on her hand when he slipped the book from her fingers to lay it on the bedside table. But she sighed in her sleep when he kissed her forehead, as he'd done countless nights before.

"Night, baby girl."

"Night, Pop."

Chapter 4

GRACE HEARD THE STACCATO OF FOOTSTEPS POUNDING up the stairs—her warning that the invasion was imminent.

"Auntie Grace! Auntie Grace!"

She braced for impact as twin juggernauts launched themselves on top of her and started to chant, "Wake up! We're here."

They bounced on her abs and patted her cheeks. They'd gotten heavier.

"Come on," little Danny pleaded.

"Please?" his twin Joey asked.

How could she resist her hooligan nephews? Pretending she'd only just woken up, she yawned loudly and opened one eye. "Oh my goodness! What are you two doing here?"

The twins giggled. She knew they would. "We're here to play with you."

They slipped off of her stomach and settled one on each side, in the curve of her arms. "Mommy said 'cause—"

"Because?" Grace placed a kiss on the top of Danny's head and the tip of Joey's nose.

"'Cause you missed us to pieces." Danny's little face was precious and his expression the mirror image of one she'd seen on her brother-in-law's face countless times.

"Have I?"

"Sure's shit."

Grace drew in a breath. She knew she should not laugh. But the sound Joey made right before he covered his mouth with both hands was too adorable. The scamp must have learned that expression from Meg.

She gave in and chuckled. "I don't think your mommy wants you to use words like that, Joey."

The mutinous expression on his face warned her that his temperament was quite real—these two little ones had lived up to every single adage—terrible twos, tantrum threes, and in six months they would be in the fearsome fours. She'd have to ask her sister what came next.

When his lip trembled and his eyes filled with tears, she hugged him closer and kissed his forehead. "We won't tell." She hugged Joey tight and asked, "Will we?"

Joey stared up at her and finally shrugged.

"Shrugging's not an answer."

"It is in our house."

Grace looked up. Meg stood in the doorway with eight-month-old Deidre on her hip, who was pointing and babbling.

"Hey there, sweet pea." Grace scooted up in bed, dragging the boys with her, and lifted her arms. Her sister softly smiled and laid Deidre in Grace's arms. She snuggled the baby close and pressed kisses on her cheek, blowing air bubbles against the baby's neck.

Her belly laughs went straight to Grace's heart. Want curled with need, twisting a knot in her belly, but she knew better than to wish for what she didn't have. Instead she said, "You're up early, Sis."

Meg laughed. "Every day. These two woke up the baby when they started chanting your name."

"Why would they do that?" Grace asked, feigning innocence. She knew perfectly well why; she'd taught the little hooligans a few singing chants when they were younger and every time she visited, they made up new ones—silly sayings and bits of old nursery rhymes. It was their favorite game—well, next to chasing their father, and a soccer ball, around the yard.

The boys got restless and slid off the bed, but Danny grabbed her elbow and tugged to get her attention. "Gran'pop's making pancakes."

Grace's day brightened. "Is he?"

"Uh-huh," Joey added. "That's why we waked you."

She looked from the twin rapscallions to their mother and nodded. "Well, I guess you two better go help. It's man's work…cooking pancakes."

"Yay!"

"Race you!"

"Do not run in the house," Meg called after her boys, but she knew they wouldn't hear her. "Is it too much to hope that Deidre learns to walk late?"

Grace cuddled her niece close to kiss her before handing her back to her sister. "Well, can you see yourself carrying her around while she's crying because she can't chase after those two?"

"I guess not." Meg kissed her daughter's cheek and lifted her gaze to meet Grace's. "Can I tell you again how glad I am that you finally broke up with Ted?"

"Jeez. I don't want to talk about him."

"I think we should," Meg insisted. "You haven't dated since you caught him cheating on you."

Grace's hands clenched. "I haven't met anyone I've wanted to date. I'm here to spend time with the family, not to rehash what happened with my ex or hear about what eligible bachelors have moved into town since I moved out."

Meg surprised her by agreeing. "See you downstairs."

"Let me grab a shower."

"Make it a quick one," Meg said, cocking her head to one side and listening. "The natives are restless."

———

Grace walked into a scene right out of her childhood: her father with his back to the room while he poured pancake batter into neat rounds in the cast iron pan, two little ones sitting on pillows so they could reach the table, each with a stack of hotcakes covered in syrup in front of them while their mother reminded them to take human-sized bites.

The ache of missing her mother would always be there.

Danny broke the spell of the past when he reached for his glass of milk and knocked it over. "Careful there, kiddo." Grace got the roll of paper towels and mopped it up.

"Can we go outside?" Danny asked around a mouthful of breakfast.

"Wait till you finish eating before talking," Meg reminded her oldest.

He looked over at Grace and rolled his eyes. Grace laughed. She used to do the same thing when Meg told her what to do.

"Reminds me of someone." Joe Mulcahy set a plate of hotcakes in front of Grace.

"Thanks, Pop, but I'm not really hungry." She pushed the plate to the side and got up.

"Since when?" His formidable glare would have set stone on fire, but Grace was used to it. His bark was worse than his bite.

She got a cup and reached for the coffee pot. "I usually just have coffee in the morning."

"Breakfast is the most—"

"Important meal of the day," Grace finished for her father. "Yeah. I know."

He crossed his arms across his massive chest and ground out, "Then slide that plate back in front of you and chow down before it gets cold."

Grace looked over at Meg, seeking support, but the way her sister was frowning at her told Grace she wouldn't be getting any help from that quarter.

With a sigh, she opened the fridge and got the milk out. Doctoring her coffee kept her hands busy while her mind raced. Would her father or sister comment on her weight gain? It had been steady, a few pounds a month, and it had been a few months since she'd seen them last. She'd never been quite as skinny as Cait, but she'd been thin most of her life.

"Grace!"

"Hmmm?" She looked up at her sister. "What?"

Meg was in the process of wiping sticky faces with a damp cloth when Grace stopped obsessing about her weight.

"I said I just heard a car pull up."

"Daddy!" The two imps struggled against their mother's hold until she'd cleaned most of the syrup off. They were laughing as they opened the screen door and raced down the steps. Grace heard the deep rumble of her brother-in-law's voice and her nephews' answering cries of "Yay! Soccer!"

"That'll keep them busy while I clean up." Meg gave her daughter a wooden spoon. The little one banged it against the tray of the same high chair Grace and her sisters had used.

"She's got rhythm." Grace smiled, watching Deidre

smack the spoon and giggle. "I'm surprised she's not crying to chase after her brothers."

Meg nodded toward their father. "Pop's here to distract her."

Joe sat down next to his granddaughter with a steaming cup of coffee. "Ahh," he said after sipping. "I've earned this cup this morning."

Meg leaned down and kissed him on the cheek. "You're the best, Pop."

Joe agreed. "It's my burden to bear."

Grace heard another car pull up. "Who else is coming today?"

Meg's face had an odd expression on it, but it was gone before Grace could decide if her sister looked guilty or happy.

"I invited Honey B. and the kids over." Meg turned to look out the window over the sink. "Grace, would you mind bringing Deidre out with you?"

Before Grace could answer, her sister was gone.

"Well, what's up with her?"

Her father's eyes twinkled for a moment, but then he cleared his throat and changed the subject. "Now, baby girl, about breakfast."

"Pop, I'm not a baby anymore," Grace grumbled, pointing to her niece. "She's the baby."

Her father chuckled and took a drink from his mug. "That she is, but you'll always be my youngest and therefore my baby girl." He whistled and Deidre stopped banging the spoon to look up at him.

"And you," he said, pressing his lips to Deidre's forehead, "are my pretty little Princess Tickle Feather."

Grace's heart just burst with love watching the way her father played with his youngest grandchild. He'd always had a heart of gold; he'd been strict with her and her sisters when they needed it and been tough on the boys that came calling once they started dating, but deep down in her father's broad chest beat a heart one hundred percent pure gold. A long buried yearning filled Grace…once upon a time she had wanted to marry a man just like her father. Reality was harsh, but so was the realization that there weren't any left out there. All the good ones were gone.

"I love you, Pop."

He looked up, and while Grace watched, his eyes filled with tears and his mouth curved up into a broad smile. "I know, baby girl, and I love you right back."

"Grace, are you coming?"

She started to answer her sister, but her father shook his head. "Best to go see what she wants. She might have had to hog-tie my grandsons."

She was laughing when she undid the strap holding her niece in the high chair. "Come on, Princess Tickle Feather." Deidre's chubby little arms were reaching for Grace, ready to be picked up. "Let's see what your big brothers are up to."

Grace didn't turn back around, so she didn't see her father's smile deepen or the way he rubbed his hands together in anticipation of what was waiting outside for his unsuspecting youngest daughter.

Patrick Garahan was trying not to step on the twin forces of destruction currently whooping like wild men while they chased after the soccer ball he was dribbling across the grass. It was hard because they were quick and coordinated. He didn't remember his sisters' kids being this good at soccer at the same age. But it had been awhile since he'd been home, and maybe he was thinking of his nieces and nephews when they were younger than the two pistols hooting and hollering as they grabbed his left leg and took him down.

Before he hit the ground, he spun and plucked the two of them off his leg and curled himself around the boys to protect them. "Can we do it again, Unca Pat?"

He was a sucker for a cute kid. His two honorary nephews were hard to ignore—and pretty damned special too. He saw more of them than he did any of his sisters' kids back in New York. For a moment, little Michael's face filled his mind then morphed into the face of the little boy he hadn't been able to save—the one who was his nephew Michael's age—as the image from his nightmare bubbled dangerously close to the surface.

Danny dug his knees into Patrick's stomach as he crawled toward his chest. Joey wasn't one to be left out, so he scrambled to his feet next to his brother. Shoving those thoughts deep, Pat made a grab for the boys—they were heavier than they looked. But they were fast and each gave a rebel yell that would have made his cousin Tyler proud as they leaped off his chest, tucking and rolling as they hit the ground.

"Ompfh," he groaned as their tiny sneakers pushed off. "Uncle!" he hollered, making his friend Dan Eagan laugh.

"You can't say I didn't warn you, Garahan," Dan told him. "Besides, you know they've been asking for you for a couple of weeks now."

Pat leaned on one elbow and watched as the two chased each other across the Mulcahys' backyard, tumbling into one another like puppies. "Did you ever imagine that you'd be a dad?"

Dan's gaze moved toward the petite, auburn-haired pixie woman he'd married.

Watching his friend, Pat chuckled. "Earth to Dan!"

"Hmmm? What?" Dan blinked and had to ask him to repeat the question.

"You seem to fit life here in Apple Grove like you were born here."

Dan agreed. "It was like coming home, you know?"

Pat did and told him so. "When I left Brooklyn, I didn't think I'd be staying. I just needed to get away"—and for the nightmares to stop—"but it grows on you. Everything just clicked and my life seemed…"

"Seemed what?" Dan asked.

Pat couldn't speak, couldn't think—he could only stare at the goddess standing in the sunlight on the Mulcahys' back porch. Her hair was clipped short, brushing against the line of her jaw, but it was the way the woman filled out her T-shirt and jeans that kicked him in the gut. "Is she real?"

Dan looked over at the woman and back, and shrugged. "Last time I checked, why?"

Pat swallowed his spit before he drooled. She had killer curves. "Aren't you going to introduce me?"

Dan's laughter had the curvaceous, strawberry-haired goddess glancing in their direction. She pressed her lips to the top of Dan and Meg's daughter's head and helped baby Deidre wave at them. "Whatever you want, Eagan, it's yours, but you've got to introduce me."

Dan turned and stared at Patrick as if his friend had lost his mind. "Introduce you," Dan said slowly then nodded toward the woman. "To her?"

Pat ran his fingers through his hair, hoping there weren't any leaves or sticks in it. "Yeah. Is that a problem?"

Dan cleared his throat and his amused expression changed to one of concern. "Yeah."

Pat felt like the bottom had dropped out of his stomach. "Come on, man," he pleaded. "I'll owe you."

Dan looked from Pat to the woman cooing at the baby in her arms. "OK."

Pat felt relief flow through him. Just then the goddess looked at Patrick and tilted her head to one side as if wondering what he and Dan were discussing.

Dan said. "Come on."

They walked across the grass, around the big old oak, and over to the bottom of the steps, where Meg was speaking to his mystery woman.

"Whoa, Meg! You cut your hair?" This was the first time Pat had seen her without her signature braid hanging down past her waistband.

"It was for a good cause." Meg turned and reached out to brush the ends of the other woman's hair. There was something familiar about her...

"I, uh—" The woman turned and her gaze connected with Pat's. The air sizzled between them, short-circuiting his brain.

"Patrick Garahan," Dan began, "I'd like you to meet my sister-in-law Grace Mulcahy."

Pat held his hand out. "Grace?" His voice cracked and Dan coughed to cover the fact that he was laughing at his friend.

"Hi, Patrick." Grace's voice was soft and soothing. "It's been awhile." She gathered Deidre in one arm and held out her hand to grasp his.

"You too," he said, reaching for her hand. "I mean— great to see you."

Her green eyes sparkled, captivating him. Then she

smiled and he noticed her dimples. *Damn, he always had a thing for curvy, green-eyed women.*

"I thought Honey B. was here," she said to Meg.

Meg shook her head. "I guess I was wrong." She turned toward the sound of her twins arguing and sighed. "Dan, can you please go be Switzerland?"

He laughed and said, "I'm on it."

While Dan settled whatever the boys were arguing about, Patrick stared at Grace. "I didn't recognize you. You look amazing."

Her eyes widened and he knew from her expression that she hadn't expected him to say that. "I like the hair," he said, making her smile at him again.

"Thanks. I donated it to a good cause."

"The two *G*s," he mumbled to himself.

"Excuse me?"

Jeez, she hadn't heard him, had she? "Nothing."

She narrowed her eyes and locked gazes with him. "What are the two *G*s?"

"Busted," he groaned. "Something my brothers and I used to say."

"When…?" she said, obviously hoping he'd fill in the blank. *Fat chance.*

"It's nothing." Pat wasn't going to elaborate.

Deidre was leaning over Grace's arm, squirming and reaching toward him. Pat said, "I'll take her."

Deidre started to fuss, so Grace handed her over. As soon as the little one was in Patrick's arms, she quieted down and laid her head on his shoulder. Warmth filled him as the littlest Eagan's breathing deepened and her tiny body went slack. Used to his nieces and nephews falling asleep on him, he pressed his lips to her ear and brushed the flyaway hair out of her eyes.

"You're wonderful with her."

He looked up and found that Grace was studying him, not quite like he was a smear on a slide but pretty damned close. "I like kids."

Joe Mulcahy chose that moment to step outside. "Grace, you didn't eat—Pat," he said, extending his hand. "Glad…er, good to see you."

If Grace caught on to her father's slip of the tongue, she didn't mention it, but her gaze went back and forth between the two men. Something was up.

"You didn't mention that anyone else was going to be here today."

Her father cleared his throat and crossed his arms in front of him. "Hmm," he said. "Meant to. Cait and Jack will be here around noon and we'll fire up the grill." He pinned Grace with the intensity of his gaze. "You're going to need to eat to keep up with everyone."

"Pop, I told you—"

"Breakfast is the most important meal of the day." Pat wondered if she'd gotten up late or if she'd been distracted by her family. "I could scramble up a mess of eggs for you."

Before she could answer, he handed off the sleeping Deidre to her grandfather, who took her and walked over toward the boys. Patrick tugged on Grace's hand. "Come on, gorgeous."

Pat wanted to yank on Grace's hand until she tumbled into his arms. But he didn't want to give her the wrong impression, and he definitely didn't want to get on the wrong side of Joe Mulcahy—the former coastguardsman was built like a linebacker. So he settled for savoring the feel of the silky smooth hand grasped in his work-roughened one.

It would have to do for now…but after seeing Grace again, he knew he wanted to do more than hold her hand. A whole lot more.

She tugged her hand free the moment they were inside. "I don't eat breakfast."

He was washing his hands in the kitchen sink and turned to look at her. "Ever?"

"Not in the last year or so."

"But how do you keep that killer body fueled?"

She groaned and stared up at the ceiling, mumbling beneath her breath.

"Hey," he said. "Are you counting?"

She blew her bangs out of her eyes. "Look, Garahan," she began, only to stop when he got into her personal space.

"Yeah, Mulcahy?"

She tried to take a step back, but he'd boxed her in, her back to the counter. "You're too close," she bit out.

"No, ma'am," he rasped. "I'm nowhere near close enough yet." He let his gaze drop to her full lips and then back up to her amazing green eyes. "But that is all about to change."

The hand in the middle of his chest surprised him.

"No."

He relaxed his stance, eased back, and held up his hands. "Any reason in particular you don't want me to kiss you, Grace? Because that's what I want to do… kiss you."

"I…you…we haven't—"

"Ah," he said, staring at her mouth. "But we could." When she ran a hand through her hair and licked her lips, he decided he'd staked enough of a claim for the moment. He'd remind her throughout the day that he was interested—all the way interested. Grace Mulcahy was a woman with a capital *W*, and he intended to sample those lips before the day was out.

"Coffee?" Her voice broke over the word and he started to feel sorry for her. He'd come on strong and knew he had a tendency to do so when he found something—or someone—he wanted. But Pat had learned that life was short and you had to grab it with both hands or take the chance that you'd lose it all.

Come hell or high water, he wasn't losing his chance to get to know Grace better. "That'd be great. Thanks."

While she made coffee, he made himself at home in the kitchen and took out a frying pan and four eggs.

"Are you going to share those with me?"

"No."

"Then one will be fine."

He shook his head at her. "You lose most of the egg when you scramble it. I'll make you two; you'll be surprised how hungry you get chasing after Danny and Joey."

She laughed and the tension in the air eased. "They like to jump on me to wake me up."

His guts twisted, imagining a slightly different version—with just him and Grace. "Really?"

"They've been doing that since they could walk," she told him. "Before I moved to Columbus, those two used to sleep over on Friday nights so that Meg and Dan would have some time together."

"Was that before Deidre was born?"

Her throaty chuckle added another knot in his gut. "Yes," she admitted. "It was."

"Thought so." He kept his tone cheerful and upbeat, despite the desperate desire rioting inside him, clawing for freedom. "My three sisters are all married with kids."

"I thought you had brothers?"

"Three of them too."

"Wow, your mom must be a saint."

He grinned and agreed. "Saint Bridget Garahan."

She poured him a cup of coffee and put it on the counter. "How do you take it?"

"Black, thanks."

"Then you're good to go," she said. "Thanks for making me breakfast."

He scooped the eggs onto her plate and handed it to her. "Crap, I forgot the toast."

"No carbs." She took the plate and set it down on the table.

"Honey, everybody needs carbs to keep the engine firing on all cylinders."

"Car talk," Joe said, walking into the house. "Whose engine needs work?"

Pat laughed and answered, "Grace's." When Joe stared at him, Pat held up his hands. "Your daughter doesn't eat breakfast or carbs."

"Well, she will today," Joe told her, turning to glare down at his youngest. "Messes up your metabolism if you don't eat at least three squares."

"Amen," Patrick added. "So, how about a piece of toast with jelly or peanut butter on it?"

Grace sighed. "All right, but no butter."

Pat held a hand to his heart in shock. "OK, that's it," he said, turning to Joe. "I accept full responsibility for teaching Grace how to eat right."

Joe laughed. "You have no idea what you're getting into."

Pat stared at the top of Grace's head until she lifted her face and his gaze meet hers. "I'm not so sure about that, Mr. Mulcahy," he told him. "I think I do."

"Auntie Grace?" Two little missiles shot through the back door, into the kitchen. "Aren't you ready to come play yet?"

"She'll be right out boys," their grandfather told them.

Grace knew when she'd been beaten; she gave in and ate the last bite of egg but left half the toast.

Pat rose from his seat when she did and handed it to her. "You can finish it outside while you watch the boys try to beat Dan and me in a game of keep-away-soccer."

―∿∿―

Grace looked from the man standing beside her to the one standing by the sink. The feeling that they knew something she didn't crawled under her skin, but before she could begin to figure out just what it might be, the boys banged on the frame to the screen door, hollering for her and Patrick to hurry up.

For a big man, Patrick Garahan was light on his feet. He moved smoothly around her as if in a choreographed dance and opened the back door for her, holding out that blasted piece of toast.

"I'm not hung—"

"Little people have big ears," he warned with a nod toward the two who were currently standing at the base of the steps looking up at them. His amber eyes twinkled with bottled-up laughter, but it wasn't until the corner of his mouth lifted and the smile slowly spread across his rugged face that she realized she was totally out of her depth with him. He'd never looked at her the way he was looking at her now. She'd always been at ease in his company. But today, things were different. It was as if they were meeting for the first time, and wasn't that crazy?

He was right—kids learn by example and by doing.

She smiled down at her nephews and held up the toast, took a big bite, and made exaggerated chewing motions and yummy sounds as she ate it.

They giggled and ran over to where Dan was bent over the front fender of the F1, her grandfather's 1950 Ford pickup. *Boys and their toys*, she thought. "Does Pop know you're messing with that engine?"

Dan's head came up like a shot and he rapped the back of it against the inside of the hood. He swore and held his hand on the back of his head.

"Daddy said a bad word. Daddy said a bad word."

Pat chuckled and leaned closer. "Troublemaker."

The depth of his voice sent a shiver up her spine, and she couldn't ignore the fact that it was one more thing that captured her attention. Why hadn't she ever noticed it before?

"Hey, you need ice?" Pat sprinted down the steps toward Dan and his boys.

Dan rubbed his head then shook it. "Hurts like a—"

Grace watched her brother-in-law pause, look down, and shake his head again.

"What does it hurt like?" Danny wanted to know.

"Yeah. What?" Joey added.

Dan's snort of laughter had his sons giggling. "A son of a gun."

Danny tilted his head to one side and asked, "Guns have kids?"

Grace ate the last bite of toast and watched them— two broad-shouldered, good-looking men standing side by side. The way Dan and Patrick were smiling down at her nephews tugged at her heart. She had a soft spot for a man who paid attention to kids—especially her hooligan nephews. Her ex—no, she wouldn't go there.

Patrick laughed at something Danny said, and the sound made her feel warm and fuzzy inside.

Lyrics to one of her dad's favorite Grateful Dead songs started playing in her head—*trouble ahead... trouble behind*. When Patrick looked up, she felt the air snap and sizzle. His amber eyes deepened in hue. Oh yeah...definitely trouble.

Chapter 5

THE GAME WAS ON AND HER NEPHEWS WERE RUNNING around, screaming like little heathens. "Watch out!" she warned as Danny nearly collided with the back of Patrick's knees, but the man seemed to have a sixth sense where little people were concerned and stepped to the side at the last minute.

Her nephew tumbled to the grass but got up like a shot, sporting a grass stain that she knew her sister wouldn't be able to remove without a fight. Two minutes later, Joey tried the same move on their honorary Uncle Pat and ended up sprawled on the grass. Their delighted laughter lightened her heart, but the added depth of the men's laughter was music to her ears.

Grace thrived here, and maybe that had been the biggest motivator to her looking for a job in the city. Deep down, she'd been afraid she couldn't exist anywhere else, afraid she'd lose the tie to her family—like the one she'd already lost when her mother died tragically.

Grace was Irish to the bone and had been raised to believe in fate, destiny, karma, and the all-important Murphy's Law. She needed to be the one to sever the chord in order to find out if Apple Grove was her destiny…or if it lay somewhere farther west in the big city.

Wisps of her childhood dream teased at the edge of her memory; she remembered dreaming of a tall and handsome man smiling at children, playing with them. Her brain struggled to pull the rest of the details from that long ago dream but got sidetracked when questions filled her heart.

Why had Patrick been here today?

Was it the Universe or someone a lot closer to Earth who arranged their meeting again this way?

Had the long and winding road brought her back to Apple Grove because of her dream?

Was she meant to stay?

Her thoughts circled around and around until she had no way of sorting them out.

"Hey?" A strong, callused hand had a hold of her elbow. "Are you all right?" The warmth of that hand snapped her out of it and down off the proverbial hamster's wheel.

The concern in Patrick's gaze added to the warmth his touch ignited. *He cared.* The trick would be figuring out whether it was caring about her as a person…or if it was the something a lot more basic that he'd hinted at when he'd gotten into her personal space earlier.

Grace finally found her voice. "Yes. Fine. Why?" *Was I staring at you like an idiot?* She sure as hell wouldn't be asking him that.

"You got quiet all of a sudden," he said. "When one of my sisters does that, it usually means she's solving the world's problems or worried about something."

She smiled. "How many sisters do you have again?"

He grinned. "Three younger sisters."

"Do they have adorable freckles across the bridge of their noses like you do?" As soon as the words left her lips, her hands flew to her mouth and her eyes opened wide. *Dork!*

Patrick's cheeks turned an interesting shade of pink. She'd embarrassed herself and him! *Way to go making*

*a great impression on the first guy who set off sparks
inside you in more than a year.*

"I'll uh…take that as a compliment?"

She blew out a breath. "I'm sorry, sometimes the
words in my head sort of slip out of my mouth."

"So you didn't mean to bring up the fact that I've got
freckles?" His tone was light and his manner endearing
as he tried to get her to fess up.

"No," she said. "But since the cat's out of the bag,
they really are adorable."

He straightened to his full height, puffed out his
broad chest, and pounded on it with a fist. "I'm a man.
Men are not adorable."

"Mommy calls Daddy 'dorable all the time," Joey
said, patting Patrick's jean-clad leg.

"Jeez," Dan hissed. "Nothing is sacred once you become a parent."

Patrick grinned and nodded. "I hear the most interesting things from my nieces and nephews…out of the
mouths of babes."

Grace realized that he'd glossed over the fact that
she thought he was adorable, but she knew he'd been
touched by her words if those intense glances he shot her
way every few minutes were any indication. Deciding to
test her theory, she took a step closer to where he stood
and watched for a reaction. His body tensed. *Oh my!*

For whatever reason, this handsome hunk of fireman
was interested in her—the youngest of the Mulcahy sisters, the only one who didn't know how to use power
tools or a plumber's wrench. The black sheep of the
family, the only one who'd left home to make a life for
herself—the only one who wasn't wand slim.

Maybe he was thinking about something else and it

wasn't a reaction to her nearness. Needing to find out, she moved to stand beside him and touched his arm. The muscles in his forearm jumped beneath her fingertips. She looked down at his arm until she heard his sharply indrawn breath. She glanced up and felt her heart skip a beat watching the desire swirling in his amber eyes. *Desire for her.*

"Patrick, I—"

"Grace, can you—" he said at the same time.

They laughed together and the tense moment eased into something she hadn't experienced yet in her life. He was focused solely on her, as if she was the most important person in the universe. The heady feeling threatened to topple her resolve not to get involved with anyone until she was good and ready to.

"I'm ready," she whispered. *Good Lord, she hadn't meant to say that!*

His eyebrow shot up. He bent his head until it was close to hers, and whispered, "If you knew what I wanted to do to you right now—"

"Am I interrupting?"

Meg's question had Patrick clearing his throat. "I, uh, no. How's little Deidre?" As easily as that, he'd distracted Meg.

What was wrong with her? She'd known Patrick for a couple of years and had shared more than one meal with him over at Meg and Dan's house. They'd always enjoyed one another's company, but there hadn't been this sizzle before. Why hadn't they noticed one another on this level until now?

He glanced her way, and sparks went zinging just beneath her skin. She fanned herself, but her heated reaction to the man just wouldn't go away.

Patrick was listening to Meg talk about Deidre but was
staring at the pulse point at the base of Grace's ivory
throat. He had to get her alone for five minutes. A clever
man could do a lot in five minutes—given the opportunity. Too bad he couldn't think of anything to say. His
mind had short-circuited from the moment their hands
had touched.

"Gracie?"

Joe Mulcahy was walking across the yard toward
them. "Can you and Pat give me hand with something
in the barn?"

If Grace thought the request was unusual, she didn't
act as though it was. Personally, Patrick had lived with
a meddling Irishwoman until he'd moved to Ohio—no
one could hold a candle to his mom when it came to
sticking her nose into other peoples' business.

He stared at Joe until the man had to look away. He
was up to something, but Pat wouldn't find out what it
was if he didn't play along. Grace seemed to be clueless.

"Sure, Pop. What's up?"

When Pat didn't move fast enough, she looked over
her shoulder and asked, "Are you coming?"

He had to bite his lip to keep from uttering the words
that came to mind. "Uh, yeah. Right behind you."

He sprinted to catch up. Joe and Grace were already
in the barn, walking toward the back. "I was sure I'd
left it here," Joe was saying while he and Grace poked
through piles of what looked like car parts to him.

"Are you looking for the grill?" Grace asked. "I
thought you kept it on the other side of the barn, by the
building supplies."

Joe looked up when Pat entered the barn. "I used to
keep it there, but it seemed easier to store it here."

Grace was shaking her head and looking behind crates stacked along one wall. "I didn't think you'd want anyone coming this close to the Model A now that it's been restored."

"I don't," Joe answered. "See that you don't bump into it."

"Yes, Pop." Grace moved further along the wall.

"Joe?" Dan called from the doorway. "Cait's on the phone for you."

"Coming." Joe hesitated and stared from Patrick to Grace and back again. "You two keep looking. This call might take a while."

And that's when Patrick knew he was being reeled in and set up, but Grace wasn't going along with her father's plans. "Oh, can I talk to her first? I just have a quick question for her—"

Joe was already halfway to the door. "She'll be over later. You can talk to her then."

"But I—" Grace began, but when her father passed by the tarp-covered antique car he and her brother-in-law had lovingly restored and kept going, she whirled around and glared at Pat. "What's going on here?"

He held his hands up and struggled not to smile. "I have no idea."

She stalked toward him and drilled her finger into the middle of his chest. "You're lying."

He clenched his jaw and tamped down the instinctive reaction those words always caused—like a match to a stick of dynamite—but he refused to lose his temper with her. "I don't lie."

Her face paled and her hand dropped to her side. "I'm sorry, Patrick—it's just that I've been..." Her words trailed off and it didn't take a rocket scientist to figure out what she'd been about to say. Someone had lied to Grace, someone important enough to have hurt her.

The need to pound the living daylights out of whoever had left such a deep mark on Grace filled him. It was a struggle to keep silent, but he sensed that his reaction to her words was important.

He wanted to reach out and touch her but shoved his hands into his pockets instead. "There are usually two reasons people lie."

Grace's eyes filled. "There's never a reason to lie."

He took his hands out of his pockets and clenched them at his sides. He almost lost the battle against his will not to touch her—yet.

She wiped the tears with the backs of her hands and lifted her chin, daring him to contradict her.

He eased a half step closer, all the while watching her expressive eyes. "In my experience," he said slowly, "people lie because they are afraid to tell the truth for fear of hurting someone's feelings."

He pressed a finger to her lips and felt their trembling in his gut. Need filled him, want nearly had him on his knees, begging. He felt his throat constrict as desire for Grace slashed through him. Strengthening his resolve, he said, "And they lie because they don't care enough to tell someone the truth."

His mother had been right when she'd told him that the eyes were the windows to the soul. He saw so much in the grass-green eyes watching him. A long-ago hurt she struggled with—from her childhood when she'd lost her mother or more recent than that? Had the guy she'd brought to Meg and Dan's the last time he'd seen her done something to hurt her?

A tiny spark of hope flickered in the depths of her

eyes. He moved to close the gap between them. He wrapped his arms around her and fought not to groan aloud as her soft curves fit against him. Did fate and destiny have more in mind for him now that he'd stopped running from his past? Reveling in the feel of Grace Mulcahy in his arms, he tried to remember the snippets of conversation he'd heard but couldn't remember how long she'd dated the guy or when it had ended. Maybe it was because he hadn't been attracted to her too-thin form. But this new womanly version caught him by the throat and wouldn't let go.

"I don't lie, Grace. My mom taught us not to, and no matter how much what I have to say might hurt someone, I won't gloss over the truth, not even for a woman with eyes the color of shamrocks and lips begging me to kiss them."

Grace slid her hands up his back and over his shoulders, pulling him flush against her. He felt her generous curves pressing against him and had to close his eyes; he didn't want to scare her away with the depth of the need raking through him.

"I'm not begging you to kiss me," she mumbled against his collarbone.

He eased her back and locked gazes with her. "Oh no?"

Her mouth curved into a smile. "Begging's not the same as wanting." She pressed her lips to his jaw and he groaned.

"Wanting could lead to begging, Grace." He slid his hand down to the base of her spine and slowly up again, delighting in the way her body quivered beneath his touch.

He stroked his hands along her shoulders and down to her wrists, manacling them. "Will you let me kiss you, Grace?"

He wanted so much more than a kiss but would be damned if he'd give in to his body's clamoring like a teenager. He'd savor every step of his seduction of Grace Mulcahy.

When she realized he'd captured her hands as effectively as if he'd handcuffed them, her eyes changed to a deeper hue as desire and want filled them.

"May I?" He brushed his thumbs against the underside of her wrists and felt her pulse pounding there.

She tilted her face up. Green eyes glowing, she whispered, "Please."

He fought against the urge to feast and gently brushed his lips tentatively across her mouth. The sexy sound she made in the back of her throat made it hard to go slow. He fitted his mouth to hers, kissing her softly. With the tip of his tongue he traced the fullness of her bottom lip, adding kindling to the fire he was building between them.

He nibbled where he'd licked, and her sharply indrawn breath told him she was right there with him.

When her tongue tangled with his, he lost all perspective and let the kiss take them to the edge of desperation. When her hands started shoving his T-shirt up, his brain kicked in and he broke the kiss and their intimate connection. They stared at one another, though neither one spoke at first. His conscience wrestled with what he wanted to do and what he should do. Needing to catch his breath and struggling for control, he rasped, "Your father would hang me from the yardarm on the ship's mast in Mr. McCormack's field."

Grace laughed.

He liked the husky sound of it. Running his hands across her shoulders and down to her hands, he grasped them, lifting them up to his lips. Pressing a kiss to the backs of her hands, he confessed, "From the moment I saw you standing on the back porch with a ray of sunlight setting fire to the red highlights in your hair, I knew I wanted to kiss you."

When she remained silent, he added, "But I had no idea you'd set me on fire." Holding her hands against his heart, he told her, "I'm going to want another taste of you, Grace. Are you going to make me beg?"

Her lilting laughter filled the barn and his heart. "I've only got today and part of tomorrow. I'm not sure when I'll be able to get back."

Patrick was determined not to let her forget him when he'd only just found her. "Dan challenged me and a couple of the guys from my firehouse to a game of soccer next weekend, but the day's still up in the air."

Grace was watching him closely when she said, "Maybe I could visit Pop again next weekend."

He chuckled. "I have a feeling your father and Meg, and maybe your other sister, might be counting on that."

—◈—

Grace had suspected something was up but hadn't been paying close enough attention to catch all of her meddling family's telltale signals—just her father's. "Are you angry with them?"

"No. I come from a long line of matchmakers, but I have a feeling you weren't in on it."

"I wasn't," she said. "But I'm glad they meddled."

She laid her head against his chest and listened to the steady beat of his heart. Grace hadn't expected romance when she'd left Columbus. Was she reacting to Patrick because she was lonely, or was it because he'd been turned on by her curves instead of put off, as she'd expected him to be? Although no one from her hometown commented on her weight, she could see the speculative looks in their eyes, leaving her to wonder if they were mentally tallying up the number of pounds she'd gained. People in the city didn't meddle—just one more thing she loved about living there—but then again, people in the city weren't as openly friendly as people in her hometown.

Patrick's hand stroked up and down her back, soothing those worries until they evaporated under the hypnotic warmth of his touch. *Maybe I'm scared.* Patrick was the walking, talking version of her childhood dream of a man who worked with his hands, liked children, and was handsome as sin. She wasn't sure yet, but she'd bet her family's farm that he had a heart of pure gold.

But I'm not looking for a man!

He slid his hand higher. Cradling the back of her neck, he tipped her face up. His eyes darkened with desire that called to her, pulling at her until she realized it didn't matter that she hadn't been looking—he was real and he was here.

He leaned down and kissed her until her eyes crossed and she melted in his arms.

"Did you two find that grill yet?"

They broke apart and started to laugh. Dan shook his head. "Good thing Joe asked me to find out what was taking so long."

"Since you're here," Pat said, "why don't you tell us where he actually hid the grill?"

Dan's grin was infectious. "On the other side of the barn—he'd never keep anything like that by the Model A."

Grace tugged on Pat's hand. "Come on. I know right where it is." With a glance over her shoulder, she called out, "Tell Pop his plan is working like a charm."

Her brother-in-law's laughter confirmed their suspicions.

"Let's get that grill," Pat said. "I'm starving."

Chapter 6

THE SCENT OF MEAT GRILLING CARRIED OVER TO WHERE Grace stood beneath one of the oak trees in her family's backyard. Drawing in a deep breath, she sighed. "I've missed this." Turning to Meg, she asked, "Did you ever lie awake at night and imagine yourself as a mom?"

Meg's smile bloomed slowly as she cuddled baby Deidre in her arms. "No, I'd spent too many years trying to be a mom to you and Cait after mom died."

Interested, Grace urged her sister to tell her about it.

"I was going to take over the business from Pop and maybe start tracking down our cousins and making them an offer they couldn't refuse." The sounds of deep male voices drifted toward where they stood. "But then Dan came to town, turned my life upside down and inside out, and well…here I am."

Watching the twins whooping it up, running in a circle like they were little wild things and the grill was their bonfire, Grace couldn't understand her sister's serenity. "I guess we never really know what life has in store for us."

Meg put her arm around Grace and squeezed her close. "Fate, dear sister," she said. "And destiny."

"Serious talk for such a beautiful afternoon."

Grace grinned as Meg smiled and said, "Cait! You made it."

Deidre held out her arms to the middle Mulcahy sister and was passed off to Cait's waiting arms. "I just had a few things to catch up on this morning. Jack's bringing the potato salad."

"Looking for me, gorgeous?" Jack Gannon set a large bowl on the table behind the sisters and wrapped his arms around his wife and their niece. Deidre was babbling a mile a minute but stopped when he kissed his wife. From the way she giggled, Grace knew the little one was used to getting her share of her uncle's kisses too.

Jack pressed his lips to Deidre's forehead and snagged the little one from Cait's arms. "My turn." Settled on his hip, the two walked over toward the group of men—tall and small—standing around the grill.

With Meg in the middle, the sisters linked arms and listened as Cait caught them up on the latest news from Honey B. and Rhonda.

"So we'll have even more donations for Love Locks." Grace couldn't be happier. "I'm so glad Kate talked me into making that appointment with Honey B. to straighten out the mess I'd made of my hair."

Cait snorted. "That's what you get for snipping while you were sipping."

Once she started giggling, Grace couldn't stop. She ended up brushing away tears from the laughter. *It feels so good to laugh like that.*

"Did you check out the town website this morning? The pics turned out great."

Grace heard Cait's question but was distracted by the deep rumbling of male voices again.

—∿∿—

Pat watched the way the sisters linked arms and started talking all at once. They made a solid unit—like he and his brothers. Now he sounded like the oldest of his brothers, Tommy. *Not gonna go there.* He shoved those thoughts deep.

The ladies' laughter floated toward him and, like a tantalizing scent on the breeze, distracted him. They were quite a trio, heart-stoppingly beautiful. Cait and Grace were tall, with the same gorgeous green eyes and strawberry-blonde hair, and although they used to have the same slender figures, Grace's had filled out to bodacious proportions while she'd been living in Columbus. The petite firebrand in the middle, Meg, had auburn hair and bright blue eyes.

It was crazy to think a blind date with Honey B. had brought him here. How he let Snelling talk him into signing up for that online dating service he couldn't really remember. It might have been an ARI—alcohol-related incident. Whatever the case, Honey B. had been his intended date that night. To his surprise and approval, she'd shown up with reinforcements, Dan and Meg, to watch her back, and he'd ended up making new friends that had filled in part of the gap leaving New York City and his family had caused.

"My girls are gorgeous." Joe's voice broke through Pat's train of thought.

Patrick answered without thinking. "Yeah."

The older man's laughter caught Pat off guard. He turned toward Joe and asked, "Did I miss the joke?"

But Joe just smiled, turned the steaks, and sent the boys over to their mother to grab the bowl of potato chips. "Don't run," he warned them as he tossed a few burgers for the kids onto the grill, "or you'll spill your share of the chips."

Enjoying their antics, Pat watched Danny and Joey walk back with the bowl between them like it was TNT and about to explode. "You always know just what to say to those two."

Joe smiled. "They're a lot like my girls were growing up."

"Your girls were that wild?"

Joe's deep laughter had Dan and Jack breaking off their conversation. "Did you just ask if the Mulcahy sisters were wild when they were younger?" Dan asked.

"Just wondering," Pat replied.

"Did you hear about the time Meg climbed up to the crow's nest?" Dan asked.

Patrick just had to ask, "At the top of the mast in McCormack's field?"

Dan nodded.

"Or the time Cait tried to dye her hair blue with Jell-O?" Jack asked.

Pat shook his head, asking, "What wild stuff did Grace do?"

Joe sighed. "She was always the one to quietly rebel."

"So she wasn't as obvious as her older sisters?" Pat filed that information away with what else he'd learned so far about the beguiling woman.

"Wow," Jack said, staring at the sisters. "Separately they are gorgeous. Together—"

"They're stunning," Dan finished for him.

"Some little girls are going to be very surprised when they receive the new wigs that Love Locks will be creating for them with all the hair my girls donated."

"Whose idea was it?" Pat asked.

"Grace's," Dan told them. "She's the catalyst that had her friend Kate calling Meg who called Honey B. Once those three started talking, the ball got rolling."

When Pat stared at him, Dan shrugged. "That's how it is in Apple Grove. One good deed leads to another, and before you know it, the town's in on it and every-one wins."

Joe smiled. "It's what I love most about living here—that and the fact that the Mulcahy family's roots go deep." He turned to watch his youngest. "Maybe not all of us feel the same way, but two thirds of my girls do." His sigh was heartfelt. Joe shook his head and added, "Everyone has to follow their own path, make their own way." He locked gazes with Patrick. "Sooner or later a man meets his destiny and either accepts the fact, or he walks away from it."

Pat wondered if Grace's father knew Pat was run-ning from his past or if the man was referring to his daughter—the blonde goddess with the killer curves. A man's destiny could be twofold, couldn't it?

"Family's important." Joe watched Patrick intently. "Do you have family in Newark?"

A completely innocuous question unless you caught the underlying tone in Joe's voice—the man was dig-ging for information. Everything Joe knew about him was surface.

Patrick watched the way Grace laughed with her sis-ters and felt the jolt go deep. This could be the one his ma had warned him he'd meet one day when he wasn't looking, a woman who'd make all the ones he'd dated before fade in comparison.

"Ma's right," Pat whispered.

"What's that?" Joe asked.

Patrick shook his head to clear it of those thoughts and said, "Thinking out loud."

"You didn't answer my question," Joe reminded him.

"If you mean other than my firefighting brothers in Newark, no, my family's in New York—Brooklyn."

Joe looked up and Patrick knew the man was asking because he was curious for his daughter's sake.

"From the way you are with my grandsons, I'd say you have nephews and nieces of your own."

Pat found his equilibrium and his smile. "My three sisters are all married with kids. Grania's got three boys and two girls, Maeve has three girls, and Kelly has four boys. None of my brothers are married—yet."

Jack and Dan were keeping the boys from eating too many chips by starting a game of keep-away with the bowl. The boys enthusiastically chased after the men— and the bowl of chips.

"Always wondered what my life would have been like if there'd been a son added into the mix," Joe said softly. "But my girls are my heart." He stared out at the field behind the house for a few moments before looking down at the grill. "Hand me that platter. These babies are done."

Pat did as he was asked, surprised when Joe spoke up. "Are you going to keep me in suspense or tell me about your brothers?"

Pat laughed and told him, "I've got three. Tommy's the oldest, then me, Mike—then come the girls, Grania, Maeve, Kelly, and the youngest—Johnny."

"Salesmen and stockbrokers I suppose," Joe said cagily.

The snort of laughter escaped before he could stop it. "We followed the family tradition; we're all firefighters."

"Smoke eaters," Joe said. "Takes a certain breed of man to walk into a fire—had them in the coast guard. Scariest thing I'd ever seen in my life was a fire aboard ship."

Before Joe could begin what Pat sensed would be an amazing tale of courage, filled with danger, the women walked over, distracting him.

"So, Pop," Grace said, "what have you been up to?"

Patrick watched Joe deftly distract his youngest to keep from letting on that he'd been subtly grilling Pat for information. The man was a master at distraction, Pat decided, watching Grace turn around and head back inside to bring out the tray of condiments Joe had left in the kitchen.

The picnic table was just long enough to fit everyone, with a high chair for the baby at the end of the table. Watching the boys sitting on their knees to reach the table top reminded him of his childhood.

Grace's laughter had him turning to watch her. He had a gut-deep feeling that she'd fit right in with his family.

Maybe what he should have been focusing on was arranging schedules with Grace so they could start to fill in the blanks. He was pretty sure he'd convinced her to come back next weekend for the soccer game. But Patrick wanted to find out if the spark that sizzled between them could be kept going until it built into a flame that would last for years.

His last girlfriend hadn't been able to handle his job and had walked out of his life when he'd hit bottom and needed her most—after that tragic fire. The nightmares that plagued him—superimposing his nephew Michael's face over that of the boy's he hadn't been able to save—had sent him in a downward spiral. The spiral ended with his ex walking out and him trying to drown in a bottle of whiskey. It had taken months of his lieutenant and brothers badgering him to get help before he would even admit he'd tried to solve the turmoil inside of him by drinking himself to sleep—every night.

His heartbreak, the nightmares, and the breakup with his ex were all tangled up in a mass of emotion he had yet to unravel. He'd learned to push those feelings deep and move on with his life—accepting that he wasn't meant to have a woman to come home to. Or so he thought until he'd seen Grace again and felt the frisson of want and need spark to life.

"So," he drawled, "what's for dessert?"

"Cait made Boston cream pie."

"I love pie," Pat said.

"I guess you've never had it before, or you wouldn't be saying that," Grace added.

"OK," he said, "I give. Because…?"

"It's not really a pie," Jack told him.

"It's our grandma's recipe," Meg added. "It's actually a buttery vanilla layer cake filled with homemade custard and topped with confectioner's sugar."

Dan shook his head. "My mom's recipe for Boston cream pie called for melted chocolate poured on top."

"That's because she didn't have my grandmother's kick-butt recipe which does not call for chocolate."

"But I like chocolate," Dan mumbled.

"Me too, Daddy!" Danny scooted close to his father's side and patted him on the arm.

"I like Auntie Cait's pie." Joey jumped off the bench and followed Cait across the yard and into the house.

Dan chuckled. "So tell me again about this sugar fixation our boys have."

"All kids have it," Meg protested. "It's not just a Mulcahy thing."

"Yeah it is," her father said.

Instead of contradicting him, she just shook her head at him. Joe turned to Patrick and asked, "So, any interesting habits in the Garahan family?"

Pat thought about the way Tom and Mike had called

a family meeting and told them they'd be getting shamrocks tattooed over their hearts to support their Texas
cousins and help raise money for the first annual Take
Pride in Pleasure Day Celebration and Rodeo. At the
last minute, only Tom and Mike had been able to fly
out to Pleasure, Texas, to take part in the finale—
the lineup of Garahans and their Colorado cousins.
Cowboys, firefighters, and lawmen on stage standing
shoulder-to-shoulder…clad in worn blue jeans and
beat-up boots and all of them shirtless showing their
Irish pride and their Kelly-green shamrocks tattooed
over their hearts.

He'd seen the pictures after the fact but had been in a
downward spiral of grief and self-recrimination for not
saving that little boy from the Projects in time. Every
minute counts when there is smoke and fire involved.
Smoke could be deadlier than flame. He'd seen it countless times; it wasn't often that he or his firehouse lost
the battle to save victims. The fact that the boy was his
nephew's age and size had stuck with him—and then the
dreams—nightmares—started. Add in his ex walking
out on him and he'd been a total basket case. Whiskey
had been the only way he could cope—until he'd come
to the realization that distance might be the answer.

"Patrick?"

The warmth of the hand on his arm shook him from
his private hell. He looked down the table and over at
the shouts of delight coming from the kitchen. "Sorry.
Was just thinking about something."

"Want to talk about it?" Grace's eyes were such a soft
and lovely shade of green. His mother would be nudging
Pat toward Grace if she were here.

"Uh, no," he said slowly. "Not right now."

"With six kids in one family," Dan began, "I bet you were always up to something."

The snort of laughter escaped before Pat could contain it. "You could say that."

"Did your sisters follow you around?" Meg smiled as she waited for him to answer.

"Not after the time we left them up in the tree house without the ladder."

"How did they get down?" Danny wanted to know.

Pat grinned. "They howled like banshees until we brought the ladder back because we knew if Ma heard them, we'd be in hot water."

"So did you get caught?" Grace asked, her smile wrapping around his heart.

"Almost." Pat grinned.

"Your smile tells me there's more to the story."

He nodded. "Garahans don't get mad; they get even."

"What did your sisters do?" Jack asked.

"Put worms in our beds."

"Makes me glad I never had sisters," Jack said, getting up to help his wife with the cake.

Joe's booming laughter filled the air. "My Maureen would have loved this."

He looked away and Pat sensed the man was struggling with emotions that would never die. In his profession, Pat understood loss of life and fought damned hard not to lose that battle.

"She'd have been so proud of the lives you've made." He smiled at Meg and Dan. "She would have loved the grandchildren." Joe's eyes filled with unshed tears.

Patrick's stomach clenched seeing the emotion the older man fought to keep bottled up—yet one more thing they had in common.

Meg got up and walked over to put her head on her father's shoulder and wrap her arms around him. Not to be left out, Cait and Grace squeezed in, forming a huddle of femininity around Joe.

"We want to hug Gran'pop too!" Before anyone could stop them, Danny and Joey launched themselves at their grandfather, knocking into Grace in their hurry to join the group hug.

Patrick was up like a shot and caught Grace as she windmilled her arms to keep from falling. "Gotcha," he whispered against her neck, breathing in the subtle scent of lavender and rain.

"Why is Unca Pat kissing Auntie Grace?" Danny asked loud enough to be heard three houses down.

"He's not kissing her," Joey said. "He's sniffing her."

The rumbling laughter surrounding him lightened his heart. It felt good to hold Grace close and to have her nephews peppering him with questions. He wanted Grace in his life. He'd start out as friends, but he didn't want it to end there. He wanted it all.

Chapter 7

GRACE TREMBLED WITH AFTERSHOCKS, DROWNING IN the sensation of warm, firm lips so close to kissing her before her nephews interfered. It seemed fast, but already she was wondering how in the world they could make a relationship work with nearly two hours of travel time between. Was she really ready for this?

She eased out of his arms so she could look up into his eyes. Her family blurred into the background as their gazes locked and she saw the need swirling in his amber eyes.

"Little peepers, Grace." Meg's voice had Grace snapping out of the trance she'd been in—the spell Patrick Garahan had put her under.

"Gracie!"

"Hmm?" She looked at Meg first and then Cait. "What?"

Her sisters were shaking their heads at her, and she realized that she was still hanging on to Patrick like he was her lifeline and she was drowning at sea. It certainly felt like that time she'd gone swimming in the river and got caught in the mud and reeds along the bank. Her mind was muddled and her thoughts fuzzy— just as they had been back then, when she'd finally struggled free and broke through the surface of the water. The strong, firm hand grasping hers squeezed gently, tugging her the rest of the way out of the childhood memory.

"Does Cait's Boston cream pie taste as good as it looks?" Patrick asked.

"Oh yeah," Jack answered. "She's come a long way in the kitchen," he teased, earning a smack on the back of the head from his wife. "And her reflexes have improved too." He swept to his feet and scooped his wife in his arms, twirling her around in a circle.

"Can we play merry-go-round too, Unca Jack?"

He winked at his wife and set her down. To his nephews' delight, he picked them up at the same time, whirling them around until Meg had to tell him to stop or they'd throw up.

"You'd think a doctor would know better," Meg said.

After they'd devoured dessert, Meg announced it was time to clean up.

"But we want to play keep-away with Unca Jack and—" Joey began.

"Unca Pat and Dad," Danny finished.

"You two are going to help with cleanup duty first, while the men go fiddle with your grandfather's antique pickup."

"Can we—" Danny's question was interrupted by his mother's fierce frown. "Never mind."

Patrick lingered while the other men headed to the barn.

Grace was surprised that he didn't tag along behind them. "Aren't you going with them?"

"I'd rather give you a hand." He grazed her shoulder with the tips of his fingers, setting off a series of sparks beneath her skin that tingled long after the contact was broken.

"I, uh…" Grace started to say, struggling to get her tongue to work properly. "That is—"

"Thanks, Pat," Meg finished for her sister. "Boys, go on inside and get the plastic containers I left on the table. Pat, could you wrestle that garbage can over here? It'll be easier to just dump everything at once."

Patrick winked at Grace and sprinted over to the smaller outbuilding where two plastic cans sat by the corner.

"I keep some of my smaller wood scraps in the left one," Cait called out. "Grab the other one."

Surprised, Grace asked, "Don't you have a workshop over at your house yet?"

Cait shrugged. "Pop said there was no use moving everything when he'd probably be hanging around with time on his hands and could help me move the bigger projects around the shop."

Meg didn't stop to look up as she asked, "Like that solid oak credenza you just finished last week for Mrs. Winter?"

Cait smiled. "Yep, it was really heavy, and Jack doesn't want me lifting things."

Grace's hands stilled and her breath caught as she whirled around and stared at her older sister. "Cait, are you and Jack—"

Before she could get the question out, happy tears filled Cait's eyes. "I'm gonna be a mom."

Meg was laughing and Grace was crying as they pulled Cait into a group hug and held on tight. "You always did know how to surprise us, Sis," Meg rasped, her voice filled with emotion.

"Unca Pat!" Danny called out, coming out of the house.

"Something's wrong with Auntie Cait!" Joey yelled, running after his brother to where the women were huddled in a tight knot.

—◦◦◦—

Patrick reacted as he'd been taught at Randall's Island during training—instinctively. He spun around and sprinted over to where Cait stood bent over, held up by her sisters. "What's wrong, where does it hurt, Cait?"

Before she could answer, he yelled, "Jack, get your ass out here!" His booming voice had all three men bursting out of the barn.

Grace was amazed at the way Patrick took charge of the situation—even though there really wasn't one. He'd reacted without thinking—or had he? While he urged her sister to sit, Grace went over everything in her head; it had happened so quickly. Patrick had answered the call for help from her nephews and, while assessing Cait's physical state, had called for backup.

"She's fine, Patrick."

But he ignored her, taking Cait's pulse, watching her breathing and her pupils. "Caitlin, I asked: where does it hurt?"

"Grace is right. I'm fine."

"Then why—"

Before Pat could finish his question, the men arrived and Jack eased past him. "Expectant mothers shouldn't be lifting heavy things," he said quietly. "Or tiring themselves out."

Joe's face lit up like a kid on Christmas morning. "A baby?" He elbowed his way past Jack and pulled Cait into his arms. "Congratulations, string bean."

"Oh, Pop." Cait dissolved into tears.

"Can't you fix her, Unca Pat?" Joey asked.

"If Unca Jack can't fix her, nobody can," Danny said. "He's the doctor, 'member?"

Joey and Danny were squeezed tight on either side

of Meg, who still had tears of joy in her eyes. "I've saved all of Joey and Danny's baby clothes—in case you needed them."

Cait sniffled and was passed back to Jack. She rested her head against Jack's shoulder and sighed. "I'm just a little tired and weepy, guys," she told the boys. "You remember how tired your mommy was before baby Deidre was born?"

They nodded and looked from their mom to their aunt and back again.

"We'll save you a spot on our peewee soccer team," Dan told Jack.

Jack was shaking his head while Pat stood off to one side, watching the joy filter through Grace's family.

"Thanks, Patrick." Grace's touch on his arm was hesitant. "Sorry the boys spooked you."

He shrugged. "It's not a problem. I thought Cait looked tired when she arrived, but when the boys started yelling, my training kicked in."

She was watching him closely when she said, "You love it."

He noticed it wasn't a question but a statement. "Most of the time." He wasn't about to tell her about the times when he would lie awake at night, going over what-ifs until he was so wired he couldn't sleep. More often than not, he had trouble sleeping. When he glanced at Grace, she was watching him like a baby bird—wide-eyed and innocent. Thoughts of his ex had him wondering if he should just walk away now, before he lost his mind and his heart. And then Grace smiled.

He wanted nothing more than to wrap her in his arms and never let her go. Craving her touch, her smile, and her warmth wasn't a surprise; Pat had the same needs as any other man...but craving the comfort of friendship with Grace was unexpected.

His mother's voice whispered in his head, *Don't let this one get away, Patrick!*

Her soft smile added a deeper warmth to her green eyes. Silently, he agreed with his mother. He was Irish enough to recognize a sign from above when he saw one—Grace Mulcahy of the curvaceous body and generous heart haloed in that shaft of sunlight had definitely been a sign. He was keeping her.

Jack tucked Caitlin against his side. "I think somebody should lie down for a little while. Come on, gorgeous."

And as quickly as that, the family dispersed, and Pat and Grace were all alone. Working together, they cleared the table and walked over to the barn. He smiled when he heard the little voices echoed by Joe's much deeper one. "Those two are pistols."

Grace laughed. "They do give my sister a run for her money, but she'd never trade a moment of her crazy life."

When she fell silent, he wondered if she was thinking that she might. Since he'd already decided she was a keeper, he asked, "Would you?"

"Trade them?" She shook her head. "Not for all the tea in China."

"Good to know, but not what I was asking." He brushed at a strand of hair that got stuck on the curve of her lashes. He asked, "Would you trade your life?"

She blinked and sighed. "What part of it?"

Was she being dense, or was it him? "The moving away from Apple Grove and making a life for yourself in a city a couple of hours away from everyone you love part."

"I've always known exactly what I wanted. From the

time I was old enough to work in the office and balance the checkbook—I knew that something bigger, grander, flashier was out there. But it wasn't till Mom died that the need to leave began to take hold." She lifted her gaze to meet his. "You know what I mean?"

He thought of his nightmares after the fire—and the long journey up from the bottom of that bottle. Some days the temptation to have more than a sip tempted him. "Yeah. I do."

"Apple Grove is so—" She looked around and then back up at him. "I don't know if I can explain what it's like compared to living in the city."

"You don't have to. I lived in New York most of my life. Even though Newark is a city, it's a speck on the map compared to New York."

"Then you do understand?"

"Yeah, I left the bigger, grander, flashier for something simpler, homier. At first I thought I found it in Newark, but then I met Honey B. and your sister and came here." He let his gaze shift from her upturned face to the barn, across the wide expanse of the yard and to the field behind the house. "A man could settle down here and make a good life."

"I know of a few single women who would jump at the chance if you're offering."

Testing his theory that she wasn't including herself but that she was tempted, he traced the line of her jaw with the tips of his fingers. When she sighed and closed her eyes, he cupped her face in his hands and brought her mouth to meet his.

"I'm not interested in other single women, Grace." He swept his finger along the curve of her jaw. "I'm interested in you."

"We live so far apart," Grace said. "Long-distance relationships never work."

"So you're going to ignore what you know we've already got between us?"

She shivered. "I don't know."

"I think I could convince you," he rasped.

"But that wouldn't be playing fair," she said.

He sighed. "Too bad because I've got one hell of an idea for convincing you." Her mouth rounded in shock and he pushed his advantage, asking, "So you haven't changed your mind about next weekend, have you?"

She sighed and took a step back, adding distance between them. "I hate to make promises I don't know if I can keep, but I won't say that I'm not tempted."

He felt like a teenager. "Can I call you?"

She smiled. "I'd like that."

He dug into his pocket for his phone and handed it to her to input her number. "And you'll think about it?"

"I will."

"I'd better go." He didn't want to, but being this close to Grace, not knowing if they'd ever do more than share a few heart-stopping kisses, was hard to accept. He turned to leave.

Grace grabbed his elbow. "Patrick?"

He turned back. "Yeah?"

"I had a great time today."

He shrugged. He needed to put some distance between them since Grace had already put the brakes on things.

"You're making it hard for me to say no."

Patrick fought against the urge to take her in his arms. "Then let's see where we are after you've had a few days to think things through." He nodded and jogged toward his truck.

The last thing he saw as he backed out was Grace Mulcahy standing in the late afternoon sunlight waving good-bye. He hoped it wasn't for good.

Chapter 8

IN COLUMBUS, GRACE SLIPPED BACK INTO HER WEEKLY routine, rising early and working late. She loved her job and enjoyed the daily challenges. But there were moments during the day when she'd find her mind drifting back to Apple Grove and the man who'd jump-started her heart after it had been fine the way it was: tucked away—safe.

She'd replayed the kisses they'd shared every night in her sleep, but it was the way he'd acted with her nephews and fit into her family as if he belonged that had her looking forward to his calls.

By Friday night, they'd had a few short conversations, but his job kept interrupting—something she'd have to consider carefully if she was going to go forward as Patrick indicated he hoped to.

When her phone rang, she picked it up and smiled. "I was hoping you'd call."

"Nothing a man likes to hear more. How was your day?"

He sounded tired. Was it his job? "Busy," she said. "But I've caught up by working late every night this week. There were two projects I've been working on. Apparently I'm the spreadsheet queen in my office."

"Everyone has gift in life, Grace."

They both laughed and then he fell silent.

When she was about to ask him what was the matter, he spoke up. "Are you going to make me ask you again?"

She laughed. He'd asked her the same question every

time he'd called this week and she'd dodged answering. She owed him an answer. "I just got off the phone with Pop. I'm leaving tomorrow after breakfast, so yes. I'll be there for the weekend—and actually, longer. I was going to spend the next two weeks here in the city but talked to my dad about spending my vacation in Apple Grove."

His sigh of contentment was hard to miss. "I'm glad. Wondering if I'd see you this weekend kept me up when I should have been sleeping. Wait—did you just say you're spending vacation time with your dad?"

"Yes."

"So you'll be forty-five minutes from where I live instead of an hour and a half?"

She laughed. "Yes. Now, can we get back to the part where you're telling me you can't sleep? In your line of work that can't be a good thing," she said. "Is that why you sound so tired?"

"It's not really a problem," he told her. "I don't need a lot of sleep."

She had the feeling there was more to it than that. It didn't make sense that someone who worked as hard as Patrick did during the day wouldn't be sleeping. For now, she'd wait. He'd tell her about whatever kept him up nights sooner or later. Her gut told her it was something else. "Well, if you aren't going to tell me what keeps you up nights, tell me about your day."

"Busy. Only three routine calls today. Thankfully everyone is fine."

"You make it sound as if it's all just a part of your day, risking your life to save others."

He paused and said, "It is."

"Were they bad?"

He was quiet for so long, she wondered if asking him specifics was a bad thing. This was the part of getting to know someone that always made her nervous. She worried that she'd asked the wrong question at the wrong time—a question that would ultimately have the man running in the other direction—and into another woman's arms.

Finally he said, "The first one was a car fire out on the highway. Melted the tires it was so hot."

Something in his voice sounded off. "You sound really tired. Maybe you should get some sleep."

"I wouldn't be able to fall asleep if I hit the sheets now," Patrick replied.

"Are you sure? Sometimes, I think I'm beyond tired, and as soon as my head hits the pillow, I drift off."

He chuckled. "We need to stop talking about pillows and beds, or I'll never get any sleep tonight."

The innuendo and heat from his comment sizzled in the air. Grace fanned herself and tried to think of something to say to redirect the conversation.

But before she could, Patrick said, "If I wasn't so tired, I'd hop in my truck and drive out to see you tonight."

"I'm not sure I'm ready for what would happen if you did," she confessed. "I thought we agreed to get to know one another first."

He cleared his throat. "Uh, that is what I had in mind." His sexy chuckle had her imagination going haywire.

"Not fair."

"True," he agreed. "Sorry. We'll take it slow," he told her. "For now."

"Good night, Patrick."

"Night, Grace."

Saturday dawned with the promise of a warm day. Grace grabbed her suitcase, tote bag, and laptop, and headed downstairs. She'd stop for coffee on the way home. The drive gave her time to mull over the things Patrick had said last night—and the things he hadn't.

Every conversation revealed just a bit more of who he was, but she still had a feeling there was something he kept to himself. She was glad she'd have some time off from work and could spend part of it with her family, but she was really hoping to spend a good chunk of it with Patrick, so they could continue with their relationship and take it to the next level. She hoped he'd trust her with whatever it was that he seemed to be holding back. But that meant that eventually she might have to talk about how things ended with Ted—something she wasn't looking forward to.

The weather was gorgeous and the music just what she needed to lift her up and brighten her mood. The drive was blessedly uneventful. She pulled into the driveway, surprised but glad to see that Patrick's truck was already there.

"Hey, Pop," she called out as her father walked toward her from the open barn door.

"Hey yourself, Gracie." He hugged her and set her back so he could look at her.

"What?"

"I'm just glad that you'll be spending time with us. There's something I wanted to talk to you about, but that can wait. Patrick's still in the barn. I left him to tighten up a few nuts and bolts."

"Finished up, Joe. Hey." Patrick's deep voice had butterflies fluttering in her belly. "I'm glad you made it." His nearness had her blood pumping and her breath hitching in her breast—the same reaction she experienced last week.

"I've got to call Mary back," Joe said, looking from Grace to Pat and then back again. "Why don't you two—visit?" He was whistling when he walked up the back steps.

"Pop's up to something."

Patrick grinned and swept her off her feet and over his shoulder in a fireman's carry.

"Hey!" she said. "What are you doing?"

"Kidnapping you," he said, taking off at a jog, past the back porch steps, heading toward the field behind her family's house.

Breathless from surprise and the warm, firm hand on the seat of her jeans, Grace started to laugh. "Are you crazy?"

His answering rumble was unintelligible, so she tried to lift and turn so she could see his face. He picked up speed, so she had no choice but to fall back against his back. "Put…me…down!"

Surprisingly her demand was answered immediately as he swept her off his back and into his arms, but he kept going. His gaze was focused on something in the distance beyond the fenced-in field. Grace tried, but she couldn't figure out what he was staring at or where they were headed.

"What are we running from?"

He chuckled. "The face plastered against the picture window. I think your father's spying on us."

The vibrations rumbling around in his chest as he spoke soothed her into relaxing against him. As if that was all he'd been waiting for, he slowed down to a jog.

"I can walk," she insisted, although she had to admit, she'd never been carried anywhere before. Was this what it felt like, being carried away, the tangle of emotions leaving her breathless?

He slowed to a walk and settled her higher in his arms, so she was right against his heart. But the beat wasn't as fast as she knew hers would be if she'd been the one running and carrying someone.

"You're not winded at all and don't look tired." She didn't mean for her words to sound like she was accusing him, so she asked, "Do you run as part of your training?"

They were halfway across the field, headed toward the woods. "Yeah, we get used to training in our turn-out gear and breathing equipment—about one hundred fifteen pounds if you're a roofman like me—then add in the weight of the hoses. Hell, I could carry you for miles, Grace."

She frowned. Was he being nice? She knew she was heavy. "I'm not a lightweight anymore."

He grinned down at her. "I think you're gorgeous."

His strength awed her. The need to wrap around him like a vine nearly overwhelmed her. After their phone conversation, anticipation had kept her up most of the night. Nestled in his arms was right where she wanted to be, but she needed to be clear headed where this man was concerned. He was important and she didn't want to screw things up.

"I can walk."

He paused and looked down at her. "I like carrying you."

He shifted his handhold and slid a hand beneath her breast, grazing it. His touch sent her spiraling into another dimension where only the two of them existed and being held in his arms was the only thing that mattered. "I can't think when you're touching me."

"You're killing me, Grace." He set her on her feet and took her by the hand.

"How much time do we have before everyone gets here for the game?"

"Oh, sorry. I forgot to tell you. The game's tomorrow. I'm here just visiting today. Dan said he and Meg will be stopping by after they run errands." He tugged on her hand. "Now's our chance for a little alone time. Your father mentioned one of your favorite spots—that looks like it."

She smiled. "My favorite meadow. It has the sweetest grass. I spent a lot of time there as a kid rolling in it and picking blades for my fairy houses."

"That's what he said. Let's go."

Pinpricks of awareness sparked between them as they walked. When they reached the meadow, he stopped to pull her against him. But instead of the tongue-tangling kiss she expected, he placed soft, tentative kisses along the arch of her brow and down the curve of her cheek. "You taste like lavender." He paused to nudge her chin up and began to nibble the underside of it. "And rain." He pressed his lips where he nibbled, leaving a trail of kisses from her neck to her collarbone. "You're delicious."

His quiet words flipped a switch inside of her, allowing her to finally give in to the overwhelming need to let him lead wherever he was going. Reveling in his every caress, she was rewarded when his lips slid along her collarbone and pressed against the hollow of her throat.

She breathed a sigh of relief and tilted her head back, giving him silent permission to do more, hoping he'd take the hint to continue down toward her breasts. She suddenly ached for more of his touch. When he pulled back again, she nearly wept with need. "You're killing me."

"Baby, you have no idea what you're doing to me."

"Tell me then." Grace didn't mean for her voice to sound so breathy.

"I want to make love to you until I'm blind, crippled, and crazy."

She couldn't control the giggle at his words.

"Trust me," he said, tipping her head back so their eyes were locked on one another. "Once I get started, there will be no stopping."

Grace wondered if it had been his intention all along to drive her to the edge of distraction and leave her wanting. "This might sound like a line, but it's not. I've never felt like this before."

———

"Ah, Grace." He tucked his head beneath her ear and inhaled the fragrance that was already imprinted on his heart. "I feel the same way."

Her soft sigh had him settling her against his heart, ignoring the demands of his body, showing her his ability to cherish and not just take. He'd been in relationships before that were all heat and no heart. He didn't want that with Grace.

But would she pass the Garahan sticking test? His ex hadn't.

Firefighters gave everything they had to their jobs, so the women in their lives had to prove that they'd stick through the tough times, picking up the slack when their men were broken and bleeding on the inside from the very jobs that they loved. His brother Mike had found that with his fiancée, Moira.

He traced his thumb along the line of her jaw and the surprising tear that slipped from the corner of her eye. "Baby, what is it?"

"Just when I've decided I'm not what any man would want until I go on a crash diet, you walk into my life and have got me so twisted up on the inside wanting you that it hurts to breathe."

The hurt she tried to hide was there deep in her eyes. "Want me to hobble him?"

She blinked. "What?"

He slowly smiled. Her tears were gone and her eyes were clear. "The guy who made you think you need to be skinny. The ancient art of hobbling leaves your enemies alive but helpless."

She tilted her head to one side. "I'm almost afraid to ask what that entails."

"*Aut vincam aut periam.*"

"Latin?"

Gorgeous and smart. "Yeah. It means 'I will either conquer or perish.' It's our Purcell ancestors' family motto. My great-grandfather liked to pass on battle stories and they always ended the same—no quarter, no prisoners. We take care of our own, so you just say the word, sweetheart."

She shook her head. "Remind me not to make you mad."

He laughed and hugged her tight. "You suit me down to the bone, Grace Mulcahy."

She laughed, a low and sensuous sound as she nibbled at his lips. He gave in and pressed his mouth to hers, tasting the honeyed sweetness of her kiss until he thought he'd spontaneously combust. The need to make love to Grace screamed through him, but he wouldn't rush things—he would savor her a little bit at a time until they were both ready to make that leap. He craved her scent and another taste of her sweet lips and, for the first time in years, was afraid that he'd want her even if she didn't pass the sticking test.

Braced against his chest, his arms holding her tight, he swung her around and around in a circle until they were both dizzy and laughing. He turned one last time and tumbled them to the ground, skimming his hands from her shoulders to her curvy backside over and over, memorizing each and every dip, until he would remember how good she felt while they were apart.

When she moaned, he lifted his head up to lock lips with her, shifting his handholds to her sides, where he tortured them both by sliding his hands up, dipping in at her waist and then slipping between them to cup her bodacious breasts.

"Your curves slay me, Grace."

She reared back and stared at him. When he nodded to emphasize his words, she planted her elbows in his pecs and rested her head on her hands. After watching him like a hawk for a few minutes, her frown smoothed out and a look of puzzlement settled on her features. "You mean it," she said, "don't you?"

Sensing that his next words were crucial, he opted for a different way to get his point across. Sliding one hand to her backside, he pressed down until she was snugged up against him. The heat from her sweet center nearly burned him alive. Lifting his torso, with his free hand he cupped the back of her head and brought her lips to meet his.

He tasted the sweetness she had in abundance before tracing the fullness of her bottom lip with the tip of his tongue. She moaned and he tangled his tongue with hers, coaxing her to take what she wanted, giving all that he could.

When they finally had to come up for air, she laughed softly. "Was that your answer?"

"Do you want me to tell you again?" he teased, knowing that there was no way he could kiss her like that again and not have it all. He ached from holding back when his body craved being buried to the hilt inside her.

"I don't want you to think that I'm like this with every guy I meet."

The urge to keep teasing her was strong, but the serious expression on her face and hint of sorrow in her eyes had him moving past the urge. "Same goes, gorgeous. I felt like I'd been poleaxed when I saw you standing there."

"Really? My dad always said that's how he felt the first time he saw mom."

"I was unable to move, speak, or think when I saw you standing in the sunlight with your killer curves and soft, sweet smile." *Jesus, did he just say that out loud? She's gonna think you're full of it, Garahan.*

Instead of the reaction he expected, she sighed and laid her head over his heart. "I know exactly what you mean. I've always been a sucker for a man with broad shoulders."

"Yeah?"

"Ummm…and broad workingman's hands."

He held her with one hand and lifted the other to look at it, but she didn't notice. Her eyes were closed, a look of bliss on her pretty face. "Really?"

"Really," she whispered. "But the part that totally had my attention—"

"My über-athletic muscles?"

"No."

"The Garahan auburn hair?"

"No."

"My height?"

She giggled. "No."

"I give up," he finally told her. "What was it?"

"The way you played with Danny and Joey."

Jeez, Ma, he thought. *You were right!*

"So—" he began, only to be interrupted by her scream of terror.

He shot to his feet with her in his arms. "What's wrong? What is it?"

She was trembling in his arms. "Big, black, hairy," she rasped, hiding her face against his chest.

Before she could say another word, he was running back toward the house.

"Aren't you going to step on it?"

He jolted to a stop. "The bear?"

She looked at him as if he'd lost his mind. "What bear?"

"The one you saw…you know, big, black, and hairy?"

She scrunched up her nose and started to laugh— deep belly laughs that made it hard to hold on to her. He set her on her feet and planted his hands on his hips. "You didn't see a bear."

She shook her head.

"Or a wolf."

"Wolves aren't usually black," she told him. "Besides, we have coyotes out here, not wolves."

"So it wasn't a coyote either."

She threw her hands up in the air and whirled around, stomping through the field toward home. "It was a spider. OK? I hate spiders!"

She'd walked about fifty feet before he finally calmed down enough to follow after her. "Don't ever scare me like that again, woman."

Grace, being Grace, laughed over her shoulder at him.

"I mean it," he said, reaching for her arm and pulling her to a stop. "Save the hysterics for serious stuff. You know, like muggers, really big wild animals—your father catching us making love in your hayloft."

She giggled as he'd intended, making him smile. "Seriously, you scared the shit out of me. My heart gets a hard enough workout on the job. How would it look if I had a heart attack all because you screamed and I scooped you up in my arms and tried to outrun a bear for five miles?"

She slipped her arm through his and tugged to get him moving. "I'm sorry. Come on," she urged. "If we don't head back now, I'll let you distract me again, and this time, I'll pick a spot without spiders. I've always heard that firefighters have an amazing amount of stamina."

He swallowed the spit pooling in his mouth rather than drool. He cleared his throat. "We do."

She leaned close and whispered, "Actions speak louder than words."

He wanted nothing more than to grab her and rip their clothes off, but he'd already made the decision not to rush things, and not just for her sake—for his sanity. Clenching his teeth, he ground out, "I'm trying to be considerate, not rushing you, but you're making it impossible."

She stared up at him with an adorable smile on her face. He wasn't in this alone. "I think we both want the same thing." He said the words slowly, giving her time to either agree or disagree.

She nodded. "But," she said, "there's more to life than the mattress mambo."

Truer words, he thought. Patrick lifted her hands and brought them to his lips, placing a chaste kiss on the back of her left hand and then the right one. "I'm looking for someone I can laugh with, cook for, play with, make love to, make babies with—I want it all, Grace. If that's not what you're interested in, then tell me now."

Her eyes widened at his confession, and before he could blink, they were glistening with unshed tears. "What if you decide a few months from now that I'm not woman enough for you?"

He slid his hands to the curve of her hips and grabbed hold of her. "Not a chance."

"What if you change your mind and want a brunette?"

"I'm not into games, Grace."

Her smile transformed her face from pretty to beautiful.

"Do you think your dad is still watching out the window?"

Grace laughed. "Probably has his binocs out."

Pat grinned. "Then let's give him something to see." He lifted her up, tossed her over his shoulder, and ran toward the house.

Chapter 9

"So," Dan drawled, "you always carry women around like a sack of potatoes?"

Pat was breathing hard but not winded, so he laughed. "Depends on the woman."

"Put me down!" Grace demanded.

"What's the magic word?"

"If you think you can haul me around and then treat me like a kid—"

"Mind your manners, Grace," Joe said. "She's been known to get grumpy without enough coffee," Joe added. "The pot's fresh and Meg stopped by the diner to pick up doughnuts."

"Please, put me—"

Before she could finish, he switched handholds and had her cradled in his arms. Grace's face was red from hanging upside down. Maybe he shouldn't have run that far with the blood rushing to her head.

She patted him on the shoulder, her signal to put her down. He hesitated, and she said, "I'm used to hanging upside down. It's how I relax."

He set her on her feet and the guilt faded. Her cheeks were flushed, but her eyes were sparkling with what his ma would say was deviltry. He shook his head. Not possible. Grace was an angel.

Joe chuckled. "When the three of them would watch TV, Meg would be sitting crossed-legged, Cait would be lying on her stomach with her elbows in front of her and her head propped up on her hands, and little Grace would be hanging off the sofa upside down. I gave up trying to get them to sit like ladies a long time ago."

Patrick enjoyed being around the Mulcahys. As a family unit, they were tight, like his. He and Dan had become friends the moment the word *soccer* had been mentioned. The first time he'd met Jack Gannon, he'd liked him.

Grace handed him a plate filled with mouth-watering sweetness. Looking from the plate to her full lips, he couldn't decide which he wanted to sample more. When someone cleared their throat, he realized he'd been staring at her without speaking. "Looks good enough to eat."

Grace's laughter tugged at his heart when she focused her dimpled smile on him. "You seemed to like the first taste you had."

Oh man! She was killing him—and she knew it.

When Grace winked at him and spun around to pass the plate around, he knew he was going to enjoy every minute spent with her. Figuring out the rest of his week in his head, he realized free time was at a premium, but if he could convince her to stay over at his place a night or two, they'd have more time together. They were both adults, and as long as they were on the same page, at the same time, then maybe a little seduction would be just what the doctor ordered.

~~~

Grace wondered what Patrick was thinking. At first she could tell by the set of his jaw and desire in his eyes, but now, he was staring into his cup of coffee—thinking deeply, like Pop sometimes did when he was thinking of mom. Did he have something tragic in his past too? Given the nature of his job, it was a definite possibility.

The urge to find out what was on his mind niggled at the back of her brain. The need to help him heal was almost as much of a surprise as wanting to know what was troubling him. She'd been in two serious relationships—serious enough to be thinking about wedding dresses and white picket fences—but since life is full of surprises and both guys had disappeared after the "where do you think our relationship is headed" chat, Grace was hesitant to think about more than just the present.

Live in the moment. That's what her best friend, Kate McCormack, always told her. Thoughts of Kate had her wondering about the latest blind date her friend had been on.

She'd have to call Kate and catch up—maybe she could stop off at the diner on her way home.

She noticed Patrick was watching her intently.

What's on his mind now? "Thanks."

Before Grace could let her mind drift much further, Patrick was holding a chocolate-covered doughnut in front of her face. She could tell it was one of the cream-filled ones. "Come on, one bite won't hurt."

She was about to refuse, but then remembered his earlier comment about her curves. *What the hell.* She opened her mouth and the combination of chocolate and cream melted on her tongue. "Mmmm." Their gazes locked and she was thinking about the last kiss they'd shared. He was delicious too. Live in the moment—she knew better than most that none of us knew how long each of us would be here.

"So, Grace," Meg said slowly, "what are you cooking for dinner tomorrow?"

"Who said I was cooking tomorrow?"

"Pop said you had some time off and were spending a few days with us. Since you are, he figured you'd want to cook for us."

Grace frowned at her sister first, her father second. "Did he?"

"Meg's beyond busy with her job and her family," Joe said. "And given Cait's news—they'll be here tomorrow too by the way—I'd think you'd be delighted to cook dinner for all of us."

His pointed look said way more than words.

"OK, how many will be here?"

Dan grinned. "We'll all be here."

"That's five of us," Meg said, "but better just count four since baby Deidre won't be eating grown-up food."

Grace rolled her eyes and said, "I guess I'll have to call Cait and ask if Jack has any house calls lined up for tomorrow after church."

"Jack is used to eating nuked food. Why don't we meet back here after church? I'm really glad you're cooking, Grace." Meg winked at her as the twins walked into the room.

"We're coming again tomorrow?" Danny asked.

"Are you gonna be here, Unca Pat?" Joey asked.

"Yes," Grace told Danny before turning toward Patrick to wait for his answer. When he merely cocked an eyebrow as if to say *Are you gonna ask me?* she laughed. "I think if we ask Patrick nicely, he might come for dinner."

Danny yanked on the hem of her T-shirt at the same time Joey said, "Ask him, ask him!"

She was still laughing when she asked, "Would you like to come to Sunday dinner tomorrow?"

Patrick's smile faded and a serious expression settled on his handsome features. "What are you having?"

Joe and Dan thought his question was hysterical and broke into guffaws of deep laughter. "I used to ask the same thing when Maureen and I were dating," Joe said.

Grace smiled. "Don't worry. I'll call Kate for some recipe ideas."

Her friend picked up on the third ring. "Hey, Grace. How's it going?"

"Great. I'm calling for two reasons—one, I just found out that I'm cooking for everyone tomorrow; and two, did you go out on another date with that guy you met through the online service?"

Kate hesitated before asking, "Would that hunky fireman be included in everyone?"

"Yeah." Grace noticed her friend ignored the second part of her question. "So I need a menu suggestion for ten for tomorrow."

"Hmmm, difficulty level?" Kate asked.

Grace sighed. "You have anything that's semi-easy that gets rave reviews?"

Her friend paused. "What's in the freezer?"

"Not sure. Can I call you back?"

"OK, I'll have a couple of ideas ready for you."

Grace walked back to the kitchen, shaking her head at her father and Patrick, who were still munching doughnuts and drinking coffee. "Did Meg and Dan leave with the boys?"

"Yes, and Dan reminded me about the game. I can't remember if I told you—I got distracted."

Their eyes met and she knew he was remembering their time together in the meadow. When he smiled, she knew he was remembering the spider.

"Great, now I'm cooking for a whole soccer team," Grace grumbled, going to the freezer.

She opened the freezer. "I have to tell Kate what's in here—wow." Everything had been labeled and dated. "Must be Mary's doing."

Her father grunted—his way of agreeing sometimes.

Sorting through everything, she realized there were a bunch of smaller frozen options, but nothing that would feed ten—maybe as many as sixteen. She shook her head, hit redial, and told Kate, "I'll have to go to the store. Not enough of any one thing in here to feed this crowd."

"I thought that might be the case," Kate said. "It's usually just your dad and Mary on weekends."

"Really?" Grace was surprised because she hadn't seen Mary yet.

As if Kate could read Grace's mind, she added, "Mary doesn't close up Murphy's Market until just before dinnertime on Saturdays."

"Ah." Grace should have figured that her father had some sort of life now that he had an empty house most of the time. That thought led to another one: Did he spend more time at home or at Mary's? She'd have to ask one of her sisters.

"Meatballs and spaghetti would easily feed a crowd, especially if you make your meatballs a little smaller than my mom does."

Grace considered the idea and realized it was the perfect solution. "Kids usually like spaghetti. I think the guys would like it too, but I just found out that they're playing soccer tomorrow too, so I'll need to feed more than I'd planned on."

"I'd go with meatball sandwiches then," Kate suggested. "If you make the meatballs a little smaller, you can stretch a single batch to feed ten. A double batch will easily feed twenty. Hey," Kate asked, "what about dessert?"

Grace groaned. What had her father gotten her into? "Darn, I didn't even think about feeding them dessert. Dinner's going to be enough of a challenge feeding so many."

Kate laughed. "Easy or hard?"

"Jeez, Kate, it's not like it's thirty years ago and I'm trying to snag a man with my cooking!"

That had them both chuckling. "Why not go super easy and pick up two boxes of brownie mix?"

"But that's not homemade." After she'd said it, Grace wondered if it mattered.

"You could always ask me nicely and I can save two pies for you."

"Wow, I didn't even think about asking you for a pie…you're offering me two? What's the occasion?"

"Nothing," Kate said far too quickly for Grace's peace of mind.

"Hmmm. I'm not sure what his favorite—"

"Whose, your dad's or Patrick's?"

"Smart-ass," Grace said. "Since you know so much, what is Patrick's favorite type of pie?"

"He'll eat any kind of pie, but I think he's partial to apple."

"Would you please bake two for me and I'll owe you?" When Kate agreed, Grace asked for a second time, "Now what happened last night?"

Her friend didn't answer.

"Kate?" Grace urged.

"Nothing," Kate insisted.

"Something happened last night, didn't it?"

Kate's sigh was just audible enough for Grace to catch. "If you don't want me coming over there right now, you'd better fill me in."

Kate sighed louder. "He just wasn't quite what I expected."

"Meaning?" Grace hoped her friend wasn't hiding something important, like she had with her last loser boyfriend—the one who knocked Kate around when he started drinking.

Her friend's refusal to talk about it convinced Grace something bad happened. "You'd tell me, wouldn't you?"

"If there was something really wrong? Maybe."

"Define *really*," Grace said.

"Drop it, or I won't text you my mom's meatball and sauce recipe."

"Fine."

"Good."

"Thanks," Grace grumbled.

"Bite me," Kate said, making Grace smile.

"I love you even when you're crabby, Katie."

"Yeah, yeah," her friend said. "Same goes."

Grace disconnected and walked outside.

"Everything OK?" Patrick's deeply rumbled question eased the stiff set of her shoulders.

She was worried about Kate. She hadn't been in town the last time Kate had ended up in a bad situation with the wrong man. But how much should she tell the man who'd just entered her life?

"We'll be having meatball sub sandwiches tomorrow—just in case we need to feed a couple of hungry firefighters."

He nodded but hadn't taken his eyes off of her. "Something has you worried."

How could he tell? "What makes you say that?"

"It's there in your eyes." He reached out a hand toward her; she waited a beat before taking it.

"Sometimes it's better to get stuff that's worrying you off your chest."

"And then again," Grace said, "some things are better kept to yourself."

"I know everything is happening at warp speed between us, but I'm a good listener and ace problem solver, being second oldest in the New York Garahan clan."

She shrugged. *What could she say? Where did she start so he wouldn't think she was worrying unnecessarily just because she had a bad feeling?*

The warmth of his hand eased another kink of tension inside of her. Maybe she should share her burden. "You might think I'm overreacting."

He tilted his head to one side. "I have three younger sisters."

What kind of a response is that? Her head started to ache with all of the thoughts and questions swirling around inside of it. She finally blurted out, "What does that have to do with anything?"

"I told you." He tugged on her hand to get her to stop. "I've had lots of practice listening without passing judgment—I always left the judging to my older brother, Tommy. He can be a real pain in the ass, but there's no one I'd rather have at my back—well, except for my younger brothers, Mike and John."

"And you never laughed at your sister's worries?"

He laughed. "And run the risk of getting clipped in the jaw?"

"Did they really punch you?"

"A couple of times, until I caught on that they really

did want a sounding board, especially after our dad died." Patrick looked off into the distance, seeing something far beyond the field.

"It's just a bad feeling I have," Grace confessed.

"In your gut, can't explain why you have it?" Pat asked. He did understand. "Yeah."

"Worst kind and usually a portent of doom if the Garahan sisters are involved. What's up? Who's in trouble?"

"I'm not sure if she's exactly in trouble—yet—but I think she might be headed that way."

"Since both of your sisters are married to great guys, whom I'm happy to call friends of mine, it must be a friend. Am I right?"

She nodded. "She'll kill me if I say anything, but then again, if she's mad at me for the rest of her life, but safe, I'd be OK with that."

Patrick frowned down at her. "Spill it, Mulcahy."

"It's just a feeling, remember?" When his frown intensified, she grumbled, "There's nothing really to spill, but, well, she's been using an online dating service."

"Didn't she check the guy out ahead of time?"

"I don't know. She didn't say much about the last guy, but apparently he liked to push her around."

"OK. Doesn't she have family in town? Friends who still live here who would kick her butt for not calling on one of them as backup for their first meeting?"

She smiled up at him and squeezed his hand. "Like Meg and Dan did for Honey B. that first time she met you?"

He nodded. "I liked Honey B. a lot but could tell her mind was on someone else. But I made a bunch of friends from that one dinner, and I felt a whole lot better knowing Honey B. had friends who cared enough to be her backup."

"You really are one of a kind, Patrick Garahan."
Grace traced circles on the back of his hand while she
thought about how to approach the subject with Kate.
"She doesn't want to talk about it, but I know the first
date didn't go according to plan. She went out with him
for the first time last night."

"And you're worried?"

"Yeah."

"Let's go." He tugged her toward his truck.

"Where?"

"Don't know. You tell me and I'll drive there. If
you're that worried about your friend, you'll have to
trust me to help. I never ignore bad feelings, Grace."

"Let me tell my dad we're leaving." She ran over to
her father and told him she and Pat were going for a ride
to pick up the groceries for their Sunday dinner.

She hopped up into Patrick's truck, and he closed
her door and got in the driver's side. Putting it in re-
verse, he let out the clutch and backed out to the street.
"Where to?"

"The diner."

"Is it Kate or Peggy?"

She should have realized he'd know both sisters.
"Kate."

"Good because I think Peggy is seeing one of the
guys from my firehouse, and I'd hate to have to beat the
crap out of a fellow firefighter."

Grace could picture Patrick punching some equally
large guy's lights out. "You would, wouldn't you?"

He kept his eyes on the road and answered, "You
betcha. Women may think they are just as strong as a
guy, but unless they're bodybuilders or weight lifters,
chances are pretty slim—different muscle mass." He

glanced at her and grinned. "By the way, I'm loving the way yours is put together."

She punched him halfheartedly and told him to keep driving. As they turned onto Main Street, she wondered how she'd get Kate to tell her the details.

As if he'd been thinking along similar lines, Pat said, "Let's just get her talking."

"She's giving me her mom's Italian meatball and sauce recipe and two apple pies."

Patrick whistled. "I really like your friends." He paused then said, "We can tell her I wanted to thank her in person for the apple pie."

"OK." Grace crossed her fingers as he parallel parked his pickup in front of the diner. "But if she starts to get pissy, you may want to wait outside."

He pressed a kiss to the tip of her nose. "I'm here as backup; use me."

Just when she thought she had the man figured out, he managed to surprise her. "I'll let you start talking, since I like the pie idea."

"Got it." Patrick opened the door for Grace and waited for her to go first.

A gentleman. Her mom would have liked that.

"Hey, Grace, Patrick," Peggy called out as they walked inside. "It's great to see you two."

Grace noticed the conspiratorial smile on Peggy's face and wondered what kind of gossip she had just spread; it usually put a smile on the older McCormack sister's face. As Peggy continued to smile at the two of them, Grace wondered if the look on Kate's sister's face had anything to do with the intrigue going on at her house. Everybody there seemed to be pushing her into Pat Garahan's arms—not that she didn't want to be there. It was an exciting place to be. And she knew it would only become more so. But still…

"Hey, Peggy," she finally said. "Is Kate in the back?"

"Yeah, go on around while I keep your boyfriend company."

"I'll wait out here for you and Kate."

Kate should have heard his voice by now. Sure enough, her friend pushed the door to the kitchen open and walked out.

Patrick grinned. "I owe you a debt of thanks."

She smiled at him. "Ah, you heard about the pies for tomorrow?"

"Yes. I'm real partial to apple."

"I told Grace you were. I've just finished the crust and was about to fill the pies. You can come on back if you can keep from snitching while I'm baking."

Grace was surprised at how easily Patrick put her friend at ease. Normally, Kate would never invite anyone in the back—well, except for Grace, but she was practically an adopted sister in the McCormack household.

"Don't touch anything unless I say you can," Kate said without turning around. "Got it?"

"Yes, ma'am," Pat said.

When Kate turned around with her hands on her hips, Grace was braced for her friend to lose her temper—Kate hated to be called ma'am—but she didn't. She just shook her head at Pat and said, "You're lucky I like you."

They walked over to one of the long counters in the back where Kate had been rolling out crust and mixing the filling. "Here." She broke off a piece of uncooked crust and handed it to Pat.

He chewed and groaned. "Amazing. It's as good as my mom's."

Kate harrumphed. "Probably better."

Pat shook his head. "Now there's where you'd be wrong, but I'd love to be the one to have one of my ma's pies right beside one of yours so I could do a taste test."

Kate grinned. "Wouldn't be the first time. We don't mind putting our pies to the test. It's our grandmother's recipe."

When she turned her back, Pat nodded at Grace. "You look tired, Kate," Grace said. "What time are you closing up?"

"Gee thanks," Kate grumbled. "You know we're always open late on Friday and Saturday nights."

"If you're not closing until eleven o'clock, is Peggy driving you home?"

Kate put her hands on her hips and leveled a glare at Grace. "Why?"

"No reason," Grace mumbled, looking at Pat, hoping he'd have a way to soften her friend up.

He was quick to say, "I'd be just as worried and give my sisters the third degree whenever I'm in Brooklyn."

"Maybe I don't like it," Kate bit out, mixing the apples, sugar, flour, and spices until they were coated evenly.

Pat chuckled good-naturedly. "They don't either, but it never stops me. When you care about your family and friends, you risk getting the sharp edge of a female's tongue."

That comment had Kate's mouth hanging open.

Grace glared at Patrick. "What about your brothers?"

"They don't snip at me; they toss punches."

"And that's so much better," Kate said, dividing the apple mix between the two lined pie plates.

"Sometimes, the punches hurt less than words—words can leave marks that fester or bleed on the inside."

Kate just shrugged and Grace knew for a fact that her friend's date had either said something or done something that had Kate worried; she wasn't normally this quiet.

"Have a nice time last night?"

Kate's head shot up and her gaze locked with Grace's. For a heartbeat they just stared at one another without speaking. Finally, Kate said, "We went out to Slater's Mill for a couple of burgers."

"Sounds like fun."

Kate's expression said it was anything but. When she lifted her arm to brush her bangs out of her eyes with her forearm, the sleeve of her blouse slipped down, revealing purple bruises on her wrist.

Patrick's face showed no expression, but his eyes were dark and dangerous. He'd seen the bruises too.

Kate was concentrating on what she was doing and didn't see the looks Grace and Pat exchanged.

"Is he someone from town?" Grace asked now that Kate was putting the tops on the pies.

"No. Is this why you stopped by?" she asked. "To give me the third degree about my date?"

Patrick shook his head. "It was to personally thank you in advance for the pies and the meatball recipe."

Kate's expression changed, and she seemed more at ease. "You're welcome. And since you're here, I'll just make a copy of ma's recipe for you, Grace."

While she went to the back room where the tiny diner office was located, Pat turned to Grace. "Those were vicious bruises."

Grace felt sick at heart, hurting for her friend. But now she was definitely going to make Kate talk. She knew she'd have to risk making her friend mad at her, but what choice did she have? "If you go out and talk to Peggy, I'll ask Kate when she gets back."

Pat pressed a kiss to her temple and walked out into the diner. Kate didn't seem surprised that Grace was alone, waiting for her. "Here's the recipe."

"Thanks." She paused, hoping that Kate would say something, but in the end her friend didn't. "Kate, you know you are my best friend in the entire world, right?"

Kate sighed. "God, you always say that right before you do or say something to piss me off."

Grace snorted. "I guess that makes me predictable."

"Pretty much," Kate said.

"I saw the bruises. He hurt you, Katie."

To Grace's shock, Kate's eyes filled. "Yeah."

Grace hesitated before asking, "Did he do more than bruise your wrist?"

Kate held up her other wrist so that Grace could see the identical bruising there. "Oh, sweetie." Grace held out her arms and Kate walked into them. She sniffled but didn't cry. Kate rarely did. "Want me to go beat the crap out of him?"

"He'd hurt you, Gracie."

"Want me to ask Patrick to go beat the crap out of him?"

Kate leaned back and started to giggle. "Maybe."

"Patrick!" Grace called out. A moment later, his broad-shouldered form stood in the doorway to the kitchen.

"You need me?" he asked, looking from one woman to the other and back.

"Kate might need you to beat someone up."

He cracked his knuckles and grinned. "I'm your man."

"Have you talked to Mitch yet? You should probably press charges."

"And tell him what? That I was stupid enough to meet a guy I didn't even know?"

"Pretty stupid not to even give Mitch a chance to do his job and question the guy or bring him in on assault charges."

Kate's gaze met hers and Grace knew her words had hit home. She waited a moment before asking, "What about Deputy Jones?"

Tears formed and fell, but Kate didn't answer Grace's question. She put her arm around Kate and told Patrick, "We're going to the powder room. Be right back."

"I'll be waiting in the diner."

"Thanks," Grace said.

When they were in the ladies' room, Kate protested, "You can't let Patrick get into a fight over my mistake."

Grace ran cool water over a towel to bathe Kate's face. "Patrick is a big boy. He'll make his own decisions. Just tell me what happened," Grace urged. "It'll make things easier when you talk to the sheriff."

"Things were going OK at first, and we were actually having a good time, but then one of the guys from high school came over and started to talk to me. You know me. I can't not talk to people—it's in my blood."

"That's why the diner does such a great business and you always know all the gossip."

"Well, I guess my date didn't like me talking to another man while he was footing the bill for dinner."

Kate filled her in on the rest, and when Grace asked if Kate wanted her to stay with her when she talked to the sheriff. Kate shook her head.

"Let's go find that big handsome firefighter of mine. We'll walk with you to see Mitch."

"So," Kate drawled as they headed out to back door, "he's your firefighter?"

Chapter 10

THEY LEFT KATE IN GOOD HANDS, NOT SURPRISED THAT she didn't want them hanging around, and drove to the next town over to the supermarket there. When they got back to the Mulcahys' house, the driveway had only two cars in it. Recognizing Mary's car, Grace wondered if they should have called to let her dad know they were on their way back. They'd been gone a lot longer than expected.

When Pat parked, she said, "Give me a minute to call my dad."

"But we're right..." Patrick's voice trailed off as he followed the direction of Grace's gaze and noticed as she had that the house was dark.

"Maybe we should drive on over to Goose Pond and call from there," Grace suggested.

They got back in the truck, backed out, and drove to the pond.

———※———

"Joe, is that a car door?" Mary eased out of his arms and cocked her head to one side to better hear.

"Probably Gracie."

"Wasn't she due home a while ago?"

"Yes, but she's with Pat Garahan. Nice man. Firefighter from Newark."

Mary was out of his bed like a shot. "Where are my clothes?"

Joe's laugh startled her into standing still. "I think

your shoes are in the kitchen...your dress on the banister...and your—"

Mary put her hand on his mouth and started to laugh with him. "You are a wicked, wicked man."

He pulled her back into bed. "And you love every minute of it."

When the phone rang a few minutes later, he let the answering machine get it. And to his dismay, Mary squirmed out of his arms a second time in ten minutes and started pulling on his arm to get him out of bed. "They'll be here in a few minutes. We've got to get my clothes."

"I'll be right behind you, sweetheart." She looked over her shoulder in time to see his wink as he added, "Just enjoying the view."

Mary laughed and headed for the stairs.

———

"The lights are on downstairs," Grace pointed out as they drove back into the driveway.

"OK," Patrick said, pulling up behind Mary's car. "Tell me again why we couldn't just shoot them a text from the driveway?"

Grace's sigh was definitely exaggerated. "Because then they'd know that we'd know what they'd been doing."

"What if they heard us pull in before?"

Grace put her fingers in her ears. "Don't want to think about OPS anymore, OK?"

Patrick chuckled as he hefted the two bags of groceries from the space behind the driver's seat. "I really don't want to ask, but damned if I know what OPS is."

Grace grit her teeth, closed her door, and walked over to the back porch. "Old. People. Sex."

Pat nearly bust a gut laughing. "Did you make that up?"

"No. It's like TMI and OPKs."

"Got it."

As they walked up the steps, Pat caught himself before he started down the dangerous path of wondering what having kids with Grace would be like. Resolving not to think so far ahead, he focused on the now.

Life could be tricky sometimes.

"Are you coming?" Grace was holding the screen door open for him.

He nodded, bracing his shoulder against the door. "Ladies first."

"I'm not the one with my arms full."

Pat leaned close and whispered in her ear, "Go with the flow, Mulcahy."

She mumbled something he could not quite hear and knew he wasn't intended to as he followed her inside. The overhead light was on, an old brass hanging lamp that had—oh boy! He looked at Grace, but she was already rooting through the grocery bags and didn't see what he had.

When she had her head in the fridge, he reached up and snagged the black lace then wondered where the hell he'd put it. Grace kept a running monologue going as she put stuff in the fridge and then the cabinets, obviously not expecting him to reply—good thing, since he was trying to find a place to stash the lacy black bra without Grace seeing him do it.

Patrick had always liked Joe Mulcahy, but now the man was elevated to hero status. His gaze shifted to the hallway and found the perfect spot—the dry sink drawer. "Be right back," he called over his shoulder.

Grace didn't turn around; she just waved a hand over

her head at him. Even better, he thought, sliding the drawer open.

"Patrick," Joe called as Pat was stuffing the bra inside.

"Joe." The men locked gazes and understanding and relief flashed through Joe's eyes.

"It's in the dry sink," he whispered to Joe. "Long ride, gotta use the bathroom," Pat said loud enough for Grace to hear.

Joe nodded and mouthed "thank you" before he said, "I'm just going to make some coffee."

Pat closed the bathroom door and leaned against it, fighting the urge to laugh out loud. Guys had to stick together; it's what separated the men from the boys. Besides, some women get funny about other women finding their underwear hanging in odd places.

Walking back toward the kitchen, he heard Mary Murphy's low voice. The conversation sounded serious, and he hoped it wasn't about what he'd hidden in the hallway. Standing in the doorway, he knew from the look on Grace's face that they were talking about Kate McCormack.

Joe glanced up. "I'll go with you once Kate gives you the bastard's address."

Patrick nodded. "Kate didn't want anyone else to get involved once we got her to agree to tell the sheriff what happened."

Mary leaned toward Grace and put her arm around her. "She'll feel better now that she's gotten it off her chest and done the right thing by filing charges."

"I hope so." Grace leaned her head on Mary's shoulder. "There are enough people involved that word will get out—I don't want people to get the wrong idea about what happened. She's my best friend."

"People will think what they will," Mary advised, smoothing a few strands of hair out of Grace's eyes. "Putting the truth out there will solve that worry and might help Mitch find the bastard."

Grace's head popped up and she laughed. "I've never heard you swear before!"

Mary's face turned a brilliant shade of pink. "I am a firm believer in not overusing words...one must use them wisely for maximum impact."

Joe raised his mug high. "Here, here!" Pat had just swallowed a mouthful when Joe asked, "Are you planning on camping out on our sofa tonight?"

Pat wasn't sure if that was a wise idea; Grace was temptation personified. "Dan's already offered his sofa and I made a deal with the boys: if there were no predawn attacks, I'd make breakfast."

Joe chuckled. "Sounds great." He turned toward Mary. "Do you want me to follow you home?"

She smiled and rose to her feet. "Here's your hat; what's your hurry?"

"Not in the least, Mary," Joe said, rising to his feet. "You're more than welcome to stay the night."

Her hand fluttered to her throat, and for a moment, Patrick wondered if she'd faint.

But she finally composed herself enough to rasp, "A lovely invitation, but thank you, no."

Joe's laugh was deep and just this side of wicked, and from the interested expression on Grace's face, Patrick wondered how he'd feel if it was his mother and her beau and not Joe and Mary. The grinding in his gut told him far more than he realized. His mom had been a widow a lot of years. Did she have a boyfriend that he didn't know about? He'd be shooting

Tommy a text asking just that when he got out to his truck.

"I'll just see you outside," Joe said, slipping his arm around Mary's waist, guiding her toward the door.

"See you at church!" Mary called out over her shoulder.

"You bet," Grace replied, but she wasn't watching her father and Mary. She was staring at Patrick.

"Have we scared you away with all of the small-town drama?"

He held out his hand to her. When she rose, he pulled her close and slid his hand up and down her spine. "New York might be a big city to grow up in, but our neighborhood in Brooklyn was a small town in itself."

She shifted so she could slide her hands around his back. Lifting her face to his, she licked her lips. "Plenty of drama?"

He cupped the back of her head in his hand and murmured, "Big time," right before he kissed her deeply, lingering over the potent flavor that rose above the hint of coffee—pure sweetness, one hundred percent pure Grace. A man could get addicted to that.

The sound of a car door closing had them shifting apart and Grace pushing him toward the door. "You'd better let me get started cooking. It sounds as if there'll be twice as many people eating here tomorrow."

"I thought you were tired."

She smiled, which did crazy things to his heart. "For some reason, being with you energizes me."

He was reaching for her as Joe opened the door behind them, whistling softly as he walked through the kitchen. "I'll leave you two to say your good-byes, then."

"Drive safely—we don't have streetlights like you're used to."

"I've been here after dark before, Grace," Pat said. "And since I'm staying at Meg and Dan's, I don't have that far to go. But it's nice that you're worried about me. It's been a while since anyone worried about me."

She placed her hand over his heart and tilted her head back. "I'm sure your mom worries about you—you're so far away."

He covered her hand with his and drank in the sweetness of the thought and the pressure of her hand lying against his chest. "My mom's a champion worrier, but that wasn't what I meant."

"See you tomorrow?"

"Count on it." He shifted his grip and lifted her up to eye level. Pouring himself into the kiss, he finally broke away, set her down, and whispered, "Dream of me."

She was still standing with her fingertips to her lips as he backed out of the driveway.

Chapter 11

THE ELBOW TO HER RIBS WOKE HER. GRACE BLINKED, surprised to realize she was sitting in a pew and that the recessional hymn was playing.

Her father was shaking his head at her. "What time did you finally stop cooking? Not that I minded falling asleep with the scent of meatballs and sauce filling the house."

Grace was mortified. "Did I really sleep through the whole service?"

The answering chuckle had her hanging her head. "What will Reverend Smith think?"

"Why don't we just go on over and you can explain what happened? I'm sure he'll understand."

"But, Pop—" She was talking to his back. He'd already stepped into the aisle. "Perfect," she grumbled, pushing to her feet, hurrying to catch up. Tapping him on the shoulder, she hissed, "This wasn't what I had in mind."

But he was either ignoring her or didn't hear her. A moment later, she was next in line to shake her pastor's hand. "Reverend Smith."

His eyes were positively twinkling. "Ah, Grace, so glad you could join us today. I hope you enjoyed my sermon."

Busted.

"I, uh…well, you see—"

"She's just so overwhelmed that she's speechless."

Mrs. McCormack slipped her arm through Grace's. "Weren't you, Grace?"

Grateful didn't begin to describe what she was feeling. "Yes. That's it," she said over her shoulder because Kate's mom was dragging her outside.

"Still staying up till all hours instead of getting enough sleep?" Mrs. McCormack asked. "I guess some things never change."

"Thanks for saving me back there."

"It's the very least I could do after what you and Patrick did for my Katie yesterday."

Grace's mouth opened and closed, but no sound came out.

"Deputy Jones drove her home last night, and I, for one, am delighted. Such a nice man—good catch if you ask me, not that my Katie is paying him enough attention."

Mrs. McCormack's smile said it all. She'd always liked him. Grace wondered if that was why her friend was so adamant about ignoring the guy.

"When I sent her to the kitchen to put the coffee on, he mentioned that he'd be keeping a very close eye on our daughter. What with everything that happened, it's such a relief. Those girls of ours keep long hours at the diner."

"But they've never had any trouble at the diner," Grace added, hoping to ease the rest of Mrs. McCormack's worry.

"Well," she said, tugging Grace's arm so she had no choice but to follow her across the parking lot, "back when I was fifteen and working the counter for my mother, there was that time the Riverdale football team showed up ready to rumble."

"Inside the diner?" Grace had trouble believing it. "How come I never heard about it?"

"It was a long time ago and fortunately Sheriff Meeks showed up in time to lay down the law." She was laughing when she added, "He had every one of those boys call their parents to come and pick them up."

"Why didn't they just leave?"

Mrs. McCormack shook her head. "Sheriff Meeks had Bob Stuart pull their ignition wires. Tough to start a car without them."

Grace smiled, imagining Bob Stuart sneaking around to each one of the cars, disabling them. "Was my pop in on it?"

An expert at evading questions she didn't want to answer, Mrs. McCormack just smiled and patted Grace on the arm, slipping hers free. "Good to have you back, Gracie dear. Don't be a stranger. Stop by the farm."

"I will," she promised.

"You 'bout ready to go, Grace?"

"Coming." Hurrying over to her father's pride and joy, the 1950 Ford F1 pickup truck, she traced the gold lettering on the door. *Mulcahys*. Grace was proud of what the last three generations of her family had accomplished.

Then why are you so fired up to live in the city? Once that question settled into her mind, she couldn't stop thinking about it.

She liked the nightlife, she reasoned, and the museums and art galleries.

Then there was the sophistication of city-bred men; they knew how to dress and treat a lady. "I'm kidding myself," she said aloud.

"About what?" her father asked.

Catching herself in time, she sighed and said, "Nothing. Do you mind driving into town? I could get what I still need for dinner at Murphy's Market."

"I have a better idea. Why don't we go on home, and I'll call Mary and ask her to come on over early with what you need?"

"She won't mind?"

He turned onto Peat Moss Road. "Not at all. We've been spending most weekends together," Joe said, pulling into their driveway, "since I've been all alone in this big old house when my baby girl moved out."

It was then that she realized she was probably cramping her father's style—and his love life. "Sorry, Pop. I didn't think that I'd be getting in the way by being here."

"Nonsense. Nothing to worry about."

~~~

Patrick stayed behind to clean up the mess he'd made in Meg's kitchen while the family went to church. Once he'd left it at least as clean as it had been before he started, he headed out to the Mulcahys'. He couldn't wait to see Grace again.

"'Bout time you got here, Garahan."

"Dan, where's your car and how'd you beat me here?"

"Meg dropped me off. I had a change of clothes in the car. She and the kids had an errand to run; we took the shortcut." His friend nodded toward the cooler sitting on the picnic table. "Would you mind asking Grace for the ice I stowed in their freezer yesterday?"

"Be right back." The sight of Grace barefoot and humming to herself caught his attention the moment he opened the door. She had her back to him and was stirring a big pot and swiveling her hips to whatever tune played in her head.

Sucker punched. That's what he would later remember. The sight of Grace Mulcahy just then felt like that time his older brother had sucker punched him over Jenny Rosenkrantz.

"Hey, Dan," Grace called out midstir. "Would you mind handing me that lid I left on the table? I just want to give this sauce a little more love before I—"

Grace looked over her shoulder and smiled. A slow, lovely smile that started with her eyes, softened her features, and added another blow to his midsection when her dimples deepened. He was a goner.

He grabbed the lid and handed it to her. "Smells amazing."

"Mmm," she murmured, stirring in random patterns. "It's Mrs. McCormack's recipe—no wait, maybe it's Katie's grandmother's—" Grace broke off and laughed at herself. "Sleep deprived, can't remember, but you'll love it. Packed with garlic and spices, the red sauce will have you singing for your supper."

Before she slid the lid in place, she opened the drawer next to the stove and pulled out a tablespoon. Dipping it in the sauce, she blew over the surface and touched it to her bottom lip—and had Patrick's libido simmering, shooting sparks of awareness and desire to places that would be better left alone. *Damn.*

She held the spoon out to him. "Taste it. It's not too hot."

He shifted so he boxed her in against the countertop. Her sharply indrawn breath was music to his ears. Her ragged sigh as he snagged the spoon and licked it clean, all the while staring at her mouth, had him leaning close and capturing her lips, savoring the combination of herbs, spices, garlic, and Grace. His head spun from the delectable delicacy he sampled.

Craving another taste, he nibbled on the fullness of her bottom lip before soothing the spot with the tip of his tongue and gorging himself with another mind-blowing kiss. She was warm, willing, and ripe for the picking. He needed air. With a swift kiss to the end of her nose, he drew in a deep breath and rested his forehead against hers.

"Hi."

She sighed. "Hi yourself."

"You kept me up last night," he said, sliding his hands up and down her arms, encouraged by way she shivered. "Cold?"

She shook her head. "I thought of you while I was cooking last night."

"Did you?" He slipped his hands into the back pockets of her jeans and tugged. She tumbled against him and sighed.

"When I finally hit the pillow, so tired I couldn't see straight, I couldn't get you out of my head."

"She fell asleep in church."

Joe's deep voice had Grace jolting and Pat moving his hands from her pockets to her generous hips. He figured a smart man like Joe would figure out he was interested in Grace; besides, Joe owed him for removing the black, lacy evidence last night.

Joe nodded and opened the freezer. "Dan's filling the cooler for the game later. Thought I'd bring the ice out."

Pat looked over his shoulder at her father, noting the grin on the man's face. "I was getting there. Grace needed my help."

Joe grabbed two bags of ice and drawled, "Taste testing?"

"Quit teasing Patrick, Pop."

The sound of a car door and voices had Joe looking out the back door and Patrick reluctantly releasing Grace. "I'll be back for another taste," he promised, staring down at her.

"Smart man," her father said.

Before Grace could think of a snappy comeback, the screen door slammed and her father was gone. "He always manages to have the last word."

"My mom's like that," Pat told her. "Used to drive me crazy."

"And now?"

"I don't get home as often as I'd like to. My baby sister's been bugging me to visit my namesake—her youngest son, Patrick. My mom's birthday's coming up in September, but I may be going home for a quick visit in between."

"Is New York like Columbus?"

"No," he answered, putting the lid on the pot for her, and taking her hand and bringing it to his lips. "It's bigger, louder. The layout and buildings look totally different—want to go with me?"

"To Brooklyn?"

"Sure." As soon as he suggested it, he ran with the idea, needing her to agree. "You'll be doing me a favor if you come with me."

"I will?"

"Yeah, between our ma, Grania, Maeve, and Kelly, there is always a single woman waiting to meet me. I'd rather bring someone I want to spend time with."

"Me?" She sounded breathless.

"Yeah. So what do you say?"

"Maybe. When are we talking?"

"I don't know, but it has to be soon."

Grace was watching him closely when she asked, "Family emergency?"

He sighed. "Yeah. I talked to my brother on the phone while you guys were at church today. Sounds like Ma's got a boyfriend."

"And you want to meet him?"

Patrick grinned. "Hell yeah. Will you think about going with me?"

"Yes. Let me get through today first, OK?"

"OK."

"Do you miss Brooklyn?"

"At times," he admitted. "I love the parades around the holidays—especially the St. Patrick's Day parade."

"Your namesake?" she teased.

"My patron saint."

"Ah, a good Irish Catholic boy." When she lifted the lid for one more stir, her T-shirt slid off her shoulder.

Thinking of nibbling his way from her shoulder to her fingertips, he shook his head. "Not as often as I should be." He'd call his mom tonight, no more putting it off; besides, knowing his mom was worried about him added another layer to the guilt.

As if she could sense there was a deeper worry, she set the spoon on the stove top and the lid on the pot. "Sometimes when we try to be all things to all people, we mess up—big time."

He knew Grace's mother had died in a car crash years before but not much else. "Sounds like you've been in my shoes."

"It was a tough decision for Pop to hire outside the family to find someone to do the office work."

He lifted one of her hands and studied the back of it before turning it over. "Your old job?"

She snatched her hand away. "What makes you ask that?"

He didn't blame her for being irritated with him; he'd been known to irritate people he cared about. "I've known Meg for a couple of years. She and Cait are the handymen in the family. You're the brains that used to run the office and keep the books balanced."

Surprise flickered in her eyes. "Meg said that?"

"Sure did," he told her. "Although she was spitting mad at the time because the high schooler they hired deleted the schedule template you'd created."

Her eyes widened and her hands flew to her breast. "When? Why didn't they tell me? I can try to recover the document and fix things."

"I'm not sure."

"Great. Now I feel like a traitor and as if I abandoned them."

"Didn't you leave them with the accounting and inventory system you'd created?"

"Well, yes, but—"

"And didn't you color code and label the files so that a fifth grader could locate whatever documents your dad needed?"

Her gaze narrowed at him. "How do you know that?"

He laughed this time. "Dan was on file duty a few months ago because the fifth high school student they'd hired had just quit—"

Grace yanked a chair out from the table and plopped onto it. "Five replacements?"

He shrugged. "I think they're up to seven by now."

"Why didn't they just hire an adult?"

"Don't know," he said, but he had an idea that it came down to not being able to pay one the going rate, given Joe's propensity for hiring part-time after-school help. "Have you asked them?"

The guilty look on her face had him pulling out the chair next to her and taking her hand in his. "Look. I didn't say anything to make you feel bad. It was just a question."

She swallowed and stared down at their hands. "I've been too wrapped up in my new job to ask how things were going."

"Have they said anything to intentionally make you feel guilty or bad?"

Her gaze lifted to meet his. Worry was replacing the guilt in her eyes. "No."

"Then they don't blame you, because you did everything you could to make sure they could continue doing business as usual after you left."

"I can't believe they didn't call me."

Pat sighed. He needed to get her thinking about something else. "That's what my ma always says whenever I call her."

Grace's eyes were the key to her thoughts. They softened with understanding. "You feel guilty that you moved away and guiltier whenever she reminds you it's been awhile since you phoned. Makes sense why you put off calling home."

He squeezed her hand. "No one else in my family understands. Why is it that you do?"

She eased her hand free and rose to check the sauce. "I'm betting no one else in your family has moved out of Brooklyn, have they?"

He shrugged. "We're the black sheep that have

moved away from everyone we should be holding near and dear to our hearts."

"We had different dreams that led us away from home."

"And needed the freedom to make decisions and a life for ourselves," he added.

"Exactly." She set the spoon down and turned off the burner. "It would have been easier to stay—less guilt—but then I would have always wondered what it would have been like, fulfilling my dream of living in the big city."

"Until it would have become the only thing you wanted." Patrick stood. "Making everything else seem unimportant—even though it wasn't."

"It shouldn't make us feel so guilty," Grace whispered.

Pat ran a hand over the softness of her hair, sliding it around her neck. "We do that all by ourselves."

Her troubled gaze lifted to his. "Why can't we stop?"

He snorted. "Damned if I know."

"Maybe we can help one another figure out a way to be everything our families need while still pursuing our dreams," Grace suggested.

"Sounds like a plan."

"I'm going to find out if they need help in the office while I'm on vacation."

He sighed. "Less time for you to spend with me."

"But you'll be at the firehouse."

"True," he agreed. "I guess I could call my ma."

"I wish I could." Grace's voice had dropped to a whisper again.

Pat eased her head onto his shoulder and let his hand stroke up and down her back until the tension eased. "Close your eyes," he told her. "Then imagine her smiling face."

"All right."

"Tell her what's on your mind and in your heart; she's still listening."

Grace lifted her head and swiped at the tears. "How did you know just what to say?"

He caught one of her tears on the tip of his finger. "I've been talking to my dad since the day my uncle Bill showed up at school with soot on his face and tears in his eyes."

"He was a firefighter too?"

Pat nodded. "I come from a long line of firefighters—both sides of the family."

"Where was your mom?"

Pat wondered at the ache that still filled him whenever he remembered that day. "She went into premature labor with the youngest—my brother, Johnny, when she heard that the roof caved in on my father's fire company."

"Yet you and your brothers all followed in his footsteps?"

"Tommy, Mike, and I were old enough to understand that it was his time. Fate and destiny have more of a say in your life than you realize." He pressed his lips to the curve of her brow. "You know?"

Grace's gaze locked on his. "I've seen it happen with first Meg and then Cait. Neither one of them were looking for love—but love found them."

"And your dad?"

She chuckled softly. "Mary's the best thing to happen to him in years. I just worry that he won't do anything to make it permanent."

"I'd say things are pretty solid between those two." He sifted his fingers through the hair curving against her jaw. It felt like corn silk. "Why mess with a good thing?"

"Because they belong together, not going back and

forth between two houses, spending stolen moments together."

"Sounds like one of the romance novels Grania reads."

"Everybody's here," Joe called out.

"Is the food ready?" Jack asked from where he stood on the other side of the door.

Patrick stared at Grace and wondered if she too sensed that their conversation had done more to cement their growing relationship than the heart-shattering kisses they'd shared.

"Yeah, but we're playing first, remember?"

"I'm hungry," Jack grumbled.

"Grace made enough to feed an army," he answered before turning back to hug Grace close, promising, "we'll talk more later."

"After the game?"

"How about that ride—down to the river, wasn't it?"

"I'd like that."

"It's a date then."

Grace's smile had him reaffirming his decision from yesterday. It still held—she was a keeper.

Chapter 12

THE GRUNT THAT FOLLOWED THE IMPACT OF TWO MALE bodies vying for the soccer ball had Grace biting her lip. "Was that move legal?"

Her sister Meg shook her head. "You're not supposed to tackle the player with the ball from behind."

"Then why did Patrick just do that?"

Meg laughed. "I guess he wanted to take the ball."

The ball shot past them down the improvised soccer field. "So do you know all of the guys' names?"

Meg turned to look at Grace and smiled. "Nicknames and last names. Today, they're only playing six on six. The number keeps changing depending on which guys are off shift at the firehouse." She pointed to the dark-haired man in the goal. "That's Finney. The defender next to your Patrick is Sledge."

Grace sighed; she liked the way that sounded—hers. "Is Sledge his last name?"

"Nickname. They just smile whenever I ask what it's short for," Meg said. "Jimmy's holding down the mid-field, while Mike and Bear are forwards."

"The home team looks a little young—except for my handsome brothers-in-law and Mitch." Grace paused, then asked, "Where is Honey B. today?"

Meg smiled. "Visiting her mom."

Grace tilted her head to one side. "The three other guys look familiar. Should I know them?"

"The tallest one with the dark hair is Jimmy Doyle—"

"I thought he was away at school."

"Graduated in May."

"Where does the time go? So I guess the guy with the fair hair and football build is his best friend Tommy Hawkins?"

Meg's smile lit her entire face. "I'm not the only one who's got a soft spot for those two. They've been working with Cait whenever they're home on break."

"And who's that?" Grace pointed to the man holding down midfield.

"Seriously? You don't recognize him?"

"Broad shoulders, nice build—probably half a dozen years younger than me…I can't place the face."

"Tim McCormack."

"No way!" Grace got up to walk closer to the sidelines. Turning back, she asked, "Kate and Peggy's cousin? Skinny little Timmy?"

Meg smiled. "One and the same. Time flies and boys grow up when they're away at college."

"I'm starting to feel old."

"It's happens to the best of us," Meg said, walking over to stand beside her sister.

When two bodies collided going for the ball, Grace grimaced. "Why do guys feel the need use their bodies like a weapon?"

"I guess it feeds an inner savage need all men have," Meg answered.

"Hmmm. Mitch isn't half bad as a goalie," Grace said and then drew in her breath. "Wow, Dan's got some moves on him. He just dribbled the ball around Patrick's teammate like he was standing still."

Meg's soft smile as she watched her husband finesse the ball and kick it into the improvised goal—between two folding chairs—and score had Grace grinning ear to ear.

"Hey, aren't you supposed to be cheering for the visiting team?" Meg asked, walking back to the table.

Grace followed, deep in thought, wondering if she had found someone to fill the missing piece of her life—a partner, a friend, a lover. "Meg, when did you know Dan was the one?"

Her sister looked back at her. "When I fell off the fence and he caught me."

"Oh, so it was love at first sight then?"

Meg sat down and leaned back against the picnic table. "It might have been lust, but love sounds better."

Their laughter had Cait wandering over to sit with them. "Something funny?"

"Lust at first sight."

Cait looked over her shoulder at the men, smiling when Jack waved to her. "Mmmm. It does have its benefits."

"The lovebug bites us in different places and at different times," Meg told her. "But one thing's for sure—once you've been bitten, you can't imagine life without him."

A shout from the field had Meg whirling around. "Cait."

Her sister ran to the sideline as Dan helped Jack to his feet. Grace watched Cait breathe a sigh of relief as she walked back. "He won't admit when his leg is bothering him," she said quietly, "but a blind woman could tell."

"He's fine," Meg reassured her as curses and the sound of bodies slamming bodies filled the air. "Oh my God! I thought this was a game?"

"Looks like they're out for blood," Grace said as one

of the players clutched his leg and started shouting at the others.

Cait shook her head. "Men and their pride," she grumbled. "Do you think Mike's OK?"

The play had stopped while a heated discussion and a lot of shoving took place. Grace sighed. "You'd think soccer was serious or something."

Patrick stepped in the middle of the fracas while Grace cringed. "I guess somebody has to be Switzerland." He helped his friend to his feet but kept his arm around Mike's back. When they walked toward the women, Grace got up and met them halfway. "Do you want to sit out for a few minutes?"

Mike shook his head. "Nah, Paddy here is helping me walk off the cramp."

Grace's eyes widened at the grass stain and raw scrape slashing across Mike's swelling knee. "Maybe Jack should look at it."

Mike and Pat laughed, then Mike said, "He's the one who tried to take me out of the game."

Grace looked at Cait, who just shook her head. Grace just had to know: "Weren't you the one with that illegal slide tackle?"

Mike tried to feign a look of innocence, but Grace wasn't buying it. "You should always play fair," Grace reminded him.

"Ah." Mike limped toward her, leaning heavily on Patrick. "So all's fair in love and war?"

Patrick reached up to smack his friend in the back of the head. "Quit looking at my girl like that."

Mike went from limping to hopping. "Your girl? Damn."

She got a funny feeling in her stomach when she looked up and their gazes met. She was toast. The man only had to look at her and smile, and she was ready to follow him anywhere.

When Mike stopped and held up his hand for his friend to stop, Pat stared at him. "Hurts that much?"

"Yeah." Mike's face contorted for a moment as he gave in to the pain before shrugging it off. "Guess I might need to sit out for a little while."

Grace moved to put her arm around Mike, leading him over to the bench, where Meg and Cait were waiting to ease him off his feet. Grace moved a folding chair over so Mike could elevate his knee.

"We can use the ice in the cooler," Cait said. "Be right back with a baggie and a towel."

Pat looked from Mike to Grace and back. And nothing surprised Grace more than the clipped tone of Patrick's voice or the warning for Mike to keep his hands to himself as he rejoined the guys on the field.

Mike's lightning quick grin would be lethal to a woman's heart if her heart wasn't already taken with another.

Grace decided to let Patrick know how she felt. Jogging to catch up to him, she grabbed his arm from behind. He spun around, and just before he could ask what she wanted, she was in arms, locking lips with him, putting everything she felt into the kiss. But he surprised her by kissing the breath out of her. When she was weak as a kitten, he brushed a knuckle across her cheek and winked at her before sprinting back onto the field to rejoin the game.

"So," Mike said as she walked back over, "I just have to ask: Are you sure you know what you're getting into?"

Grace considered his question for a moment before answering, "Absolutely. Why?"

The expression on Mike's face changed from teasing

to concerned. "Garahan loves his job as much as I do, maybe more. It's in his blood."

"I know. He doesn't have a girlfriend," Grace said. "And from what he's said about his job and the long hours, not much time for one. Are you trying to warn me away?"

Mike waited until she'd sat beside him to answer. "Maybe I'm thinking of warning him to stay away from you."

Grace couldn't keep the censure from her voice when she said, "I thought he was your friend."

Mike grimaced as he shifted his weight. "He's a brother."

"Oh." Mike didn't have to say the words for her to know he wasn't ready to approve of her. Maybe when he got to know her better. Changing the subject, she asked, "So, have you two been in the same firehouse long?"

"Since he came on board," Mike said. "We were lucky to have a man with his experience. His firehouse was one of the busiest in New York. I wonder if he ever did more than eat, sleep, and fight fires."

Cait came back outside and walked over to the cooler, preparing the ice bag for Mike. When it was ready, she eased it onto Mike's knee. He smiled at her through gritted teeth.

She hesitated. "Do you want Jack to look at it?"

Mike shook his head. "It's an old injury, flares up now and again."

Grace got him a glass of water and some aspirin. Despite the fact that he didn't think she was the right woman for his friend, she couldn't fault him for that. She'd been in his shoes with Kate more than once over the years. "After you take this, you're sticking to water or switching to soda—no more beer." She wasn't about to take no for an answer.

Her father and Mary walked around the front of the house with the twins tagging along behind. Jack walked over as Joe was asking what happened. His son-in-law's shrug said more than words.

"I can't believe you kicked him, Doc."

"Hey," Jack said, raising his hands in the air. "I was going for the ball—not his knee."

"From the side," Mike said. "He missed."

"Ah," her father said. "Old sports injury?" Mike nodded. "Gracie, there's pain reliever—"

"Already gave it to him."

"No more beer." Jack frowned, watching the way Mike shifted on the bench. "You might need an X-ray."

"This from the man responsible," Mike quipped.

The others walked over and huddled around the injured man. "We taking a break?" Sledge asked.

"Is the game over?" Jimmy wanted to know.

Bear and Finney muscled their way through the crowd to squat next to Mike's knee. Neither one was smiling.

"Not much fun without Mike trying to take everybody out," Bear said.

"Hey, I was only trying to take the ball away from Jack, well, and then Doyle—"

"Yeah, yeah," Pat said. "You know what they say about payback."

Mike hung his head. "I guess I had it coming."

"Let me wash up and get my bag." Jack didn't wait for a response; he sprinted up the steps, slamming the door behind him.

"One of these days, I'll get a real door that will stay closed when you shut it," Joe grumbled.

"I like the screen door," Mary said. "It suits the house. Besides," she continued, "new isn't always better."

"Hey, Grace!" Timmy McCormack swiped the sweat dripping into his eyes. "Heard from my cousin that you're back in town. Katie's really missed you."

"She's too busy at the diner to miss me."

Timmy was shaking his head as Tommy Hawkins tossed him a beer.

Dan stuck his hand out and snagged the beer midair. "Your mom would have my hide—no beer for you until you're legal."

"Come on, Coach," Timmy groaned. "I drank all the time out at school."

"That was then; this is now. I'm responsible for you three as long as you're with me."

"We drove," Hawkins reminded him.

"You're twenty-one"—Dan narrowed his gaze at his former students—"and only having one—as long as you're staying to eat."

"Damn, Coach," Doyle grumbled. "His birthday's next week."

Dan grinned. "And I'll buy him his first beer at Slater's Mill, just like I did for you and Hawkins."

The boys shrugged and tossed Timmy a soda. "Guess you'll have to deal," Doyle told him.

Jack grinned. "My brother-in-law's a hard-ass, but he's right." He set his bag on the ground and squatted down to examine the damage to Mike's knee. Dan and Pat passed around cold bottles of beer and the bowl of chips while they waited for Jack to finish.

"You cannot be on active duty with your knee like that," Bear reminded him.

The other firefighters agreed, and Patrick said, "You'd better call Big Jim now, so he can move people around and we can start filling your shifts."

Mike leaned back and closed his eyes. "My next one is tonight."

"With me," Pat added.

Grace wondered what the next two weeks would be like if Pat would be filling in for Mike. "Do you have more than one person to cover open shifts?"

Pat nodded. "And there's a set number of hours you can work. Big Jim's careful not to overwork his men. We're the best of the best." She noticed Patrick was smiling and could hear the pride in his voice when he said, "Nobody's beat our record in the firefighter Olympics yet."

"You have games?"

"Yeah," Mike answered. "Because different towns host the games every year, they aren't always held the same weekend or month."

"When are they this year?"

"The first weekend in August."

"You'll be back to work long before then," Jack reassured him.

"Hey, Grace," Mike said, "wanna go with me?"

Pat thumped Mike on the head as he walked past him to join his friends on the field. "Go find your own woman," he warned.

Mike looked at Meg and then Cait. "But they're all taken."

To keep from laughing at the sad look on Mike's face—and the reason for it—Grace sought out Patrick in the group of men talking. The cutoffs he'd worn to play soccer were ragged and hit his leg midthigh, leaving a lot of exposed bronzed skin and a fair amount of scars along one leg that wrapped around to the back of his knee.

"Do you need us to drive him to the hospital for an X-ray?" Pat asked. When he noticed the direction of

Grace's gaze he said, "Not job related. I earned those when I got pushed out of our tree house."

Incredulous, she asked, "Did you say earned them?"

"Yep." He slipped away from the group and walked toward her. "Half the scars on my body are from growing up second in line of seven kids."

What could she possibly say to that? "We, um, didn't fight much as kids."

His grin was quick and lethal to her heart, and from the expression on his face, he knew the power of his smile. "That's 'cause you're a girl and you only had sisters."

Grace had a snappy comeback about his sexist comment but decided to let it go for now. Why spoil a good thing? Right now, what they had going was definitely great. "If you wash up, you can help me serve the meatball sandwiches." She was already in the kitchen, washing her hands in the sink when he started to nudge her aside with his hip.

"Oh no. Men as dirty as you have to wash up in the bathroom."

"Seriously?"

"Ask Pop if you don't believe me."

"Ask me what?" Her father ushered the twins inside and down the hallway.

"Only Grace can wash up in the kitchen?"

Joe grinned. "The cook calls the shots around these parts. Come on, boys," he said. "Time to wash up."

They raced down the hallway after their grandfather, leaving Grace and Patrick alone for another moment.

He leaned close to capture her lips in a kiss just this side of scorching.

"I'd touch you," he rasped before he eased back,

"but my hands are dirty." He held them up and laughed as he danced down the hallway toward the bathroom.

"Men," Grace grumbled.

"Can't live with 'em," Meg said, walking into the kitchen. "No fun trying to live without 'em."

"Amen," Cait said, joining them. "The guys said they're too dirty to come in and clean up and are asking for special dispensation to gorge on your meatball sandwiches outside—grass, dirt, blood, and all."

Jack stood on the other side of the screen door, grinning like a loon. "Can we, please, Gracie?" he asked in a high-pitched youthful voice. "Just this once?"

She laughed and shook her head at him. "Go and take care of your patient, and don't let him have any beer!"

"Too late!" Dan hollered.

"Will you be driving Mike home?" Grace asked, handing Patrick the hot stockpot.

"Not part of my plans for later. Bear and Sledge will make sure he gets home." Pat took the pot and used his shoulder to open the door. "Besides, we've got a date to go for a drive after this." The look he shot her way was dark, dangerous, and had her heart pumping double time.

Grace couldn't speak—her tongue was stuck to the roof of her mouth—so she nodded and followed after him with a huge basket filled with Italian rolls.

"This tastes great, Grace," Mike told her. Everyone agreed.

"I can't take credit; it's Kate's mom's recipe."

Timmy shook his head. "It's Gram's recipe, but she never follows it, says recipes are a guideline and every cook adds their own special ingredients."

"McCormack likes to cook," Doyle teased his friend.

"So?" Timmy asked. "I'll probably be working over at the diner—and not waiting tables."

Grace smiled. "Your cousins have been holding down the fort ever since their mom retired. I'm sure they'd appreciate your help."

"Yeah," Timmy said. "They wanted me to serve people, but that's woman's work. I can cook."

Cait and Meg were laughing when Grace set down her sandwich and turned to stare at Timmy. "Is that so?" Grace asked. "And where did you hear that?"

Timmy must have realized he'd said something to upset her; he paled and every single one of his freckles stood out. "I, uh, well…that is—"

"Best just to keep eating," Joe advised. "A wise man never tries to tell a woman what to do."

The answering rumble of laughter among the men had Grace taking pity on the white-faced young man sitting across from her.

"I'm sorry, Gracie," he said, using Kate's nickname for her. "Mom says I talk before I think."

Grace leaned across the table toward him and asked, "Who should Mulcahys send to your house the next time your furnace stops working or your plumbing springs a leak?"

Timmy looked from Meg to Cait and back to Grace and said, "Just ignore the freckle-faced kid," earning a nod of approval from Joe.

"I taught my girls everything they know about fixing things, woodworking, plumbing—"

"Too bad they're all spoken for," Finney said from his end of the table.

Patrick slid his arm around Grace's neck and ate

one-handed, licking the excess sauce before it had a chance to spill out of the roll. "You should stop at the Apple Grove Diner on your way back to the firehouse—Kate and Peggy are amazing cooks. And Kate's single."

Bear leaned toward Sledge and said, "Notice he didn't say anything about what they looked like."

Finney grinned. "Maybe we can sweet-talk Peggy into being single. Besides if they can cook—it doesn't matter what they look like."

Timmy's head shot up. "My cousins are real lookers, right, Coach?"

Dan nodded. "Pretty blonde, and curves that go on for—" He ducked as Meg took a swing at his head. "Hey, it's always best to tell the truth," he said, snagging her arm and tucking her against his side. "Beauty is in the eye of the beholder," he told Meg, "and I'm beholdin' a beauty right now."

Grace watched the fight go out of her oldest sister. The love that shone between Dan and Meg warmed Grace's heart, but she didn't get to think about it too long because Sledge and Bear started a heated debate.

When Bear shot to his feet, Grace looked up at the size of him and decided whatever the man wanted to do, she'd let him.

"I said I'm going to the diner," Sledge said, pushing Bear, but the man didn't budge.

Patrick leaned close and asked, "Are you going to finish that?"

Grace stared down at the half a sandwich left on her plate and shook her head. "I'm full. You want it?"

He slid his hand along the curve of her shoulder and down the length of her arm to her wrist. His hand expertly slipped to the inside of her wrist and he grinned. "Thinking about me or worried about those two goons?"

Grace had trouble concentrating when his voice dropped to that low seductive rumble. He must have taken her silence as a yes. He lifted her limp hand to his lips and pressed a kiss to one knuckle at a time.

"Maybe we should stay a little longer," Bear said, nodding toward Patrick.

Sledge nudged Finney, who elbowed Jimmy before saying, "I'm thinking we should ask Grace if she'd like to come to the firehouse and cook for us."

Grace heard her name, but nothing else because Patrick had turned her hand over and placed a kiss on the center of her palm. Who knew that the palm of one's hand was an erogenous zone?

"No deal, guys. Grace only comes to the firehouse if I'm there."

The hard, clipped tone of Patrick's voice had her looking up to see every one of the Newark firefighters staring at her and smiling.

"What?" she asked, looking at her sisters and realizing everyone had stopped talking. "Maybe we should get the apple pie," she said, rising to her feet.

"I'll give you a hand," Patrick offered.

"Five bucks says he proposes by Christmas," Finney said as the pair walked away.

Jimmy reached into his pocket, whipped out a ten, and slapped it to the table. "Ten bucks says he caves by Thanksgiving."

Joe tried not to smile. "That's my baby girl you're betting on."

The five firefighters shook their heads. "We're betting on Garahan, Mr. Mulcahy," Finney explained.

"He's never been so far gone over a woman," Bear added.

"Not in the four years he's been with the Newark Fire Department," Sledge added.

"What about my daughter?" Joe glared at his sons-in-law until they stopped laughing.

Dan was the first to reach into his pocket. "My money's on Grace. She's an amazing woman—she just doesn't realize it. He'll be proposing, all right."

Jack stood and reached into his pocket but came up empty. He turned to Cait and held out his hand. She shook her head. "Come on, babe, we're betting on a sure thing here. Don't you want your baby sister to be as happy as we are?"

Cait punched him in the shoulder and stood up to reach in her jeans pocket. "If you tell Gracie that I bet money on her and Patrick, I'm moving in with my pop."

Joe chuckled. "You're always welcome here, Caitlin."

"Pop!" Meg said. "Don't encourage their betting. Come on, boys," she said to her sons. "Let's go see if Deidre's awake."

"I'm coming too," Cait said, following her sister.

Joe shook his head. "You men are on dangerous ground. You have no idea what it's like when one of my darling girls gets her Irish up."

Finney chuckled. "My ma's got a tongue that'd clip a hedge when she's mad."

Sledge and Bear were watching the back door. "What's keeping them with the pie?"

Dan and Jack started to laugh until Mary stood up and they both fell silent.

"I'll go and see if your girls need help."

Joe waited until she left before standing up and reaching into his pocket. "Twenty bucks says my darling girl captures his heart before the summer's over."

There was a good deal of discussion between the men before Finney nodded. "We'll take that bet."

Jimmy grumbled, "Who's gonna keep the money until Thanksgiving?"

"Christmas," Finney interrupted.

"You're both wrong," Joe said. "Labor Day."

Dan and Jack just smiled. "Never bet against a Mulcahy, my friends," Dan said.

"You'll lose every time," Jack added.

Before anyone could protest, Grace and Patrick came back outside. "The lovely Kate McCormack baked these pies for you."

Finney nudged Jimmy. "Let's let Bear and Sledge drive Mike home—we're stopping at the diner."

Chapter 13

PATRICK DROVE OVER THE RAILROAD TRACKS. "WHICH way?"

Grace snickered. "You already asked me that."

He sat at the intersection and seriously considered rolling his eyes the way his sisters always did when they couldn't believe he'd said something. "OK, and did you tell me left or right? I can't remember."

"Right. Sorry."

"I like your family."

Grace patted his hand. "You've said that before."

"Grace…"

Her laughter filled the cab of his truck. "I couldn't resist."

For the first time in a long while, Pat had found a woman he could relax with and be himself—not some kind of firefighting hero the woman had made him out to be. Expectations could be a real pain in the ass.

"That's where we go to church," she said as they drove past Apple Grove Methodist Church.

Of course, church was the last thing on his mind at the moment. A nice drive in the country at the end of the day, some passionate necking, and maybe getting to second base—God help him, she had him thinking like a randy sixteen-year-old. But he wouldn't push for more than Grace was ready to give.

"If we drive a little farther, you can see the railroad trestle bridge that Dan jumped off of saving Charlie and Tommy."

She wasn't on the same page as him yet, but she

would be soon. "I do remember hearing that story, but your brother-in-law doesn't like to talk about it."

"So what did you think of them?"

Patrick's mind was filled with thoughts of kissing the side of Grace's neck and working his way to the hollow of her throat and wasn't following the conversation. "Them who?"

"The two boys he rescued that day."

When he didn't say anything else, she added, "Charlie Doyle and Tommy Hawkins—you played soccer with them today."

"Those college kids?"

"Uh-huh. They haven't changed much, just filled out a little bit."

"It's the typical college diet—beer."

"I didn't drink much beer when I was in school. You can take this turn," Grace told him, "and park by that stand of pine trees."

The breeze picked up as he parked, carrying in the scent of sun-warmed pines with it. He breathed deeply. "Don't have many of these back home in Brooklyn." He got out and closed his door, walking around to open Grace's for her.

"What kind of trees do you have?"

He held out his hand to help her down. She hesitated for a second before putting her hand in his. Unable to resist making her laugh, he said, "Big ones with green leaves in the summer that turn color and fall off when winter starts."

Instead of the light laughter he expected to hear, Grace made that huffy sound his sister Grania made whenever she was about to correct him. "You don't know what kind of trees they were?"

"Honestly? They could have been oak trees or maple trees for all I know. If you really want to know, I'll text one of my sisters. They know that kind of stuff because my nephews are always asking questions like that."

She hadn't let go of his hand. He liked that. The breeze shifted and something hauntingly familiar blew past his face. "What's that smell?"

Grace sniffed and smiled. "Slightly sweet and tugs at your mind like something you remember from childhood?"

"How did you know?" After their conversation this morning—black sheep leaving home—he'd felt as if a lock had clicked open inside of him. They were headed in the direction he was planning to go—forward. He needed Grace at his side and in his life.

"Come on." She tugged on his hand and he followed her lead. "See that farmer's wall over there?"

He stopped and nudged her chin up. "What kind of wall?"

"Those stones over there."

"Looks like it was an old stone wall."

"Exactly. Farmers used them to delineate their property lines."

He traced the curve of her cheek and the line of her jaw with the tips of his fingers, pleased when her gaze shifted from his eyes to his mouth. Seizing the opportunity, he bent and captured her lips, pouring everything he'd come to feel for her into his kiss.

When he finally eased back, her arms were wrapped around his neck and his hands were cupping her sweet derriere.

She licked her lips and cleared her throat. "Um, that's why they're called farmer's walls."

"What does that have to do with that smell?"

"There used to be a farm here, alongside the river, before the railroad went through. All that's left is the fieldstone foundation and a few overgrown Privet hedges." Grace traced his bottom lip with her pointer finger, distracting him. "That's the amazing scent." She tapped the fullest part before slowly, lazily, tracing the outline of his lip again.

The woman was driving him crazy. "Grace—" The words slid down his throat when she leaned forward and used the tip of her tongue to follow the same path her fingertip had. His good intentions wavering and his control in shreds, he gave in to the need grabbing him by the throat.

He lifted her up. "Put your legs around my waist." When she did, he groaned, reveling in the feeling of her million-dollar legs locking around him. "Baby, you're killing me."

Much more of her lips on his and her sweet spot blasting heat against the top of his zipper, and his legs would give out. His lips never left hers as he backtracked, walking toward the stand of pines by his truck. He backed her up against a tree, giving him the advantage, and shifted so his erection was nestled where she was hot, moist, and ready for more.

"You're so damn hot." He was hanging on to his last thread of control. He'd lost his mind somewhere around daylight, lying in his bed alone, wishing she was there with him. Sinking into her, letting his fingers explore her ripe curves, had been in the back of his mind all day. Knowing that she'd be closer and he'd be able to spend more time with her for the next little while short-circuited his brain.

"Patrick," she moaned, taking control of the kiss,

tangling her tongue with his before delving deep again and again.

"Tell me to stop," he ground out. "Or I'm making you mine right here—right now."

Her slumberous gaze met his as her hands slid between them and she fumbled with the snap of his cutoffs and the tab of his zipper. "Don't stop."

She had him freed by the time he'd eased her legs—and her zipper—down. "Wait!" he bit out. "We both want this, right?"

She nodded and he let his forehead fall against hers while he caught his breath and shoved her jeans down over her hips and swept the swath of lace to one side.

"Back left pocket."

Reaching behind him, she found the tiny foil packet and opened it with her teeth. Before he could find his voice, she'd covered him with protection from tip to base.

"Your turn," she whispered, watching him like a hawk about to dive on its prey as he shifted his stance and his shorts slid to his feet. He kicked them aside and lifted her up, hesitating when her moist warmth brushed the tip of his erection. "Take me inside you," he rasped. "Please?"

Grace spread her legs wider and locked her ankles at the base of his spine, forcing Patrick so deep his head spun and his heart thundered in his chest.

———

Hard and hot, Patrick drove into her again and again. Grace arched back to accept more of him—all of him. She swore he touched her heart when she felt him touch her womb. "More," she urged, using her pelvic muscles to receive and then give back more of herself with each measured thrust.

The bark rubbed under her T-shirt, but she couldn't think about that now. Patrick moaned low in his throat and drove into her—faster, harder, longer. She couldn't take much more. "I can't wait!" she keened.

"I'm right behind you, baby," he rasped against her ear. "Grab it, baby, take what you want and I'll give you more."

He thrust and she shattered around him, her inner muscles grasping at him to hold him deep inside, but he wasn't through with her. Again and again, he thrust hard and deep until she felt him stiffen and he threw back his head. He swept his hand down between them and played her until she sang out, her groan of pleasure in harmony with his own. They came together in a blinding flash of fire and she went limp in his arms.

"Jesus, Grace." Patrick shifted his hold to tighten his grip. "Are you all right?"

She couldn't think. She couldn't speak, but she could feel. Heat-tangled sparks were still zinging from her center, shooting out to her fingertips. She moaned low in her throat, a garbled sound. It was the best she could do.

"Come on, baby," he urged, shaking her until she lifted her head and looked up at him.

"Hi," she managed.

Worry lines eased into a slow and seductive smile as he realized she was all right. "Hi."

"Wow." Good Lord, she could only think in one-word sentences.

"You pack a punch, Mulcahy."

She sighed and felt her throat loosen until it was as relaxed as the rest of her. "That was amazing."

"Once you started moving your hips, my brain shut off."

His eyes distracted her. They'd changed from warm, deep amber to molten caramel. Desire shimmered in their depths and she knew she'd be a fool not to take him up on the silent offer in his gaze. "I stopped thinking when your hands grabbed my backside—but I felt everything."

She licked her lips and was rewarded with another of his mind-numbing kisses. "How am I going to let you leave?"

He chuckled. "Baby, I've only just gotten started." He slipped free and carried her over to the truck. Setting her on her feet, he looked around and found his shorts and her pants. "Here," he said, holding hers out. They each slipped into their pants but didn't bother fastening them. Patrick grabbed her by the hand, walked to his truck, and leaned her against the side.

His tongue tangled with hers and traced the rim of her mouth, delving deep, before he came up for air. Air-soft kisses feathered along her cheek and down to the hollow of her throat. "Patrick, I—"

"Shhh," he urged, opening the door before turning to her and stripping her bare. "Let me show you how I feel, Grace." He shoved at his shorts until they fell to his feet. He kicked them off and backed her into the cab and across the bench seat before crawling in after her, holding himself up so he wouldn't crush her.

"I wish I had a mattress in the back of my truck. We could camp out here under the stars."

Grace let her fingers grip and knead his powerful shoulders, reveling in his strength. "I've camped out before, but never in the bed of a truck." She ran her fingers down to where his biceps bulged.

He closed his eyes and sighed. "I love the way you touch me."

She obliged by slipping her fingers across his pecs and down to his abs.

"If you go any lower, this show will be over before you get warmed up."

She giggled and slid her hands to his taut backside and held on as if he were her life raft and they were in a storm-tossed sea. "Shut up and kiss me, Garahan."

His grin faded as he leaned toward her. She met him halfway, losing herself in the taste and feel of him. He stroked the fire inside of her until she was writhing beneath him, begging him to make love to her.

She was half out of her mind by the time he reached into his glove box and pulled out another foil packet. "Hurry," she begged as he covered himself and thrust home.

Wave after wave of ecstasy swept over her, and still he kept up the pace, all the while raining kisses along her shoulder and beneath her ear, coaxing her back from the edge until she was right there with him, thrust for thrust. Kiss for kiss.

He tensed and she squeezed her inner muscles hoping to send him over the edge. His hands slipped beneath her backside and lifted her impossibly closer, sending him impossibly deeper. They rose together and descended into madness locked as one.

Moonlight filtered through the pines, setting his hair on fire. "I love red hair."

He chuckled. "I was hoping your first words might be more along the lines of what an amazing lover I am."

She was on top now and settled her elbows against his chest, absorbing every ounce of feeling she could derive from their time together. "But your hair's got moonlight in it and it looks like it's alive—on fire."

He trailed his fingertips up the backs of her legs,

drawing circles and then switching to long, lazy strokes. She shivered at his touch.

"Mmmm," she breathed. "Without sounding like an idiot, it's never been like that for me before."

His hands stilled at the base of her cheeks before continuing on their journey up and over her backside, tracing more circles, driving her daft. "Patrick!"

He stopped, palming her cheeks in his big, callused hands. "What's wrong?"

"I can't think when you touch me."

He was back to chuckling, the rumble setting off sparks deep in her belly. "Thinking's highly overrated."

"You said that before." She shifted beneath his questing fingers as he slipped them up to her waist and eased her one hip up so he could slide his hand between them.

With unerring accuracy, he found the spot he was looking for and toyed with her until her breathing grew choppy and she was begging him for more.

"That's it, Grace," he urged, slipping first one, then two fingers deep inside of her. "Ride my hand, baby. I've only got one condom left."

She was mindless to everything except the pleasure he gave her. His touch masterful, his kisses devastating; she followed where he led, screaming out his name as she came again for him.

He eased his hand free and reached for the last of his protection. "Ever go around the world in a pickup truck?"

She giggled. "No."

"Want to?"

She hesitated. "I've never—"

"Let me be the first for you. Say the words, Grace, because I need to make love to you from behind and go as deep inside you as I can go."

Her mouth rounded in shock and he kissed her, tangling tongues with her. "Come on, baby, let's go around the world."

How could she say no? "Ye—"

———₩₩₩———

The word hadn't even left her lips when he flipped her onto her knees and buried himself to the hilt, her warm, wet passage pulsing around him for all he was worth.

"Not yet," he ground out, hanging on to his control with every fiber of his being as he pounded into her sweet sheathe over and over again. Harder. Faster. Deeper.

He could feel the way she stiffened beneath him and knew she was about to climax. He let go and wished there was nothing between them—skin to skin, his essence mixing with hers, making the baby girl he knew would look just like Grace.

When he could think again, he said, "My dad always said that if you want a boy, go deep."

Grace laughed. "My dad warned me that boys would want to sweet talk me into their pickups, but that I shouldn't go."

Pat's arms tightened around Grace. They were still naked in his truck, her excellent curves pressed back against him as she sat in his lap. "I'm glad you're here with me, Grace."

He tried to stop thinking about making babies with her, because it was too soon to start that kind of talk. But at his age, he couldn't deny that he was ready to settle down with the right woman and start a family. He hadn't realized the need had been so close to the surface, waiting for Grace Mulcahy to burst into his life.

"Did you ever get serious enough to start making

plans for the future?" He had, but the woman hadn't been the one for him.

"Yes," she said, scooting her backside until he shifted and she settled down. "But I guess he wasn't the man I thought he was."

"I should probably tell you where my thoughts are headed," he warned. "I'm not getting any younger—"

She tried to turn around and ended up squashing him beneath her hand. "Jesus, Mulcahy!"

"Sorry! I didn't mean to…"

She moved again and he bit out a curse. "Hold still, damn it!"

She froze and he adjusted her in his lap. "Don't move."

"OK," she said. "Sorry—"

"And quit saying you're sorry, damn it."

"But I didn't mean to hurt you. I just wanted to get a better look at your face."

"What for?"

"To see if you were teasing me or being serious," she explained.

"About what?" His brains were rattled and his parts ached from the squashing they'd just taken.

"That you're not getting any younger," she said.

"Oh," he said. "That. I'm on the downside of thirty-two," he grumbled. "Hell, I don't know. I hadn't been thinking what I'm thinking until I met you."

Grace sighed. "What are you thinking?"

He was keeping her. Should he tell her that or that he was pretty sure he was falling in love with her? Nah, neither one sounded like the kind of declaration a woman'd want to hear. He'd made that mistake before with disastrous results, because being pretty sure he was in love wasn't the same as saying he was in love.

Better to be cautious. "Damned if it makes sense to me." He'd have to figure out a way to tell her what was in his heart without scaring her away or pissing her off. He'd done that with the one other woman he thought he wanted to spend the rest of his life with. But she wasn't anything like the woman sitting naked in his lap. This woman meant more. She'd opened her life and her heart to him and met him fire for fire. She trusted him to make love to her in a position she'd never tried before.

He shook his head. "When I figure it out, I'll let you know."

She shivered in his arms and he realized it was probably time to drive her home. He'd already been tempted once to make love to her without restrictions or barriers, but he didn't think she was quite ready to start making little Garahans—at least not before they got married.

"Damn."

"What?" she asked.

"I want to spend the rest of the night with you, but I'm out of protection and don't think you're ready to make babies with me."

She shifted in his arms until she could see his face. She stared at him for a long time until she seemed to satisfy her curiosity. "You aren't making fun of me?"

"Not on your life."

"You're really thinking about babies?"

He grinned. "I'm the second oldest of seven children," he said. "What do you think?"

She kissed his cheek and scooted off his lap. "That it must be time to take me home."

It hurt, but he had to ask, "Don't you want to make babies with me?"

"There's a whole lot more to it than that, but yes, I

think I might," she said, putting a hand to his chest as he moved closer. "Do not put those lethal lips on mine until we're both dressed."

She slipped out the passenger door. "Where are my jeans?"

His heart was stuck in his throat and he couldn't speak. He pointed to his side of the truck. When his heart was back where it belonged and the knot in his tongue loosened, he asked, "So you might?"

She smiled. "Can we talk about it later?"

He shrugged, feeling better by the moment. "OK. We can talk about it more tomorrow."

She growled at him as he opened his door to retrieve his shorts. He brushed the pine needles off her jeans and handed them to her. "Truce?"

She rolled her eyes at him as she pulled on her jeans. "Truce."

After they were dressed, Pat pulled her into his arms and hugged her against his heart and breathed in her scent. He could still smell the lavender and rain, but it was mixed with the heady scent of their lovemaking and something earthier—his scent.

"I like the way you smell right now," he confessed.

She lifted her head and he brushed the arch of her brow with his thumb. "It's been a long day. I can't imagine there is anything left of my perfume."

"You don't need perfume."

Her grip tightened around his waist as she let her head fall against his shoulder. "You're a keeper, Patrick."

"I was thinking the same thing about you."

"So we're on the same page?" she asked.

"I think so." He held the door for her and waited until she slid across to the middle, then he put the truck in gear. He slid his arm around her, pulling her flush against his side. When she linked their fingers, he said, "Can you shift it into third for me—standard H pattern?"

Grace did as he asked before teasing him. "What makes you think I know what an H pattern is?"

"Perfect," he said. "Good to know I can work the clutch while you shift. Fourth, please," he said before answering her question. "You're dad's a car guy, the company car is a 1950s vintage Ford F1 pickup, and I'm betting he taught you the importance of learning to drive a stick."

"I never know what you'll say or do next, Patrick."

"Is that a problem?" He had to work to keep the worry from his voice.

She shook her head and he glanced her way to watch the way her hair slipped across her jaw and then back. "I really like your hair." He reached over to fiddle with the ends of it, giving it a tug when she remained silent.

"What?" she asked. "I was thinking."

He tried not to sound desperate when he asked, "About me?"

"Maybe." She eased her hand free from his and slid it across his abs, heading toward his zipper.

"Don't," he warned, staying her hand.

She sighed. "I just wanted to touch you again."

"I'm normally a strong man, but I've reached my limit with you."

"Your limit?" The tone of her voice tipped him off that she wasn't happy with that statement.

"Yeah," he said, before she had a chance to work up to a good mad like his ma would have. "It's taking all of my control not to pull over, toss you into the bed of my truck, and make love to you until you can't see, speak, or hear."

"Mmm."

The humming sound she made deep in her throat turned him on. Hell, everything about her turned him on. "Quit trying to drive me crazy until tomorrow after I stock up at the pharmacy."

"You're planning to see me tomorrow?" The hope in her voice wrapped around his heart like a hug.

"I've got a regular shift, not a twenty-four. If you don't mind driving out to meet me at my place, then yeah, I plan to see you tomorrow."

"Maybe I'll save you a trip to the pharmacy and pick up some supplies myself."

He slid a hand to the back of her neck and massaged gently. "Grace, I know it seems like everything's happening fast and furious, but it's not just me wanting you in my bed."

"I wouldn't be here with you if I thought that—same page, remember? Besides," she said, "we haven't tried out your bed yet. That's tomorrow."

His laughter was deep and delighted. "You suit me down to the ground, Grace Mulcahy. I'm—" He broke off before he could say "keeping you."

"You're what?" She waited for him to finish.

He concentrated on driving, and finally said, "It'll keep. Let's get you home so you can rest up for tomorrow night."

"Big talk," she teased.

"If you're gonna dream, dream big. I spent the night dreaming of you...the things we did would make you blush."

Grace softly smiled. "Try me."

He swallowed against the lump constricting his throat. "That's the plan," he said, turning onto Eden

Church Road. "Now behave, so I can drop you off and can drive back to Newark without any distractions."

He pulled into her driveway and parked, leaving both his hands free to caress her, satisfying a small part of the desire that had built up on the drive back to her house. When he finally had the strength to ease his hold on her, he peppered soft, fluttery kisses across her brow and down the side of her face. "Dream of me, Grace."

She trailed the tips of her fingers along his jaw. "I will. Drive safe, Patrick."

"Count on it," he reassured her as she started to slide across the seat to the passenger side. "If I get out, I'll walk you to your door and start kissing you again...I won't want to stop."

He could hear her breath snagging in her chest. "Oh, well...you'd better say good-bye here." She leaned back toward him to kiss his cheek.

"Tomorrow," she said.

"Tomorrow," he promised.

Chapter 14

GRACE WOKE TO THE SOUND OF HAMMERING AND THE delicious aroma of freshly brewed coffee. Opening her eyes, she blinked then focused them. Sitting up in bed, she reached for the mug. "Not a dream," she murmured, sipping the fragrant brew and listening to the steady pound of a hammer somewhere downstairs.

A glance at the clock told her the first official day of her vacation was starting a couple of hours before she'd intended. "Not happening. I'm not getting up at six thirty on my vacation."

The pounding stopped for a few minutes and she enjoyed the blissful silence of early morning. Laughing, she listened to the trill of a songbird nearby. "Well, not quite silent," she amended. Joining the songbird—she was pretty sure it was a red-winged blackbird—was the steady staccato of a woodpecker. Since it wasn't too loud, she knew it wasn't one of the larger ones living in the woods across their field.

Woods where she and Patrick had walked and discovered their first taste of one another. That thought led to the subject of her dreams—the man who'd taken her to the stars last night. "God help me, did we really make love standing up with my back to a tree?"

Pleased with herself and the loose-limbed way she felt this morning, she knew she'd do it again in a heartbeat if Patrick asked. Savoring her first cup of coffee for the day, she knew she would have to go see what her father was up to when she finished. The gift of coffee before she opened her eyes usually meant he had a favor to ask.

Revved from two days spent with the family and the new man in her life, Grace decided to grab a quick shower, since the hammering had started up again—Pop's signal that she had a few more minutes before he came looking for her.

Clean, dressed, and ready to meet the day, she walked downstairs but didn't see her father in the living room. "Must be in the kitchen."

And there he was, big as life, spatula in hand, frying eggs. "Mornin', baby girl." His eyes were bright with amusement.

"Thanks for the coffee, Pop. What's up?"

"I knew you'd catch on. Your sisters never could follow along as quickly as you."

Grace got out the bread and put two slices in the toaster while her father checked the eggs. "We're about ready here, Gracie. Got the plates?"

She reached above her head and got out two. "Coming up."

When the toast popped, she buttered them and brought them to the table. "So what are you building this morning?"

His grin was infectious and she found herself smiling back. "A board."

She paused with a forkful of egg halfway to her mouth. "That doesn't make sense."

"Well." Her father shifted in his seat and rubbed his hands on his jean-clad legs. "You weren't waking up fast enough—even after I put that coffee on your bedside table."

Her laughter bubbled up from deep inside. "So you were hammering so I would wake up?"

"Yeah." He grinned and raised his coffee mug high, toasting her. "To my youngest and smartest daughter."

"All right," she said, setting down her cup. "What do you need?"

He patted her hand and leaned back in his chair. "I'm in a bind, Gracie, and wouldn't ask you otherwise."

"I can't help if you don't tell me what you need." As soon as she said the words, her gaze met her father's. He had said those words to Grace and her sisters countless times over the years. It was her turn.

He nodded. "That's my girl. Your latest replacement left a voice mail on the office line. She won't be coming to work."

Grace sensed there was a bit more to the message than that. "Just today?"

"No." He spread his hands on either side of his plate and stared down at them. "At all. I'm not sure what's so hard about the job, Gracie." He looked up at her. "You held down the fort for us for years—since you figured out how to work that computer, you insisted I needed to keep the business up and running—still think the business would be fine without the darned thing."

She smiled. "I think I was twelve."

"And smart as a whip." His smile was open and contagious.

"So you need help at the office?"

He sighed and sat back in his chair. "We do…"

"I'm sensing there's a but here."

"I wasn't going to say anything, but you're bound to notice as soon as you sit down in front of the computer," he told her.

She took pity on her dad. "I know about the schedule template. Why didn't you call me?"

"And have you running back to Apple Grove to fix something I should have been able to handle?"

"Pop, you're a whiz at fixing things that are broken," she began, "but don't know your ass from your elbow where computers are concerned."

His face darkened and for a moment she wondered if she'd made him angry by being so forthright. Instead, he leveled his gaze at her and asked, "Is that a fact?"

"You know it, but since I love you," she said meeting his gaze, "I'm going to share a little secret with you that could have saved you a headache."

His eyebrows shot up. "Really? What?"

"I've got all of the templates I created for Mulcahys backed up on a memory stick—well," she admitted, "two of them…my backup has a backup."

"Do you mean that you can fix the schedule?"

"No, but I can upload the template so we can enter in any new data. All I have to do is plug the memory stick in the USB port, select the file I need, and upload it to your computer."

"So all of this time—"

"Your pride kept you from asking me to help," she told him.

"Ah, baby girl," he said. "Pride was the furthest thing from my mind. I didn't want you to spoil your dreams worrying about mine."

Tears filled her eyes as his words wrapped around her heart. She got up and walked around the table to hug him. "You're the best, Pop."

His voice was gruff when he rumbled, "I know."

She pressed a kiss to the top of his head before reaching for her empty plate. "So when do you want to leave?"

He got up and cleared the rest of the table, putting it in the sink. "We can do those later," he said, motioning her to step aside. "Now would be great. We've got a handwritten list of calls that haven't been added to the schedule yet."

Grace nodded. "Who's working what hours?"

"Cait and Meg are both on part-time hours, that's why the list of repairs is getting a little out of control."

"Have you thought about hiring anyone full-time?"

He frowned. "Your brothers-in-law have been after me to hire help."

"Have they?" Grace knew it wasn't because her sisters had complained about the hours. Her sisters loved the work—and hated to admit they weren't up to the task of working full-time between Meg and Dan's growing family and Cait and Jack with a baby on the way.

"Don't tell your sisters. They'd skin those men alive if they knew."

Grace laughed. "They won't hear about it from me, Pop. Let me get my purse. I'll meet you outside."

"I don't suppose you have one of those memory things with you."

"I've always got my memory sticks with me. Once a geek…"

She dashed upstairs, energized at the thought of recreating the database she'd updated before she left—and a time or two since then. Hopefully their database wasn't too badly damaged. She'd know once they got to the shop.

He father was in the F1 waiting for her. He smiled as she opened the passenger door and hopped in. "Glad to have your help."

"Next time," she told him, "just ask me."

He was focused on backing up as he agreed.

"Promise me, Pop."

"All right, I promise."

On the short drive to town, they talked about the most recent repair calls. "So you're not really sure how many people are waiting?" Grace couldn't believe that her father wouldn't know this.

"Hell, Gracie," he grumbled, turning onto Dog Hollow Road, "you are the only reason I knew what was going on. You ran a tight ship, baby girl, and are a hard act to follow."

Grace didn't know whether to be flattered by her father's compliment or upset that the family business was suffering while she was off chasing a future that wasn't quite as rosy as she had thought it would be—one she wasn't even sure she wanted now.

Joe turned right onto Main Street and parked in front of their shop. As she got out, Grace felt a bone-deep satisfaction that the exterior of their shop looked the same. Parking the F1 out front was something her dad used to do in between calls—but this time of day the truck should be with one of her sisters—out on the job.

"How come Cait's not driving the truck?"

He unlocked the front door and shrugged. "She's feeling poorly this morning. That's why I needed your help. I have no idea who's waiting on us today."

Grace shook her head as she walked inside and froze. "Oh my God! What happened in here?"

The office was littered with open boxes of plumbing

supplies and, worse, files on every available surface, some piles tilting precariously. "What happened to my desk?"

Joe snorted out a laugh. "Your desk?"

Grace tried to hide the fact that although she no longer worked at Mulcahys, she'd always think of some things as hers. "While I'm uploading the schedule template for you"—she looked around and sighed—"and straightening this place out so we can get some work done, it is my desk."

Her father smiled. "What do you need me to do?"

"For starters, can you find me that handwritten list of repair requests?" She walked toward the desk that she'd spent so much of her time running the family business from.

Grace waited for him to find it, unaware that she'd been holding her breath until her head felt light. With a whoosh, she let it go, telling herself to breathe. He held it up and said, "OK, now what?"

"Seriously? You're asking me? It's your business."

"Used to be," he reminded her. "I retired five years ago."

The reminder had her wondering who, then, was at the helm. "Has Meg been doing the books?"

He stared at her as if she'd lost her mind. "I doubt it."

"Cait?"

"Gracie, no one has touched them since you left."

"But that was over a year ago! How did you pay your bills?"

"I took care of the utilities and suppliers that called me, but the rest…"

This wasn't her worry and certainly not her fault, but somehow she couldn't let herself off the hook. Maybe she could come back once a month and take care of things in the office, or at least set up a system and find someone competent enough to do the filing and answer phones when she went back to her real job.

She looked at her father and noticed his frown of frustration. "Tell you what, Pop," she said, wanting to make up for the fact that his dream appeared to be going down the toilet, "why don't you go next door and get us a couple of really big coffees while I get started?"

His expression changed from frustrated to relieved. "You don't need my help?"

"I do," she said, shooing him toward the door. "But I really need that coffee if I'm going to dive into this list you gave me."

"Be right back."

Needing him to take his time so she could at least uncover her desk and get started on the schedule, she asked, "Would you see if Mary's got any fresh strawberries and Greek yogurt?"

He paused in the doorway and looked over his shoulder at her. "You still hungry?"

"No," she laughed. "I'm planning to work through lunch and can if you don't mind stopping at Murphy's Market for me."

He smiled. "You're a trouper, Gracie."

"Wait until I get the schedule going for you before you say that," she warned.

He waved and was gone.

Alone, she looked around her, wondering how things could go from streamlined and organized to disaster so quickly. *Well*, she thought, *not that quickly.* It had been a few months since she'd been inside the shop.

"The shop!" Scooting around the boxes, she opened

the door to the back and sighed in relief. "At least the supplies in the back are organized." Laughing to herself, she realized her sisters wouldn't care about the office side of things, but mess with their carpentry and plumbing supplies and you'd be in trouble.

Bracing herself, she walked back into the office, wondering if maybe it was just her initial reaction and maybe it wasn't that bad. "Holy crap!" It was.

Grace started by going to the closet and pulling out the folding table she kept for year-end file-sorting purposes. "I doubt anyone's used this since me." With a huge sigh, she leaned it against the front of her desk and went in search of paper towels to get rid of the dust on it.

Satisfied that it was clean, she set it up and started shifting the stacks of files off the top of her desk. Heading back to the supply closet, she pulled out the multisurface spray cleaner and shook it. "Still full." With a glance around the office, she knew why. "Guess I'm the only one who cared about the office."

Shaking her head, she got to work, cleaning and straightening until she had the piles of files looking organized. Although her hands itched with the need to sort through them, she left them for now. She had a clean place to get started on that schedule.

She fired the computer up and saw the antivirus warning. With a huge sigh, she picked up her cell phone and texted her dad: I need my laptop—office computer's a disaster.

He texted her back right away: Got coffee and your lunch. Be right there.

Ignoring the computer, she spread the list out and started organizing the schedule the old-fashioned way—with paper and pen.

Her dad walked in a few minutes later. She looked up at him and saw the surprise on his face. "You were busy while I was gone."

She agreed. "The office computer is in desperate need of a defragging—"

"Hold it right there," he warned. "You know I have no idea what you're talking about. Where's your laptop?"

"In my bedroom." His slow smile had her realizing how much she missed being home. "Don't get any ideas, Pop—it's just habit calling it my room."

He lifted his coffee in toast to her, and in his best Schwarzenegger imitation said, "I'll be back."

She was laughing as she cross-checked her new list with the chicken scratch that passed for her father's list. "We're going to need to call for reinforcements to get to these customers."

Taking matters in her own hands—after all, her father had just reminded her that he was retired—she hit the speed dial for Meg.

"Hey, Sis," she said when Meg answered. "We've got a problem and I think I have the answer."

"Where are you?" Meg asked.

"The office."

There was a slight pause before her sister said, "I can explain—"

"I saw the shop too," Grace told her, "and know where you and Cait have spent any spare time when you're not on repair calls. I understand."

"You're not mad?"

"I was the one who left," Grace told her. "But that's not why I'm calling. We've got a big list of repair calls—"

"You fixed the computer?"

Grace snorted. "I'm not sure I can resurrect your

database. I sent Pop home to get my laptop. I've got the templates saved on it and on memory sticks—but I'm not plugging them into the disaster that passes for your office computer."

"Oh."

"I've got a working list, and from the number of requests, we'll need someone to give you and Cait a hand."

"We're working as fast as we can," Meg began.

"I know. That's not what this is about and you should realize that."

"OK," Meg said. "What do you have in mind?"

"I'm here for the next two weeks and will straighten things out in the office, but I think we should ask Charlie Doyle and Tommy Hawkins if they want to work for us again this summer."

"They know how to patch a roof, change out broken hardware, hang a door—"

"That's perfect," Grace said. "Do you think they'd do it if you asked them?"

"Yeah," Meg said. "I'll call them now."

"Great," Grace said. "Gotta call Cait next."

"Grace?" Meg said.

Her mind was already on what she wanted to say to her other sister. "Hmmm?"

"Thank you. This means a lot to us."

Grace felt her throat tighten. "It's the least I can do," she said. "We're family. Gotta call Cait, bye!"

"Bye."

The phone call to Cait met with the same enthusiasm and thanks, leaving Grace to wonder why neither of her sisters bothered to call her when they knew they were desperate for her help. But she didn't have time to think; she had work to do.

The list was finalized and summer help lined up by the time her father came back.

"Hey, Pop, I've got good news."

He handed her the laptop and waited.

"I've got the list and talked to Meg and Cait. They've agreed to hire—"

"Anybody home?" The deep voice had Grace looking toward the door.

"Come in, guys," she said. "I was just about to tell Pop about you two."

Charlie and Tommy walked in.

"When Meg called, it was like a dream come true," Charlie told them.

"Yeah," Tommy said. "We've always wanted to work for Mulcahys."

Her father shook their outstretched hands. "Welcome aboard, boys."

"Pop," Grace admonished. "They're not boys anymore."

He grunted. "To me they are—they're younger than you!"

She smiled. "I'm glad you came so quickly. We have two calls that I need you to handle right away."

After sending Charlie and Tommy on their way, the rest of the day was spent sorting and filing while the desktop ran through the cleanup programs Grace initiated.

Lunchtime came and went, and it wasn't until she noticed the ache in her empty stomach that she stopped to eat the fruit and yogurt her dad had brought her earlier.

The phone hadn't stopped ringing with calls to welcome her back interspersed with service calls. Grace's geeky side was delighted down to her toes to be able to add their names and repair requests to her color-coded spreadsheet.

With a sigh, she got up to stretch the kink between her shoulder blades. Satisfaction filled her as she glanced around the room. She'd made a good-sized dent in the work that needed to be done. Granted, there was still a ton of work to do—probably more than she'd have time to do in the two weeks she'd be in Apple Grove—but the most important tasks had been checked off her list: organizing and prioritizing the repair schedule and hiring help.

When her cell phone rang, she answered it without looking at the screen. "Hello?"

"Hey, gorgeous." Patrick's deep voice sent a shiver up her spine and sparks of awareness to the tips of her fingers.

"Hey yourself."

"Just got back from a call and had five minutes to myself and all I could think of was hearing the sound of your voice."

She was toast. "I could use a break," she told him.

"Been busy?"

"Actually, I have. My dad asked me to help out at the shop—it looked like a bomb went off inside here."

"But not now?" He sounded as tired as she felt.

"Nope, I got a handle on things, but I'll have my work cut out for me while I'm here."

"You sound pleased with yourself."

She laughed. "Wait until you see the before and after pics I took."

He chuckled. "What time can you get here?"

"When do you get off shift?"

"At six o'clock, but there's some cleanup that I have to do before I leave tonight."

She didn't want him to think she was desperate, so

she asked, "Do you want me to wait until you get home before I head out?"

Patrick's answer surprised her. "I can't wait to get my hands—er, see you."

She chuckled. "Should I bring food?"

"I haven't even thought about what's in my fridge," he confided. "With Mike out on the injured list, I haven't had time to think about what I'll feed you when you get here."

"Tell you what," Grace said. "I'll bring dinner with me and you can pour the wine while you tell me how your day was."

"Sounds amazing." There was a brief pause before he said, "I can't wait to be with you again, Grace, but I'm dead on my feet."

Feeling bold, she suggested, "Maybe I should stay over—and drive back in the morning."

"Pretty, smart, and a mind reader," Patrick quipped. "What are you bringing to feed me?"

"Something easy," she warned, "so don't expect anything gourmet after the full day I've put in here at the office."

"I'm an easy man to please," he rumbled, sending pinpricks of awareness to some very intimate places.

She swallowed the saliva pooling in her mouth. "I'll need directions."

He gave them to her and then said, "Oh, and don't worry, I stopped at the pharmacy on my way home last night."

"I, uh—" Grace's mind went on a side trip to last night's lovemaking. "Good."

His laughter was just this side of wicked as he told her good-bye and disconnected.

She was still staring at her phone when her father walked back in the shop.

"Wow!" His face lit up like a kid at Christmas as his gaze swept the room. Grace realized that for this reason alone, she'd nearly killed herself today straightening up and getting their database up and running. She couldn't handle looking at the lost and overwhelmed expression he'd had on his face that morning again.

"It's better," she said, glancing around her. "Isn't it?"

He cleared his throat. "Thanks, baby girl."

She blinked back the moisture in her eyes and smiled back at him.

"Had a couple of calls from Charlie and Tommy earlier." As quickly as that, he was back to business.

"Oh? I didn't realize they would be calling you." She hadn't thought that far ahead.

"Not a problem. They needed some quick advice and knew that Meg and Cait had their hands full at their repair calls."

She could tell there was something else on his mind, so she waited him out while she powered down her laptop and the desktop.

He finally admitted, "I should have hired help long before now."

She walked over to put her arms around him. "It's gonna work, Pop," she told him. She realized how big a step this was for him, to have someone other than a Mulcahy going out to fix what was broken in Apple Grove. "We're still on the job," she reassured him. "The fact that you're training two of Apple Grove's own, trusting them to uphold our family tradition and name, will mean so much more to the town—and Charlie and Tommy—than I think you know."

He hugged her tight before releasing her. "Funny thing," he told her. "Mary said the same thing about an hour ago when I stopped in to complain."

Grace laughed. "I love you, Pop."

"I love you back, baby girl." He hesitated before adding, "I, uh, have plans for dinner."

Grace giggled. "Me too. Patrick's expecting me to feed him."

Without missing a beat, he said, "I worry about you driving back home after such a long day. Those roads are dark. Will Patrick let you stay over?"

Grace's mouth hung open a heartbeat before closing. "Who are you and what did you do with my father?"

Joe's laughter was rich and deep. "A man can change, you know."

She could hardly wrap her brain around the two major changes Joe Mulcahy had endured today: hiring outsiders to work for the family and his all but pushing her to spend the night with Patrick.

She finally found her voice. "Change is good for us, Pop."

"Amen to that. Mary's fixing to close. Do you need anything from the market?"

"I haven't had time to figure it out yet." What could she feed a tired, hungry firefighter that would fill the hole in his belly and knock his taste buds for a loop?

"Maybe I could make Grandma's cheddar cheese fondue? It's quick, tasty, and not what he'll be expecting."

Her father laughed. "Better bring some burgers for backup."

"You're right. Let me get my purse."

"I'll meet you across the street and have Mary start setting aside what you need."

"You remember what's in it?"

"Yeah," he laughed. "Cheddar cheese!"

Grace was smiling while she finished packing up and headed for the door. "Men."

———∿∿∿———

"Are you going to talk to her about today?" Mike asked as Pat eased back against the kitchen chair.

The firehouse kitchen was empty, save for the two of them. "No. We've only just started seeing each other. I don't want to scare her away."

"Even if I have my doubts about her, she might surprise you," Mike told him. "Didn't you always say that you wished you'd met Meg before Dan did?"

Patrick shrugged and pushed to his feet. "Hey, our job's a tough one. Sometimes there's good things that we can't wait to tell people about, and then…" His voice trailed off. It had been rough arriving at the scene of an accident too late to do anything to help the senior citizen who'd had a heart attack and driven into a telephone pole.

Mike groaned when he stood up, calling Patrick's attention back to him. "You shouldn't be standing on that knee yet."

His friend grinned. "It's not as bad as we thought yesterday. The swelling's down. Besides, I got a special dispensation if I showed up for work today."

Patrick shook his head. "We need you one hundred percent, my friend. That won't happen if you don't let that knee heal."

"You sound like my mother," Mike grumbled.

"Yeah?" Patrick asked. "I like your mom." He finished straightening up the kitchen from the late lunch the guys had just finished because of that last emergency call.

Mike loaded the last of the dishes into the dishwasher and shut the door. "I hope the rest of our shift is quiet."

Pat was about to agree when the alarm sounded. His friend shrugged while Pat ran down the hall, toward the lockers. "Suit up, Garahan," his lieutenant ordered.

"What do we have?" He stepped into his pants and tugged the suspenders up, shrugging into his turnout gear.

"Duplex fire—over on Kennedy."

Patrick's gut clenched, but he showed no emotion on the outside; he'd trained himself to do the job at all costs—and keep the memories bundled tight inside him, praying this next fire wouldn't leave him raw and bleeding as the memory of that night threatened to rip free.

Focused on the job, he was ready when they arrived at the burning building and did what he did so well— walked straight into hell.

Chapter 15

GRACE PULLED INTO THE LOT RIGHT BEHIND HIM. "Hey!" She waved and got out of her car. "I thought you were going to be late?"

He dragged his sorry butt out of his truck, digging deep past the body aches and soul-deep tiredness. "You have no idea how glad I am to see you." He walked over to her car, tugged on her hand, and twirled her into his arms.

"Mmmm," he murmured, burying his face in the crook of her neck, inhaling the scent he was coming to crave. "Are you supper?"

She chuckled and stroked a hand up and down his back as if she sensed he needed soothing. "Rough day?"

He eased back and captured her lips in a kiss that wouldn't satisfy the need churning inside him but would have to do until he could get her inside. "Yeah. Can we talk later? I'm starved."

She reached into her backseat and pulled out an over-stuffed grocery bag. "I've got just the cure."

"Hell, we don't need groceries for that."

She closed the car door and frowned up at him. "I'm hungry too, so everything else will just have to wait."

His groan had her shaking her head at him. "Why don't you take a nice hot shower while I make dinner?"

"Already took one at the firehouse—do I smell like smoke?"

She leaned close and gave an exaggerated sniff. "No. I thought it might help relax your sore muscles."

"Mind reader, eh?" He led the way upstairs, unlocking the door to his apartment. Holding the door open for her, he said, "Come on in."

The sun was bright in his kitchen, his favorite room. "What kind of pots and pans do you need?"

She set her bag in the middle of the table and started to unpack it. "Do you have a double boiler?"

He opened his cabinets, knowing he had the top of one somewhere; he used the bottom pan all the time. "Here it is." He handed it to her and watched as she filled the bottom with hot tap water, before going back to the cabinet to find the top pan for the double boiler.

"It'll heat up faster than using cold water." She hummed as she took out two blocks of cheddar cheese, a can of crushed tomatoes, some garlic, basil, Italian bread, butter, and a bottle of red wine.

He handed her the smaller pot and frowned at the ingredients she'd set out on his counter. "Where's the meat?"

"Right here." She pulled out the burgers and rolls.

"Whoa!" he said when she pulled out lettuce, cucumbers, and tomatoes. "That looks like the *V* word."

She giggled. "You sound like Pop. He's not a fan of vegetables, but they're good for you."

She looked around the kitchen until he asked, "What?"

"If you have a paring knife and cutting board, that's all I need."

He found them for her and opened another drawer, pulling out a corkscrew. "Cabernet Sauvignon?"

"Mmmm. I like to drink it and it tastes great in the fondue."

"I'm glad you brought meat—firefighters eat a lot of meat."

She smiled. "Why don't you take a glass of wine and crash in front of the TV while I make dinner? It won't take long."

He poured two glasses of the robust red wine and handed one to her. "I like seeing you in my kitchen, Grace. Can we have the burgers first?"

She shook her head at him. "You're going to love this, I guarantee. Where's your sense of adventure?"

"I save it for the day job."

She met his gaze and set her glass down. "How 'bout if I join you on the couch as soon as I toss everything together. If I set the timer, it won't stick to the pot."

When he just stared at her, she tugged on his arm to get him moving to the living room. "Isn't there a baseball game on?"

He sat down and flipped through the channels while a tantalizing aroma started to waft in from the kitchen. "Smells amazing."

"Tastes better," she called out.

A little while later, she walked into the room and sat beside him. "All it has to do is heat through so the flavors get happy."

"You sound like my favorite chef." He put his arms around her and slipped further into the sofa, relaxing for the first time today.

"You feel good," he said, drinking in her curvaceous warmth. "Fit good too," he mumbled, drifting off to sleep.

-∾∾-

Patrick didn't move when the timer rang, so she eased out of his arms to check the fondue. She dipped a square of crusty bread into the bubbling mixture, touched it to the tip of her tongue, and popped it into her mouth.

The flavors exploded on her tongue. "Mmmm," she sighed. "Perfect."

She tossed the salad and found a hot pad for the table. Refilling their wine glasses, she walked back to the living room and stared at the big man sleeping so peacefully. "Maybe I should let him sleep."

"Hungry," he mumbled, opening one eye.

"I thought you were asleep."

"Was," he grumbled. "Till somebody moved and left a cold spot."

He sounded like a little boy. Unexpectedly moved by the softer side of him, she leaned down and kissed his forehead. "Come on," she urged, taking his hand. "I'll feed you."

The dubious expression was back on his face. "If I try the fondue, can you fry up two burgers for me?"

She laughed, delighted with the grumpy-little-boy side of him. "Yes, but prepare to be surprised."

He eyed the pot in the middle of his table and reached for the wineglasses, handing one to her before taking a sip from his. "Thanks for coming, Grace. I'm not always good company after a day like today."

"My pleasure. Now sit down and eat," she told him. "No more stalling."

He chuckled. "There's no fooling you, is there?"

She shook her head at him. "I have very wily nephews."

He laughed and held out her chair. Once she was seated, he scooted closer to her. "OK, now how the heck do I eat this?"

"You've really never had fondue before?"

He shrugged. "Not in my ma's repertoire."

Patrick was being such a good sport after what she sensed had been a grueling day. "My grandmother Mulcahy used to pile up chunks of bread on a plate and pour the fondue on top—my favorite way to have it—but my sisters always liked spearing the bread with a fork then doing the dip and twirl."

He looked at the fork and the pot, and asked, "Can we have it Grandma's way?"

"Absolutely." She passed him the bowl of bread and stood up. "I tend to spill if I try this sitting down."

She fixed his plate then hers before sitting. When he just watched her, she finally laughed. "OK, I'll be your royal taste tester."

She stabbed a cheese-covered cube of bread and started to eat. Patrick did the same, only his eyes widened as he chewed. He dug in after that first bite, pleasing her immensely when he asked for more.

He finished a second helping when she passed the salad to him. "Repeat after me," she said. "Green things are my friends."

He laughed as he scooped out generous portions of salad on both of their plates. "I like frogs."

Their shared laughter warmed her heart. "You're fun to cook for, even if you are a little grumpy when you're hungry."

He hooked his hand around her neck and brushed his lips across hers. He tasted of garlic, cheese, and red wine. She licked her lips, delighted when he softly moaned. "You taste great in grandma's fondue."

"I'll taste better after I have those burgers."

She got up and turned on the pan. "How done do you want 'em?"

"Rare."

When they'd eaten their fill, they sat at the small table in his tiny kitchen, sipping wine. She couldn't recall ever feeling this content…and wasn't sure if she was comfortable with the feeling; she was used to the highs and lows a relationship went through at the beginning, but not the sense of companionship and abiding affection she also felt for Patrick. Afraid to jinx things, she didn't want to admit—even to herself—that she was sliding toward love.

He brought her back to the present with a jolt when he asked, "What's for dessert?"

"Don't you need to digest first?"

He stretched and patted his stomach. "Look," he said. "I just made more room."

She laughed at his antics and got up. "Well, I just happen to have something—in case you were hungry in a couple of hours."

He got up and followed her to the fridge. "Does it have chocolate in it?"

"No."

"Oh."

She tried not to laugh at how disappointed he sounded. "I brought you a slice of whiskey cake."

His eyes lit up. "Seriously? When did you have time to bake today?"

Grace narrowed her gaze at him. "I didn't."

"Who baked it?"

"Who do you think?"

"One of the McCormack sisters?"

"Wrong," she said. "Mary Murphy."

"I've never been to her store," he told her, holding the door while she slipped the cake out of the fridge.

"She carries a little bit of everything and always has one or two of her specialties on hand for special occasions."

He took the cake from her and set it on the counter. "Am I a special occasion, Grace?"

She bumped the door to the fridge with her hip to close it. "Very special," she whispered, walking into his open arms.

"Maybe I can hold off on dessert for a little while." He nibbled her earlobe.

She slid her arms around his waist and lifted her face for his kiss. "Maybe we could."

"Can it sit out on the counter?"

"Yes, why?"

He swept her off her feet and walked down the hallway.

She gasped as his grip squeezed most of the air out of her lungs. "Are you in a hurry?"

"Oh yeah," he rasped. "Let me show you what I've been dreaming of doing since last night."

He opened the door to his bedroom with his shoulder and knelt on the bed, with Grace still tucked in his arms. "Don't go anywhere." He eased her onto the bed and stepped back, staring at her.

Nerves had her licking her dry lips. "What?"

"You look like you belong," he told her.

His words wrapped around her like a hug. "Do I?"

He reached for the hem of his T-shirt, grabbed it, and yanked it off. "Yeah."

His body was perfection, as if each and every muscle had been lovingly sculpted for her viewing pleasure. The wide span of his shoulders, the depth of his chest with all of those lovely muscles—"You have a shamrock tattooed over your heart?"

He grinned. "Yeah. You should have seen the look we got when the four of us walked into Shotzie's Tattoo Parlor asking for them."

But she was only half listening; the bright Kelly-green symbol of their shared heritage just added another check in the what-will-he-do-next-to-surprise-me column.

"Grace." Her name on his lips had her looking up to meet his gaze. "You're not leaving tonight."

She immediately agreed. "No."

He shucked off his jeans and stalked toward the bed. "You're overdressed." He tugged her shirt off first, her jeans next, until she was naked in his bed.

"That's better," he growled.

She shivered, about to ask what was wrong, but lost the ability to speak when she saw the predatory gleam in his eyes as his gaze raked her from head to toe.

"You're like a dream—every one of my teenaged fantasies rolled into one beautiful package, just waiting for me to unwrap it."

She finally found her voice. "I think you already did that part."

His snort of disbelief had her watching for a clue to what was going on in his head. His words surprised her. "I love your sense of humor."

"Are you going to stare at me all night?" she asked.

He knelt on the edge of the bed. "I promise not to bite you too hard." Nudging her legs apart, he pinned her to the mattress with his hips.

"You're skin's so hot." She trailed her fingers up and down the line of his spine, twirling her fingertip along the top of his pelvis.

He pressed down, capturing her attention when he bent to kiss a path along her collarbone. When he playfully bit at her shoulders, she pinched his taut backside.

"How flexible are you, Grace?"

She stared up at him and waited a heartbeat for an

explanation. When it didn't come, she asked, "Physically or mentally?"

He snorted. "I guess both."

"Mentally, I try to be open to new experiences." The dark desire swirling in his amber eyes had her lady parts twitching.

He swooped down and tongued a new path from the base of her throat to her navel, dipping his tongue in before retreating, sweeping to the left to nip at her hip-bone…and then to the right.

"Is that so?" He scooted down until his breath fanned out over her belly. "Let me taste you, baby."

As she started to nod, he gripped her hips with his hands and lifted her hips toward his mouth. Breathing on the soft curls hiding her center, his eyes promised everything—his lips, teeth, and tongue delivered.

She was a quivering mass as he speared her again and again with his questing tongue. His name was a whispered benediction on her lips as he nibbled his way to the very heart of her. Cupping her backside, he pulled her closer and tongued her deep, drawing every ounce of moisture from her sheathe.

She screamed his name and shattered.

Grace sensed movement, but her eyes refused to focus. Her heart pounded and her breath snagged in her breast. She closed her eyes and felt the bed shift beneath his weight.

"You taste like wild honey," he said slipping into her wet warmth. "A man could die happy with your essence on his lips."

No one had ever said such things to her before. No one had ever craved her as Patrick seemed to crave her taste, her scent, her touch.

He moaned out loud when she cupped his cheeks in her hands and pistoned her hips to meet his every thrust.

———⁓———

"Again," he chanted as a keening moan began in the back of her throat.

"I can't—" The protest strangled on a gut-wrenching moan. Her eyes rolled back in her head and she went limp in his arms.

"Not yet, baby." He arched back and cupped her breasts in his hands, flicking and teasing them until she started to writhe beneath him again. "That's it," he crooned. "Come on, baby, I need you to come with me just once more."

Her eyes opened, and her gaze locked on his. "Patrick, I—" She lifted her hips as he drove into her, the force of his thrust, moving the bed into the wall. The sound and her body rippling with shock wave after shock wave sent him over the edge into madness.

He couldn't move but was afraid he was crushing her. "Grace?"

"Mmmm."

"Look at me?"

"Can't," she breathed. "Too tired."

"Baby, did I hurt you?"

She opened one eye, closed it, and softly smiled. "You destroyed me."

Pulling her against his heart, he rolled until she was on top. "You devastate me, Grace."

She sighed and he felt her body go lax. "Grace?"

The sound of his lover's whisper-soft snore warmed his heart. Since she couldn't hear him, he rasped, "I'm keeping you."

She shivered as he ran his fingertips along the length of her spine and over the generous curve of her backside. The urge to bite her there was hard to suppress, but he didn't want to wake her, so he continued to stroke and caress her until he drifted off to sleep.

A long while later, he felt her stirring and shifted so they were lying like two spoons in a drawer. Nestled with her sweet backside in his lap, he pressed a hand to her belly and fell asleep wondering what it would be like falling asleep with her like this every night.

"Keeping you," he mumbled.

"Hmm?" she murmured, sounding as if she was about to rouse from the deep sleep she'd been in.

He kept one hand low on her belly while the other lazily stroked up and down between her breasts, relaxing her until she quieted once more in his arms. His breathing slowed to match hers as he let go and fell back to sleep.

Chapter 16

GRACE WOKE TO DARKNESS AND THE OVERWHELMING sense of belonging as Patrick's arm curved protectively around her. She shifted and he grumbled in his sleep, tightening his grip on her. Pleasure curled inside of her. Snuggling in his arms, she accepted the fact that there was no going back.

She linked her fingers with Patrick's, wondering what lie ahead for them. Grace was a planner and liked things neat and tidy, organized in color-coded spreadsheets. But she had no control over his work schedule, so she set her ingrained need to organize aside—for now.

When Patrick shifted and rolled, she drew in a breath and had no choice but to roll with him—he had yet to let go of her. Even in sleep, the man was fitting her into his life. He was on his back and she was now on top of him. If he could make room for her as he slept, he could probably make room for her in his busy life as a firefighter. She had already made the first step toward fitting him into her life by spending her two weeks off in Apple Grove, closer to where Patrick lived.

The time they'd already spent together—in bed and out—had her thinking about white picket fences and forever. She'd always thought she was a city girl at heart. But as the sounds of the street below echoed, she already missed the birdcalls she'd heard at her family's house just that morning—she was a country girl.

Maybe there were more changes ahead for her. She

needed to make a new list of goals. That's where she'd find the answers she sought. Grace imagined Patrick's work schedule highlighted in red and smiled; hers would be green—the overlap would be brownish-purple, but it could work. She relaxed, realizing that her mind and the unsettled business of work schedules had roused her from a deep sleep.

Envisioning the spreadsheet eased the tension she'd been feeling—well, that and the heat from Patrick's body. The man was a veritable furnace, putting off an amazing amount of heat. Placing a hand over his heart and her head in the crook of his arm, she laughed softly as one arm hooked around her waist and he toyed with the ends of her hair.

"I guess you're awake too," he rumbled, stroking the tips of his fingers to the underside of her ear and along her neck.

Grace closed her eyes as the deep baritone resonated beneath her hand and cheek. "Sorry. I didn't mean to wake you up."

He slid his fingers along the top of her shoulder and down the length of her arm. "I started to get hungry." His clever fingers slipped around to toy with her breast. "Are you hungry, Grace?" His breath was warm against her ear, his hands heating her skin as they traveled from her neck to her knees, gently skimming, teasing devastatingly.

She sighed and his hands moved to cup her backside and the words got caught in her throat. Tipping up her head, her gaze met his and she realized he was waiting for her to answer. Good Lord, she thought. A drop-dead gorgeous hunk of man wanted to make love to her— again—but was waiting for her to say yes.

Contemplating the fact that he was a considerate lover, she almost missed the glint of mischief in his eyes. He chuckled and that's when she noticed the gleam of amused arousal swirling in the depths of his caramel-colored eyes. The combination captivated her as he lowered his mouth to hers. Taking his time, he kissed her deeply, tracing the rim of her mouth, tangling his tongue with hers. Pinpricks of awareness, coupled with desperate desire, erupted wherever his hands molded and his lips touched.

"I have to find out," he murmured.

Before she could ask, he changed his handhold, slipped out from beneath her, and bent to scoop her in his arms. "Taste test," he said, carrying her to the kitchen.

Excitement tingled beneath her skin as he set her in the middle of the table. It was cool…and she was not. She shifted from cheek to cheek, wondering what he intended to do. "Patrick?"

He snagged the cake from the countertop and a fork from the drawer. Moving the chair out of his way, he leaned close. "Which is sweeter?" he asked, lifting a fork-ful of cake to her lips, silently urging her to take a bite.

Unable to deny him, she opened her mouth and let him feed her. She chewed, savoring the flavor—it had been nearly a year since she'd had whiskey cake. He placed the cake on the table by her hip as she said, "It's deli—"

His tongue swept into her mouth as his hands unerringly followed the curve of her spine, pulling her to the edge of the tabletop. The kiss was openly carnal. Never had anything she'd tasted before compared to the lush flavor of his kiss.

Her heart raced as skin met skin, heat met heat. He eased back, leaving her on fire and uncertain. He lifted a forkful to his mouth, chewed, and slowly smiled. "It's good," he said, leaning close enough to circle the tip of his tongue on first one breast and then the other. "But not as delectable as you."

Words were no longer necessary as she looped her arms around his neck, drawing him closer. His lethal lips and talented tongue feasted on her while her thoughts swirled and her head spun.

When Patrick lifted the fork to her lips, she shook her head. "Not yet." It was time for her to take back control of their lovemaking. She slipped off the table and urged him to sit.

He hesitated and actually pouted. "But I didn't get to Point Pleasant."

She almost choked on the mouthful of cake. "Where?"

"It's a town on the Jersey shore," he said, grabbing ahold of her hips. "And where you keep your wild honey, just for me."

The blood rushed through her veins as her heart began to pound. "No fair," she rasped, moving between his legs. "I haven't tasted you yet."

Every muscle in his body tensed in response to her words. Power sang through her body as she bent her head and let her lips first and then her tongue test the strength and sensitivity of his pecs. "I read an article that said a man's nipples don't have as much feeling as a woman's." She flicked the tip of her tongue across one and then the other. His breath rushed out at her touch.

"Maybe their research was flawed," she said, kneading his shoulders, trailing her hands down to his powerful biceps—delighting in the way they tensed beneath her fingertips. Leaning close, she licked a path from his breastbone to his navel.

"Grace," he growled.

She lifted her head and met the intensity of his gaze with determination—to make his head spin and his heart leap. Going down on her knees, she caressed his quads before grasping his hips.

"My turn." With a featherlight caress, she traced the length and breadth of him with her tongue, awed by his strength and size.

"I want—" Patrick's words ended on a strangled groan as she took him in her mouth and suckled him, her hands in constant motion as her tongue and lips moved over him.

He speared his hands in her hair. The gentle way he eased himself free added one more reason why she was not going to let this man walk out of her life. A look was all it took before she was once again in his arms. As he strode to the bedroom, his hands and lips spoke volumes. As he placed her in the middle of his bed and opened the drawer to his bedside table, she knelt on the bed and reached for his hand.

"Let me." When she'd rolled the protection over him, he knelt in front of her and swept his hands from her hips to the undersides of her breasts, teasing her to distraction. One callused hand moved slowly down her spine. He buried himself to the hilt as his big hands grabbed hold of her backside and held her tight against him.

She moved her hands to mirror his, hanging on to his glutes as she pulsated around him. Tilting her head back, she saw the raw desire in his eyes and knew he was holding on to his control by a thread.

"Go with it," she urged. "Let me watch you come," she whispered.

The veins in his throat stood out as he threw his

head back and moaned out her name. His body looked as if he was stretched out on the rack, with each and every muscle tensed. He answered with a thrust of his hips and a growl deep in his throat. His hands vised against her butt cheeks as he gave in and let his orgasm take him.

———

She'd wrung every last drop from him. Spent, he tumbled them to the bed with one hand cupping the back of her head and the other her backside. "Need sleep." He couldn't form more than a few words at a time. She'd destroyed his control with a look and taken him to paradise with her lips and tongue.

But it wasn't just the way she'd teased him to arousal, he realized; it was the look in her eyes and the reverence in her touch that had him nearly coming in her mouth. He'd rushed the normal boundaries he placed on relationships, unable to resist tasting her honeyed essence, but he never expected her to respond in kind.

When he could finally speak again, he told her, "Give me a moment, and I'll return the favor." He needed her to fall asleep as fulfilled as he was.

"You don't have to—" He covered her lips with his and let his hands do the talking, stroking then delving deep into her sheathe. She came apart in his arms moments later. She'd been that close to climaxing when she'd urged him to let go, putting his pleasure before hers.

A beautiful, giving woman. How the hell had he managed to find her after giving up on his search for a woman to spend the rest of his life loving? Slowly, slipping his fingers free, he wrapped his arms around her and let sleep take him.

—◦◦◦—

Morning came too soon as the annoying strains of his alarm woke him. He reached for the offending object and smacked at it until it stopped. Moving back to the middle of the bed, he wasn't surprised to see Grace awake, but he was uneasy with the directness of her gaze. What was going on in that beautiful head of hers?

And then she smiled and everything was right with his world once again. "Morning, handsome."

He laughed. "Morning, gorgeous."

She kissed his shoulder and slipped out of bed. "I'm hungry and I desperately want a hot shower."

"Oh yeah?" He followed her down the hallway. "We could save water and shower together."

She laughed and shook her head at him. "You go get the first shower. I'll start the coffee. Do you have eggs?"

He grabbed for her hand and tugged, tumbling her against him. "So was that a no?"

She reached up, traced the line of his jaw, and tapped the tip of her finger on his bottom lip. "I'll never get to work on time and neither will you if I said anything but no."

He kissed her tenderly. "So it's not no because you don't want to?"

She was laughing as she looked up at him. "Go get a shower before I change my mind and go back to bed and let you make the coffee and—"

His mouth cut off what she was going to say with a tender kiss. "You're not hardwired that way, Grace. That's why we're going to be amazing together—neither am I."

When she melted in his arms, he just had to kiss her again. With a friendly pat on her backside, he let her go and walked into the bathroom. "I'm going to need half a pot just to get my brain in gear this morning."

"Maybe I won't drink the whole pot if you answer a question."

He stuck his head out of the bathroom door. "What's the question?"

She hesitated, and that's when he noticed her expression was unreadable. "Did I dream last night?"

He walked toward her and wrapped her in his arms. Holding tight, he rasped, "I'm the one who should be asking you that because, baby, you are a dream come true." Sensing she needed to be held, he waited until she sighed. "We're going to have to talk about things soon," he warned, letting her go.

"What kind of things?"

He bent down to put the bath mat on the floor by the tub. When he stood up and looked over his shoulder, he caught the expression on her face. "Were you staring at my butt?"

She flushed a bright pink. "Guilty."

He laughed. Taking pity on her, he finally answered her original question, "The you-and-me kind."

"Oh." She backed away from him and practically ran down the hall, leaving him to wonder if she was frightened of the prospect, or if she was having trouble sticking to her plan not to join him in the shower.

He preferred thinking it was the latter, so he did while he let the hot water ease the tension between his shoulder blades. Trying not to think about Grace while he lathered up was definitely a challenge. The woman had opened her heart to him in so many ways last night. He didn't plan to take advantage of her or her giving heart.

As he stared at his reflection, deciding not to take a

razor to his face, he felt his earlier energy drain out of him, leaving him weak. "Blood sugar needs a boost," he told the face staring at him. "Gotta have protein."

The angel in his kitchen was humming off-key, adding one more endearing quality to savor. Instead of pulling her into his arms, he pulled out a chair. "I've got this little problem I forgot to tell you about."

She handed him a mug of coffee. "Sounds serious."

"It is and it isn't," he told her.

"OK," she said, studying him closely—too close for comfort. "Looks like it's serious right now."

When he didn't drink any coffee, her look morphed into one of concern. Before she could work herself up, he told her, "If I overexert myself and don't eat right, my blood sugar gets out of whack and my energy takes a dive."

She turned off the burner and scooped fluffy scrambled eggs onto his plate. "Eat," she said, handing him a fork. "No caffeine until you've finished every bite." Damned if the woman didn't take his mug back.

"Wait—"

She lifted the spatula and pointed it at his plate.

He knew what she wanted him to do. Somewhere he found the strength to grin. "Yes, ma'am."

"And don't call me ma'am," she grumbled. "Makes me feel old."

When he opened his mouth to speak, she picked up the spatula again. He laughed and continued to eat, grateful when she placed two slices of toast on a paper towel next to his plate and slid the jar of peanut butter next to his hand.

"How do you know what I need to eat?"

She shrugged. "Low blood sugar runs in our family,

so I don't have to think about what will get me back on track fast. I know without thinking."

He was already feeling better as the eggs hit his stomach.

As his system leveled out, he noticed her mug was nearly empty and got up to pour her more.

"Thanks."

Her sweet smile did things to his heart that he'd never really felt before. With a blinding flash of insight, he realized he'd found the one his ma had always told him was out there waiting for him.

He got his mug and sat across from her, watching the way she brushed her bangs out of her eyes before lifting the cup to her lips and blowing across it to cool it. Lifting his mug in a silent toast to her, he waited for her smile to reach her pretty green eyes.

He couldn't wait to bring her home to meet his family.

Chapter 17

GRACE DROVE HOME, TRYING HARD TO KEEP HER MIND on the road and not on the man who'd wrapped himself around her heart so quickly it felt as if they'd been together for years.

"How is that possible?" Needing to focus on where she was going and not where she'd been, she set thoughts of Patrick Garahan aside, to be taken out later and savored like a giant-sized chocolate bar. Both were drool worthy, but the former wouldn't add any inches to her hips.

Chuckling to herself as she drove, she was in a great mood by the time she'd parked in front of Mulcahys. It was later than she'd hoped to arrive. "Locked." *No matter*, she thought. She could probably still get in through the back unless somebody moved the spare key Grace kept above the door.

Walking through the alley between her family's shop and the Apple Grove Diner, her mind was focused on a broad-shouldered hunk with auburn hair. She didn't notice that she wasn't alone until she walked into something solid and felt the cruel grip manacling her right wrist.

"Hey!" She struggled against his hold before looking up. Ice began to form in her blood. A dark-haired stranger was glaring at her. Instincts had her digging deep to remember the moves her father had taught her and her sisters.

The stranger mistakenly thought he had the advantage

when she let her arm go slack in his grip. He started to smile. She stomped on his foot and plowed her fist into his nose. The satisfying cracking sound eased the pain singing up her arm from the impact.

"You bitch!" he roared, releasing his hold on her.

She drew in a deep breath and did something she hadn't done since sixth grade; she screamed for help. The sound of heavy footfalls headed her way, and she turned away from her attacker—a mistake, because a shove from behind sent her down hard on both knees.

Deep voices answering her call gave her the strength to get up and start to give chase, knowing there was only one direction to go—toward the Main Street end of the alley. She stumbled but kept going, ignoring the pain in her knees.

"Call Mitch!" Charlie shouted, tossing his cell phone at her as he and Tommy sprinted past her.

Grateful for a moment to catch her breath, she leaned against the wall and dialed 911. When Cindy Harrington answered, she cleared her throat and told her what had happened. While Cindy kept her talking, Kate and Peggy were already running toward her.

"Grace!" Peggy called to her.

"Oh my God!" Kate shrieked. "You're bleeding."

Grace looked from her friend's horrified face to the front of the T-shirt she'd borrowed from Patrick. The block letters spelling out FDNY were covered with blood. The sight of it left her light-headed. "Not mine," she managed.

"Come on, honey," Peggy crooned, putting an arm around Grace's waist.

"You need to sit," Kate told her, slipping her arm around Grace from the other side. "Your poor knees."

Grace looked down and swore. "These jeans weren't even broken in yet." Sandwiched between the McCormack sisters, Grace let herself be led to the diner.

Inside, they pushed her onto a chair by the front window. Peggy went to fetch her first-aid kit, while Kate asked, "Who did this to you?"

"I've never seen him before."

Peggy returned with a bowl of steaming water, peroxide, and a bag of cotton balls. "Doc's on his way," Peggy told her.

"I don't need a doctor."

"Tough," Peggy grumbled.

"Wait!" Kate called out. "I should probably take a picture in case Mitch needs it."

Grace was about to tell Kate she watched too much TV when the pain in her wrists had her remembering the bruises on Kate's. They hadn't caught the guy who assaulted her friend. What were the odds that he'd come back?

Mulling it over, she waited while Kate took the picture and Peggy started cleaning her knees. She sucked in a breath as the peroxide started doing its job. "That stings."

Peggy glanced up but kept working. "That's how you know it's getting rid of the dirt and stones and whatever else got ground into your knees when you landed in the alley."

Before her friend could switch to the other knee, Jack burst through the open door. "Grace! What happened?"

The concern in his tone felt like a hug. Despite the fact that she said she didn't want anyone to call him, she did feel better knowing that someone from her family was here for her.

"She was attacked," Kate told him.

Jack looked from Kate to Peggy and back to Grace. "Thanks, Peggy. I'll take it from here."

With a deft hand and light touch, he had her other knee cleansed and free of debris by the time Charlie and Tommy walked into the diner. Both young men were out of breath and covered in sweat. "We almost caught him," Charlie told her.

"Yeah, but he'd parked a car behind the *Gazette* and had one of those key chains that you can start your car with."

"Bastard was a few steps ahead of us when he leaped in the car and drove away."

"Did you get the license plate number?" Grace asked, hoping they had at least that much.

"I only got the first three numbers," Charlie said.

"He was driving a Crown Vic," Tommy told them. "You know, like one of those undercover cop cars on TV."

Kate had grabbed one of the pads they used to take orders and started jotting down whatever was said. "OK," she said, turning toward Grace. "What did the son of a bitch look like?"

Grace described him as best she could, but other than his height, build, and hair color, she hadn't had time to get a good look at him.

Rhonda showed up a few minutes later with Grace's father and Mary. The room was buzzing with conjecture and offers of getting a posse together—that would be her dad's idea. It made Grace smile.

While Charlie and Tommy took Rhonda out to the alley to take pictures, Mitch told them to wait for Deputy Jones. They grumbled but did as he asked. A few minutes later, the four of them went outside.

Mary waited until Jack was finished checking out

Grace's hands and knees before she shooed him to the side. "Let's get the blood off that shirt." As she was leading Grace to the ladies' room, Mitch walked into the diner and told them to wait.

"I brought a spare shirt with me." He handed it to Grace. "I need yours for evidence."

She was hesitant to turn the shirt that still had a hint of Patrick's scent on it over to him but knew it would be important if they could identify her attacker's blood type. "It's not mine," she warned.

Mitch nodded. "You can tell Patrick he can have it back when we're through."

She froze in her tracks. "I didn't say who it belonged to."

He looked up at the ceiling for a moment before his gaze met hers. "And that's why I'm the sheriff around these parts," he told her, making her smile. "I know things."

"I took notes, Mitch," Kate said, handing them over while Mary tugged on Grace's arm to get her moving again.

"What you need is a cup of my special tea," Mary told her, holding the door to the ladies' room open for Grace. "Do you want any help?"

Grace shook her head. "I'm fine."

"You don't look fine," Mary told her, handing her the clean shirt Mitch had brought. "But you will be."

A few minutes later, Grace opened the door and nearly tripped over Mary. "You didn't have to wait."

"It was either me or your father," Mary said.

"Thanks," she said and meant it, feeling another knot of tension loosen. "I guess I could use a cup of tea after all."

"I'll just ask your father to run across the street to my shop for the bottle."

"Bottle?" Grace had no idea what she was talking about.

"A splash of the Irish in a hot cup of tea will set you to rights," Mary promised. "You'll see."

Winding their way around the tables, Mary called out, "Joseph!"

Her father's grim expression softened when his gaze met Grace's and he started walking toward them. "You punched him good, baby girl."

Grace smiled. "He didn't start bleeding right away, though," she told him.

Joe's mouth twitched as he fought to keep a straight face. "All of my girls know how to throw a solid punch," he told Mary. "Taught them myself."

Mary tut-tutted and made shooing motions at Joe. "Gracie needs me to fix her up with a special cup of tea."

His eyes softened as understanding flowed between them. "Be right back."

"Such a dear man." Mary sighed.

Her father returned with the bottle and let Mary doctor Grace's tea while his daughter gave the bloody shirt to Mitch.

A fan of TV crime dramas, Grace wasn't surprised that Mitch didn't handle the shirt, merely holding open a Ziploc bag that Peggy had given to him to be used as an evidence bag.

"I'll need to call Pat to get his blood type."

"Is that really necessary?" She hadn't planned on talking to Pat until this evening.

"He's got the kind of job where bleeding is part of the territory. If you'd rather call him and explain why you need to know, that's fine with me as long as you call him right now."

What should she do? She didn't want to interrupt him

on the job. He needed to focus in order to save lives and keep himself and his fellow firefighters safe.

"Can't you call his lieutenant and explain why you want to know?" Grace asked Mitch. "I don't want Patrick to be distracted on the job."

Mitch nodded at the wisdom of her request. "I'll have Cindy put the call through to dispatch and handle it that way." He paused in the doorway. "If I were you," he said, "I'd either call the man or send him a text message."

With that threat left hanging in the air, Kate settled next to Grace in the booth and picked up Grace's mug, taking a sip and then promptly choking on the sip. "What's in there?"

Grace grinned. "Mary fixed it for me."

Kate rolled her eyes. "Tastes like my grandmother's cure-all."

Peggy was laughing when she poured another round of coffee for the people still hanging around the diner waiting to hear the latest update on Grace's attacker.

Grace was surprised when her father walked over and handed her his cell phone. "It's for you."

"Who'd call me on your phone when I have my own..." Her voice trailed off. "I guess it's still in my car."

Her father's gaze held hers for a moment. "Cindy must have already gotten through to the Newark Fire Department. Patrick needs to talk to you."

"Your words," she asked, "or his?"

"Both," her father bit out, shoving the phone into her hands. "Talk to the man."

Grace wasn't ready for Patrick to be worried about her safety. *Funny how relationships unfold*, she thought. *Getting to know one another physically first, then the intimate details of what's in your head and your heart.*

"Grace?" The deep voice had her concentration shifting to matters closer at hand.

"Hey. Sorry, my phone's in the car and I didn't have a chance to—"

"Are you all right? Where are you hurt? Did they catch the bastard yet?"

Patrick's quickly fired questions left her feeling a bit shaky as the moment of panic in the alleyway washed over her.

"Grace?" he pleaded. "Talk to me."

"I'm sorry, I got blood on your shirt, but you'll get it back all cleaned up after Mitch is through with it."

"I don't care about my shirt—did you say blood?" She could hear the click as he swallowed. "I'll be there in a half hour," he ground out.

"It's not mine," she said, "and it's at least a forty-five-minute drive from Newark."

"He hurt you," Patrick rasped.

"Peggy and Doc Gannon patched me up. Mary Murphy is plying me with spiked hot tea. You need to stay at work; people are counting on you."

"It's been quiet," he told her. "We've been catching up on cleaning the rig and the firehouse."

"I'm sure that won't last all day," she said. "Trust me to know that I'm OK and that you shouldn't worry."

When he didn't answer her, she motioned for her father to come back over. "Pop, please tell Patrick that I really am fine and that he doesn't need to drive all the way over here to see for himself."

Her father talked to Patrick for a few minutes before

disconnecting. Grace was about to thank him when her father told her to sit still. "Smile, damn it."

She laughed and her father took a picture. "So that's how you're convincing him not to leave work?"

His nod of agreement actually eased one of the knots in her belly. "He'll be picking you up at seven o'clock."

"But, Pop…"

Her father shook his head and told her to deal with it. "The man cares about you. Let him."

"So," Kate said when her father and Mary left the diner, "what's up for the rest of the day?"

Grace got to her feet, surprised that her knees weren't quite as painful as she thought they'd be. "I've got tons of work next door. I'd better get moving."

"Come back for lunch," Kate urged.

"Only if you can eat lunch with me," Grace told her friend. "It's no fun if I'm eating and you're working."

"Lunchtime is our busiest time," Kate protested.

Grace put her hands on her hips. "Breakfast is."

Peggy poured another round of coffee for some stragglers. "It's always busy here."

"Fine, I'll come over and you can take five minutes to eat a chicken salad sandwich with me."

"Fine," Kate answered.

"Good," Grace said.

"Bye." Kate's eyes sparkled with laughter, but Grace refused to let her friend have the last word.

"Be back later."

Before Kate could say anything else, Grace rushed through the door and onto the sidewalk. She had just reached the now-open front door to Mulcahys when a voice called out, "Don't be late."

They were both laughing as they headed back to work.

Grace decided that the best way to put thoughts of the alley out of her head was to dive right back in where she left off yesterday. Rolling up the sleeves of Mitch's worn work shirt, she started with the first stack of boxes she'd moved yesterday, vowing to make a dent in the filing.

Grace wondered how she'd ever thought working at Mulcahys was dull. It was so diverse. How could she have thought it boring? While she worked, she compared her job in the city with the one she was doing right now, admitting—if only to herself—that she preferred what she was doing now. By the time she'd fielded a dozen or so phone calls from concerned friends and neighbors, her father walked in and asked, "Did you eat yet?"

"What time is it?" She hadn't stopped for a break since she'd left the diner.

"One thirty."

"Time flies."

"Helps to be busy doing something you enjoy."

She suspected her father was hoping Grace's love for tackling big projects and reorganizing things would keep her coming back long after her vacation ended. "Did you have time for a cup of coffee after lunch?"

"Now what makes you think I ate already?"

"You're not all grumpy and grumbling," Grace said, stifling her laughter. "A sure sign."

"Hmphf," Joe snorted. "All three of my girls have such smart mouths."

Grace gave in and chuckled. "Just like our Pop." He held the door and then closed and locked it behind her. "I'm coming right back."

"You're going to eat with Kate, remember?"

"That won't take that long," she began, wondering at the dark look on her father's face. "What's happened?"

He drew in a deep breath. "I'll let Kate tell you."

It was then that she noticed he was sticking close. Something was definitely up.

Walking in through the open door, the scent of coffee, burgers, and fries almost had her going for the comfort food instead of the healthier chicken salad.

"Grace." Kate looked worn out and hadn't earlier.

"Busy afternoon?"

Kate shrugged and Joe went over to the counter to speak to Peggy, but whatever he and Peggy were talking about was discussed in hushed tones.

"All right," Grace said, taking her friend by the arm and leading her to the farthest table in the back of the diner. "What's going on?"

Kate sank onto the vinyl bench and Grace's worry doubled as she watched the way her friend nearly folded herself in half, bracing an arm across her stomach. "Brian caught up with the man from the alley."

Grace noticed Kate was using Deputy Jones's first name. *Interesting*. "Since when is he Brian?"

Kate glared at her. "Would you please focus on what is important?"

"I like him," Grace said. "Your mom does too."

When it became clear that Kate had said all that she intended to, Grace slid in beside her friend and nudged Kate with her elbow. "Talk."

Kate sighed. "You know how Brian likes to off-road in his truck?"

Grace smiled. "When he was young and reckless, he always said the quickest way to get where you're headed is a straight line, whether it's through a cornfield or a stream."

Kate's eyes lost the desolate look as she agreed. "Well, that's what he did."

"Where?"

Kate gripped her hands together and Grace felt the tension return. "He saw the car Charlie and Tommy described up ahead and cut through the north corner of Mr. Parrish's cornfield. He ran the guy off the road right before it intersects with Cherry Valley Road."

Grace's eyes widened. "Mr. Parrish is going to be pissed."

Kate snorted. "Good thing it wasn't my daddy's field."

Grace's hands flew to her mouth to keep from bursting out laughing.

Kate nodded. "He's carried a shotgun filled with birdshot ever since that time Steve and Nick went joy riding through our cornfield."

"Fifteen years is a long time to carry a grudge."

Kate rolled her eyes. "Not according to my dad."

"So isn't it good news that the caught the guy? And why didn't Mitch ask me to come down and identify him?"

Kate reached for her hand and squeezed it. "I was delivering lunch to Honey B. when Brian got back. It was him."

Fear scraped Grace's gut raw. "Him who?"

A tear slipped past Kate's guard and Grace knew that it had been the same man who'd assaulted her friend the other night. "Did he walk into the police station under his own power?"

Kate sniffed in her tears and wiped her eyes. "Yes, but he had two black eyes and a broken nose—oh wait," Kate said. "You did that to him."

Satisfaction filled Grace. "And I'd do it again."

Kate sniffed loudly and Grace put her arm around her. "Don't cry, Katy-did," she urged.

Kate rested her head on Grace's shoulder and sighed. "Brian is one of the good guys."

Thoughtful, Grace waited a few minutes before she asked, "Is that why you won't date him?"

Kate's head shot up and she glared at Grace. "Fat lot you know."

Grace crossed her arms in front of her and glared back. "Our deputy isn't a loser."

"I never said he was," Kate said. "Hey!" Kate shot to her feet. "Are you saying I only date losers?"

Grace did the same. "If the shoe fits."

"Will you two shut up?" Peggy hissed. "You're causing a scene and scaring away the customers."

"They'll be back with reinforcements to watch us argue," Kate grumbled. "Good for business."

"Whatever you were arguing about, finish it," Peggy demanded.

"You should go talk to him," Grace said.

"Why bother?" Kate wanted to know.

"Because he's still stuck on you," Peggy added.

Kate whirled around to stare at her sister. "I thought you didn't know what we were arguing about."

Peggy grinned. "Lucky guess. Take your break now," she told her sister. "Mitch just called. He wants to talk to both of you."

"But I'm hungry," Kate protested.

"I'll have two burgers, medium rare; a basket of fries, well done; and two root beer floats waiting. Now get going."

Kate looked at Grace and frowned. "I don't just date losers."

Grace frowned back. "Then ask him to drive you home tonight."

"But—"

"Please?" Grace asked. "Do it because you're my best friend and I want you to be as happy as I am."

"Are you?" Kate asked. "You haven't been seeing him all that long."

"Sometimes," Grace whispered, "you just know."

As they wended their way around the tables, Kate tapped Grace on the back. Grace looked over her shoulder. "What?"

"If I ask Brian to take the long way home, will you tell me something wicked about Patrick?"

Grace shook her head at her friend. When they were almost to the sheriff's office, she whispered, "His stamina is amazing and the things he can do with his mouth are probably against the law in Ohio."

Kate grabbed ahold of Grace's arm and put a hand to her heart. Eyes wide, she whispered back, "Fib or truth?"

Grace made an X over her heart. "God's honest."

Kate squared her shoulders. "Thanks," she said. "I needed that."

Grace hoped that Kate didn't shoot herself in the foot where Deputy Jones was concerned. Brian tended to be a Boy Scout where Kate was concerned. Maybe it was because he usually happened to be nearby whenever one of Kate's loser boyfriends took a swing at her or left her stranded.

Mitch's dispatcher, Cindy, greeted them as they walked in. "Good," she said. "You're both here. Mitch is in the back with the prisoner right now, getting him settled."

Grace wondered how she would react seeing the man from the alley again, but the way Kate started breathing the moment they stepped inside had her more worried that her friend would hyperventilate.

"Sit down, Kate." She pushed her friend into the nearest chair and helped Kate cup her hands in front of her mouth and nose. "Cindy, do you have a paper bag?"

Mitch's dispatcher for a number of years, Cindy, was prepared for anything. She reached into the bottom drawer of her desk and whipped one out, handing it to Grace. Kate had lost that wild look in her eyes by the time Grace had coaxed her to hold the bag over her mouth and nose in place of her hands.

"That's it, nice and slow, in and out."

Cindy handed Kate a cup of water while Grace kept an eye on her friend. Kate hadn't had a panic attack in years, at least not that Grace knew of. Kate was staring down the hallway to Mitch's office and Grace had an uneasy feeling she knew what was bothering her friend.

"Did you tell Mitch the whole story?"

"What?"

Grace sighed and told Cindy, "We're just going to take a quick walk outside."

They walked in silence, circling the brick building twice before Kate spoke. "I told him enough. It's not my fault they couldn't find Jim—but it is my fault that Jim attacked you too."

Grace's gut clenched as one ugly possibility entered her thoughts. More worried about her friend's state of health than her own, Grace grabbed ahold of Kate's hand. "It is not your fault. You had no control of that bastard's actions. But I need to know, did you go to the ER and get checked out?"

While she waited for Kate to answer, she looked up and noticed Deputy Jones frozen by the back door. From the look on his face, he'd heard Grace's question and was waiting for Kate's answer. She met his gaze before looking back at her friend.

"Kate, answer my damn question. Did you go to the ER and did they do a rape kit?"

"No."

Grace hoped that Brian wouldn't make any sudden moves. "Katy-did, you know that I love you dearly, right?"

Kate nodded as she stared out over the fields separating the sheriff's office and the high school. "Sisters of the heart," Kate whispered.

"We tell each other things we wouldn't tell anyone else." Grace prayed that Kate would still be speaking to her if she found out that Grace knew they had an audience. "So tell me why you didn't go to the ER."

Grace waited, hoping the less she said, the more Kate would want to tell her.

"I didn't need to. Things didn't get that far. But I got tired of being pushed around by loser guys," Kate confessed. "I kneed him as hard as I could. I surprised him."

"So you got out of the car, but how did you outrun him?"

"I didn't." Kate chuckled. "I outclimbed him."

Grace sensed that Deputy Jones had heard all he needed and would either slip away or call out to them. "One of the pine trees by that old farmer's wall?"

"Yep. He tried to follow me, but I'm lighter and don't care about pine pitch getting on my hands."

"That's what baby oil's for," Grace said.

"Exactly. I guess he got tired of yelling at me to come down because after a half hour, he got in his car and drove away."

"How'd you get home?"

"I called Peggy."

"So she knows what happened?"

"More or less."

"Which is it?" Grace asked. "More or less?"

Kate shrugged. "Less."

"He was waiting for me this morning," Kate told her. "When I opened the back door to take the garbage out, he was waiting in the alley."

"Did you call for help?"

"I swung the garbage bag at his head and ran inside and locked the door. A few minutes later I heard you screaming for help." Kate's gaze met Grace's. "I'm so sorry, Gracie. I had no idea he'd go after you, and I was so worried about you, I never thought to put two and two together—that he was the one who attacked you."

Grace hugged her tight before urging her to turn around. "Don't worry about it, Kate. Come on, let's go talk to Mitch so he can book this guy on two counts of assault!"

"Hey, Kate. Grace." Deputy Jones walked toward them. "Mitch is ready to talk to you ladies."

"Brian," Grace said, tugging on her friend's arm. "Kate has a question for you."

He looked down at Kate and waited.

But Kate was too busy glaring at her friend to notice. "No, I don't."

"Yes," Grace said with a smile for the deputy. "You do."

Kate threw her hands up in the air and whirled around to face the lawman. "Grace wants to know if you can give me a ride home."

His facial expression didn't change, but his lips twitched. "Does she?"

Grace really liked Brian and decided to give her

friend a nudge in the right direction. "Only because Kate's too timid to ask you herself."

Kate's mouth opened and closed, but no words came out. But if looks could kill…

"Come on, Kate," Grace said. "Mitch is waiting."

Chapter 18

"PATRICK, I'M GLAD YOU'RE HERE." JOE MULCAHY
opened the door and motioned for Pat to sit down at the
kitchen table.

"How is she?" Patrick had struggled with the full
gamut of emotions all day. "Did they catch the guy?"

"Yes. I was so busy trying to keep her occupied so
she wouldn't have time to dwell on the attack, I forgot
to call you."

Patrick wanted to tell Joe it was all right, but in his
gut he knew it wasn't. Every moment not spent fighting the warehouse fire, he'd been waging a silent war
within himself—and the overwhelming need to hop in
his truck and drive to Apple Grove to see Grace.

"It's the same man who assaulted Kate McCormack."

His gut roiled as the acidity level rose. Battling the
urge to rip something apart with his bare hands, he
rubbed his palms on his thighs.

"They transferred him to Licking County Jail after
Grace and Kate ID'd him."

"Were you there when they did?"

"No. Grace and Kate went together. They've been
thick as thieves since they could walk."

He wished he'd been there for Grace. "Do you
think she needs to get away from here for a couple
of days?"

"Not sure. Why?"

"I'm working a twenty-four starting tomorrow

morning, so if she stayed in Newark, I'd be gone most of the time she was there."

"I don't want her to be alone," Joe said. "She might start—"

Grace walked into the kitchen. "What are you two talking about?" She looked at her father first and then Patrick. "If you are worried about me, don't be. I gave as good as I got. I shouldn't have turned my back on the guy."

"I thought he—"

She cut him off. "Can we talk about this later? It's been a long day and I'm really hungry."

Patrick bit down on the inside of his cheek to keep from disagreeing with her. If he couldn't get his hands on the guy and beat him bloody for attacking both Grace and Kate, the least Grace could do was fill him in on the details. Joe was a bit sketchy on them. Her father stared from one to the other. "Best feed her before she gets cranky."

Grace frowned at her father first and Patrick second before saying, "Don't wait up, Pop."

When they were outside, Patrick asked, "Anywhere to get takeout in town?"

"I'm an idiot. I haven't even asked how your day was or how many calls you had after I talked to you. You're probably tired and want to turn in early."

"Once I eat, I'll get my second wind," he promised.

"No takeout, but the diner's fast. Let's go there." She tugged on his arm to get him moving toward his truck. "I'll follow you in my car."

"Not part of the plan." He hauled her into his arms. He'd satisfy at least one of the needs churning inside of him—the rest would have to wait. "Kissing me hello is."

Her lips softening beneath his as she kissed him back filled the emptiness that had been plaguing him all day. This was right. This was where he belonged.

He loosened his hold on her and ended the kiss. "I missed you today."

She trailed the tips of her fingers along the line of his jaw. "When did you have time?"

"In between the last two calls." He didn't particularly want to talk about his day. He wanted to find out about the attacker. "I have to be honest here," he began. "I've waited all damn day to see you and to find out what the hell happened."

"I understand, but I've gone over it at least a half a dozen times today. I'm hungry and you are too. Let's eat."

His frown was fierce enough to have her sighing. "If I tell you, do you promise to drop it so we can eat?"

His sigh was exaggerated—and loud. "All right."

"OK," she told him. "Here's the 411: I was in the alley—not paying attention, thinking about you—and I ran into someone. He grabbed me; it pissed me off. I punched him in the nose—think I broke it—and he pushed me to the ground."

"Son of a bitch!"

She held up her hand. "No," she told him. "Do not go there—you're more like Pop than I thought, but I'm a big girl and can take care of myself. Besides, he's been arrested and charged for what he did to Katie and me."

When he reached out a hand to stroke the side of her face, she leaned into his touch. "Grace, I wish I had been there to protect you."

She sighed. "I know, but I'm pretty good at taking care of myself."

"But he hurt you."

"And his butt's in jail for it. So," she said, linking her arm through his, "now you know everything that happened. I'm really hungry."

He sighed. "A deal's a deal." They got into his truck and drove to the diner.

———

"How are the burgers here?" Patrick asked Peggy after they'd settled into a booth.

"Amazing," Peggy said, walking toward them. "How many do you want?"

Patrick laughed. "Am I that transparent?"

Peggy smiled. "After a putting in a full day at the firehouse, a big guy like you can probably put away at least two of our double-burger platters."

He looked over at Grace. "What would you like?"

"I'll have the chicken salad platter—easy on the mayo."

"All right." Peggy made a note on her pad. "Coffee?"

"Please."

When she left to fill their order, he asked Grace if Peggy was upset about something.

"No, why?"

"She didn't really stop to talk."

"It's been insanely busy here today. She and Kate put in a long day."

"Where is Kate?"

"In the kitchen. She serves in the morning, since Peggy's specialties are breakfast and cakes, and cooks in the afternoons and evenings."

They both relaxed for the first time that day as they talked about the diner and the differences between working all day behind a desk, as opposed to standing on your feet serving food or running into a burning building.

"I'm on a twenty-four-hour shift at the firehouse starting tomorrow morning," Patrick told her.

The reminder that his job was an important one, and busy, had her facing a fact she'd forgotten—work schedules had yet to be factored into their relationship. "I did forget. So," she said, "I guess I won't see you until Thursday?"

"I tried to switch shifts, but Mike's not ready for a twenty-four."

"I guess it will give me time to miss you." Grace tried to force a smile, but she wasn't entirely sure she'd succeeded.

When they'd finished eating and Patrick had paid their bill, he stood and held out his hand. "I'm not ready to leave yet. Want to take a walk?"

The night was warm and the breeze soft. Hand in hand, they walked down to the bank and crossed the street so she could show him the gazebo. "Nice," he said. "I like the flowers."

"Miss Trudi plants them every year."

"Is it usually this quiet so early?"

"People get up pretty early around here," she explained. "Well, at least the ones who have farms or jobs that have them opening up before eight o'clock."

"Like the diner?" he suggested.

"And Mulcahys," she added.

"Is that why you wanted to work in an office environment—so you wouldn't be starting your day so early?"

She thought about it. "That was part of it, but I was tired of working in an environment that included plumbing and lumber supplies."

"And now that you've been to where the grass is greener?"

Grace found herself telling him about her job and her

epiphany today—that she really missed working for the family and the diversity of the job.

"Did you tell your dad?"

When she didn't answer him right away, he tugged on her hair.

"What?"

"You didn't answer me, Grace. Does your dad know?"

"No. He'd be rubbing his hands together anticipating my moving back here." She looked down at her hands. "I hate knowing that I've failed."

"How have you failed?"

She lifted her gaze to meet his. "All I talked about for the last few years was leaving town and working in the city. I was pretty crappy about it, but Pop just kept nodding, telling me I had to follow my dream. And now…" Her voice trailed off.

"Now?" he prompted.

"I loved the challenge of recreating the computer files and databases—"

"You could do that as a side job or maybe as a way to help friends struggling with their own databases, while you work at whichever job you decide is the one for you."

His suggestion was one she'd never considered before.

"Give yourself a break, and remember, just because you've discovered your dream job isn't what you thought you always wanted, it doesn't equate to failure. Didn't you say they promoted you?"

She sighed. "Well, yes, but—"

"No buts, Mulcahy. They don't promote people who aren't doing their jobs."

She smiled. "I wasn't thinking of it that way."

"That's because you were thinking of it the wrong way," he teased.

She didn't mind though; he'd given her something positive to think about and a reason to contemplate moving back, working for the family, and contributing to the town in her own way—one that didn't involve power tools or plumbing supplies.

"Thanks for listening, Patrick."

The silence grew between them, having her wonder what had been behind his move to the Midwest from the city he loved. He'd been so willing to talk about her dream job, she finally just asked, "So, is your move here permanent, or will you be moving back to New York City?"

He stared at her. Her question must have caught him off guard. Darn, she'd been hoping he'd open up about his life and his plans. Now that she thought about it, he knew far more about her than she knew about him.

"You never really mentioned why you left New York."

Before he could answer, Grace's cell phone buzzed. She read the text and chuckled before telling him, "It's Kate. She said she promises to be nice to Deputy Jones when he drives her home."

He stood and held out his hand, enveloping her much smaller one in the warmth of his. "I'd better drive you home now—or I'll be tempted to take you with me—and I can't tonight."

Patrick's manners and innate kindness added another layer to the growing bond between them, but his withdrawal and refusal to answer her question worried her. Was there something he was hiding? Was there a part of him she couldn't reach or wouldn't understand? She really needed to sleep, and if he didn't answer her, she'd be up all night wondering why and what it meant.

She'd miss not seeing him and would definitely be lonely in bed without him but wouldn't be telling him that now. She had bigger fish to fry. They walked down the sidewalk and along the street side of the building instead of the alleyway.

He was silent but still held her hand. She tugged on his hand, forcing him to stop and look down at her. "What?"

"You didn't answer my question." She wasn't going to back down and she wasn't giving up on him.

He reached out and touched the tip of his finger to her cheek, tracing the curve of it. "Grace. There are some things I can't talk about."

"Now or ever?" He shrugged again, irritating her. "My dad does that and it drives me nuts."

"What?"

"Shrugs instead of verbalizing his answer."

"A shrug is an answer."

She threw her hands up in the air and groaned. "Now you sound like my brother-in-law."

"Which one?"

She thought about leaving him there on the sidewalk. Instead, she huffed out a breath and walked to his truck, wrenching open the passenger door. Grace wanted to be mad at him, but more than that, wanted him to talk to her. But she couldn't make him talk to her. "I'm tired," she explained, "and I want to soak in a hot tub."

He cupped her elbow in his callused hand and started to stroke it slowly, gently, as if he were holding something fragile—precious. She looked up at him and was struck by the turmoil in his amber eyes. There was so much emotion there, it was hard to sort out. He helped her into the truck and walked around to the driver's side and got in.

The silence while he drove back to her house wasn't as comfortable as it had been. Finally, as he pulled into her driveway and parked, he said, "There are reasons I can't talk about New York. Can we please let it go at that?"

She started to shake her head and walk away, but he pulled her into his embrace and rested his chin on top of her head. "I need you in my life, Grace. Don't give up on me."

She relaxed in his arms, hugging him back. "I'm not."

He sighed. "Thanks."

"It's obvious you love your job—and your family. You miss them."

"Yeah."

"Sooner or later, whatever your reasons are will catch up to you. When they do, I'll be there, waiting to listen."

His arms tightened around her. "I'm not letting you go, Grace."

She guessed that was his way of saying OK.

She rose up on her toes and kissed his cheek. "Only until your shift is over."

Pat rubbed the back of his fingers on her cheek. "Dream of me."

Grace watched him getting into his truck and suddenly wished she were going with him, even if it was just for tonight—he'd be sleeping at the firehouse tomorrow night. "I will."

Chapter 19

THE NEXT TWO DAYS HAD GRACE WONDERING WHY she'd thought she missed living in a small town. Visitors started dropping by the shop, beginning with Honey B. and her boys, just checking up on her. The steady stream of concerned friends and neighbors kept up. Had someone scheduled their visits?

After spending time she didn't have convincing Mrs. Winter she was fine, Miss Trudi stopped by to look in on her. She was slowly making progress where the filing was concerned, but her nerves were frazzled and she hadn't slept well in two nights. The worry that something really awful had happened to make Patrick leave the family and city he loved—the possibility that it was horrific and job related—was very possible.

She felt as if she were marking time and working at projects to keep her occupied until she could get back to what was important—being with Patrick. The anticipation building inside of her as the hours ticked by was driving her quietly insane. By the time Thursday evening rolled around, Grace checked her phone for the fifth time…no word from him all day.

The last text from him had been on Wednesday when he went off shift, promising to see her today. Wondering if she was worried for no reason, she nearly called her brother-in-law to ask if he'd heard from Patrick. But she'd never been so impatient in her life and she wasn't about to start now.

She was stocking shelves in the supply room when she heard a familiar deep voice call her name and suddenly the world made sense again. "In here!" She was halfway down the ladder when strong hands grabbed her hips and swept her off her feet and into his arms.

"God, I missed you." Patrick's lips were kissing the breath out of her, but she was too busy kissing him back to worry about a silly thing like breathing.

When they broke apart, they were both talking at once. Laughing, she brushed her hair out of her eyes. "I missed you too."

He held her while he told her about the tanker fire out on the highway and the one behind one of the elementary schools. "Kids are getting bored earlier than normal this year."

"Do you usually have problems with kids setting fires?"

"Not as many as we had when I was in New York."

"More people," she suggested as he set her on her feet.

"Maybe that was the reason."

"So how long do we have? I need to finish putting these parts away before I close up for the day."

"I'm not due back until Saturday night. Then I'm on for two night shifts in a row."

When she didn't respond right away, he rubbed her back and said, "Let me give you a hand with that and we can figure out what to do with our time until then."

Working together, they finished emptying the PVC pipe and copper tubing that Meg had ordered for an upcoming plumbing job. "I'm working tomorrow," she reminded him.

"I guess you can't take the day off."

The tone of his voice had her fighting not to laugh as she answered, "No. I promised my dad I'd be here."

"What would you do if we were working in the same city?"

His question was a valid one, but she couldn't believe he didn't realize her answer would be the same. "I'd still have to go to work tomorrow."

He sighed. "That's the biggest challenge with my job," he said. "The hours."

She brushed her hands on her jeans. "And here I thought it was walking toward the fire instead of the other direction."

He laughed as she'd meant him to.

"Give me a sec to lock up out back."

Patrick was right behind her. "What have you been up to?"

While she filled him in on nosy neighbors dropping by Mulcahys, they locked up and walked back into the office. Powering down her computer, she let her gaze sweep the room one last time. She sighed when she saw the last stack of boxes. "I guess that's all for tonight."

"It looks amazing in here. You've done so much in just a few days. No wonder your father was glad to have you back for a little while."

"You already know I'm addicted to color-coded spreadsheets." She locked the front door to the shop.

"It's a good thing you told me." He put his arm around her neck. "I'd hate to have found that out a month from now."

She laughed and he told her he was hungry.

"You're always hungry."

"Ma says it's my two hollow legs."

Grace giggled.

"All Garahan men have them. Ma's been tell-ing us that since we were kids. We have the Garahan metabolism like our dad did—as soon as we eat, we're burning it up."

"I wish I had that problem," she murmured.

Patrick heard her and was shaking his head at her as he opened the passenger door. "You are perfect." He brushed his lips on the top of her head and helped her inside.

Grace's heart acknowledged what her head was slow to recognize: he was the first man—aside from her father—to accept her for who and what she was—and she was head over heels in love with him. He didn't seem to want to change anything about her.

How refreshing! But for how long? And what about New York? When would he trust her with whatever was haunting him?

Trying to keep things light, she asked if he wanted to go to her house.

"Only long enough for you to grab a few things so you can spend the next two nights with me. We can grab something to eat on the road."

"But I have to be at work tomorrow."

He laughed. "Yeah. OK, how about this? You spend tonight at my place and I drive you to work and pick you up tomorrow so you can spend the night with me."

"I can't imagine what we'll do with our time," she teased as visions of a very naked Patrick flitted through her brain.

"We never did get to take a shower together," he said. "I've been thinking about getting you naked—and keeping you that way until I have to drive you back home."

Her tongue got stuck to the roof of her mouth as every ounce of spit dried up.

His chuckle told her that he knew exactly the effect

his words would have on her. Finally, she was able to work up enough moisture in her mouth to loosen her tongue and speak. "I've never spent more time naked than how long it takes to shower and dry off."

The way he clenched his jaw had her staring at his profile. His looks would stop traffic, he was that good-looking. When he didn't speak, she prodded him. "You've seriously spent more time than that without your clothes on?"

"Hell yeah."

She crossed her arms in front of her. "And when would you have had the time?"

"My last real vacation."

When he didn't say anything else, she realized he probably hadn't spent that time alone. Opting out of that particular discussion, she asked, "How long ago was that?"

"A couple of years ago."

"Sounds serious." Wishing she hadn't started the conversation in that particular direction, she felt her insecurities building back up again. Inching away from him to stare out her window, she watched as they passed Bob's Gas and Gears. They were near the turnoff for Cherry Valley Road. When he put on his signal, she said, "There's a shortcut if you drive just a little further and turn onto Goose Pond Road."

"Weren't we there the other night?"

"Yes, when we interrupted my dad and Mary."

"I like her," Patrick said.

"I do too, but I think both of them might be happier if they got married and stopped going back and forth between their houses. I'm getting tired just watching them."

There was a long pause, leaving her to wonder what he was thinking.

"You don't have to come back with me to Newark."

She scooted back close to his side. "Of course I do. What makes you think I don't want to?"

"Well, you just said you were tired of the back and forth."

"I distinctly remember mentioning my dad and Mary when I said that."

"But maybe you meant us as well," he added.

Fighting to control her temper, and nearly failing, she snipped, "Don't put words in my mouth, Patrick."

He slanted a look in her direction before saying, "Yes, ma'am." Waiting a beat he asked, "I guess I'll have to be careful."

"About what?"

"Trying to figure out what you mean when you're saying something."

"I thought what I said was pretty straightforward."

"You didn't grow up in our house." He chuckled. "My ma would say one thing when she really meant something entirely different."

Grace forgot all about being annoyed and sympathized. "That must have been rough."

Patrick shrugged. "You get used to it." They pulled in the driveway and he put it in park. "I don't get home often enough to suit my mother and sisters."

"What about your brothers?" she asked, getting out.

"We're usually arguing or pushing each other around whenever we get together."

"Sounds lovely." *Not.*

"Now you sound like my mother."

They were laughing when they walked into the kitchen.

Joe and Mary looked up from where they sat at the table. "We were just talking about you," Mary told them.

Joe got up and brushed a kiss on the top of Mary's head. "You weren't supposed to tell them that."

Grace laughed. "I already figured you two would talk about us, but that's OK, because we were just talking about the two of you."

That had her father freezing in his tracks and turning around to face his daughter. "Really? What were you saying?"

She was smiling when she countered with, "What were you?"

They stared at one another for long minutes before her father shrugged and Mary changed the subject. "We're going to have another Bake-Off for the Fourth of July celebration."

Grace was definitely interested since she'd missed it last year. Hell or high water, she would be here this year. "What's the main ingredient?"

"You'll be home for the Fourth?" Her father seemed surprised.

Grace nodded. She'd have to tell him soon that she was thinking of leaving her job in Columbus.

Mary looked from father to daughter before answering, "Triple berry. Local and fresh!"

"What the heck is a triple berry?" Patrick wanted to know.

"Whatever berry is in season," Grace said.

"Only you need to use three of them," Mary added.

Patrick shook his head. "How do you know what will be in season? And won't everyone just make pie?"

Grace took pity on him and explained, "Depending

on how wet or dry it has been, there could be a bumper crop of strawberries—they really like it wet and warm. If it's been warmer than normal, the wild raspberries might be ready in time. It is a bit early for currant berries, but then there are blueberries."

"So basically, since it's been warm and we've had rain, it could be any of the above?"

Grace and Mary were smiling at him as if he'd just solved a difficult puzzle.

"Exactly," Mary said. "The true test is to see how creative our bakers will be with what is native around Apple Grove," she told him. "Coming up with new or recycling family recipes, adding a new twist to them is just part of the fun."

"I don't remember having berries in anything but pie," he said.

Joe smiled as he told Patrick, "The Fourth is serious business around here. We have a parade and then the judging for the Bake-Off, and we end the evening with fireworks over behind the football field at the high school." He waited a moment before asking Patrick, "Think you can make it?"

Patrick looked at Grace first. "I'm not sure. That's three weeks away and as of right now, I'm off-shift that day, but things could change if someone gets hurt on the job or an emergency happens."

"You'll definitely be back for the celebration?" Grace's father asked her. "You won't change your mind?"

"Absolutely," she said. "And I'm going to be baking something to enter in the Bake-Off."

"Against Peggy?" Mary wanted to know.

Grace frowned. "Why not?"

"Aside from the fact that she's won for the last three years in a row?" her father asked.

"Yes," Grace hissed. "Just because she's been winning, doesn't mean she will continue to do so."

When she looked at Patrick, he spoke up. "True. You could come up with something truly amazing—and to prove that I have faith in you, I'll volunteer to be your official taste tester."

They were laughing as Grace swept past them. "I need to get a few things together," she said. "Why don't you and Pop write down a few ideas for me, and I'll see if I can whip up a recipe for the contest?"

―∾―

"Is she serious?" Patrick asked, watching her leave.

"As a heart attack," her father said. "I'm a big fan of blueberry pandowdy, how about you?"

Patrick was watching him as if he expected Joe to laugh. When he didn't, he said, "I don't even know what that is."

"It's got blueberries on the bottom and cake on top. My mom used to bake it when blueberries were in season."

"Hey how about cobbler?" Patrick suggested. "My sister's got a great recipe."

Mary smiled. "Wait, we need to start writing these suggestions down."

By the time Grace returned, the men—with Mary's help—had a list of ten ideas for her. "Not bad," she said, going over their list. "But do you really want me to come up with a relish recipe? That's technically not baking; it's cooking."

"I ran out of ideas," her father grumbled. "So sue me."

"The rest look interesting enough to give them a try." She hugged Mary first and then her father, promising, "I'll see you tomorrow at the shop."

"Drive safely," they both reminded the couple as they left.

"I think it's working," Mary said, leaning against Joe as they waved good-bye.

"Honey B. and Meg were right about those two—and the sparks."

"Why don't we give them a call now and tell them their plan is working splendidly?"

Joe had his arms around Mary's waist and was pulling her close when their eyes met. As his lips lowered toward hers, he rasped, "Later."

———

Patrick felt a bone-deep satisfaction having the woman he loved riding beside him, knowing that they'd be together for the next two days—well, except for when Grace would be at work tomorrow during the day. Maybe after he dropped Grace off for work, he'd stop by and see what Dan was up to; there was always something going on at their house, especially with his three kids. That way, he and Grace could have lunch together tomorrow.

"You're awfully quiet."

"Hmmm?" His thoughts changed direction as they drove closer to Newark. He'd straightened his apartment, done the laundry, changed his sheets—everything was ready for alone time with his curvaceous cutie.

"Are you having second thoughts about me staying over again?"

He snickered. "Just wishing there was a way to keep you here—naked—for forty-eight hours straight."

She turned toward him but didn't say anything.

"What?"

"You sound like you really mean that."

He shrugged. "I usually say what I mean."

"Unlike your mom?"

She hit that one on the nose. "Yeah. I'm more like my dad was—well, at least that's what my uncles tell me."

"On your mother's side?"

"Both sides. Two and two."

"Do they live close by?"

He was pulling into the Bob Evans in Newark when he told her, "Brooklyn."

"You must miss seeing everyone if they all live so close to one another."

"It could get a little dicey at times, since all of our uncles decided to keep an extra set of eyes on us after our dad died."

"So it wasn't as easy to get away with stuff," she said with a soft smile. "Meg was always getting into trouble until our mom died—then everything changed."

Sensing she was about to sink into the past, he parked and held out his hand to her. "Come on. Let's eat."

When she smiled, he couldn't help but smile back. Being with Grace was so easy; talking to her wasn't a chore like it had been with previous girlfriends. He didn't have to worry about what to talk about—and she'd agreed for the moment not to ask him about New York. They just talked like friends. Being friends was important if their relationship was going to last. His mother and father had been childhood friends.

They sat down at an open booth and ordered. He was a fan of their chicken-fried steak and would be ordering that. Grace was trying to decide between one diet plate and another. Finally, he grumbled, "The sausage gravy and biscuits here are amazing."

Her head shot up and her cheeks flushed a delicate pink. "What makes you think I want that?"

He swallowed the laughter, knowing that she might misunderstand and think he was laughing at her. He had his work cut out for him if he was going to convince the lovely Grace that he would never do that. He meant it when he complimented her. She was his ideal woman.

Searching for just the right thing to say, he blurted out, "You've been staring down at that side of the menu for a while now and it's got a picture of it right there." He tapped the photo and sat back. "So?"

She sighed. "I did have yogurt and fruit for lunch."

"Which is why you're hungry."

The waitress walked over with the water pitcher and, while she filled their glasses, told them about the specials.

Once they'd ordered, they started talking about his last trip home to Brooklyn.

"Was it really a whole year ago?"

He was holding her hand, rubbing the back of it, wondering how she kept them so silky soft. "Yeah, for our mother's birthday."

"What about the holidays?"

"I had to work."

Wanting to change the subject, he asked, "It sounds like it's been a while since you spent time at home too."

She sighed. "I'd been working longer hours up until I got the promotion—and when I did, there was so much work to do, I've kept to my longer hours."

"So you spent more time working and less time recharging your batteries in Apple Grove."

"What makes you think they needed recharging?"

He brought her hand to his lips and pressed a kiss to

her middle knuckle. "If you had a mirror, you wouldn't be asking me that."

"I don't understand—"

The waitress delivered their orders and left with the promise of checking on them soon. When she'd gone, he leaned close and told her, "You looked exhausted when I first saw you. There were dark circles beneath your eyes and your shoulders were slumping."

She was picking at her food with her fork when he added, "By Sunday, your eyes were brighter, the dark circles were gone, and you seemed relaxed…happy."

She was still playing with her food when he ground out, "Eat it and forget about the calories. I plan to work them off you."

Her mouth went slack. He reached over and tapped beneath her chin until she realized what she was doing and closed her mouth. Eyes sparkling, cheeks flushed, Grace picked up her fork and dug in.

Patrick pushed her spoon toward her. "I've learned not to miss a drop of their gravy—I always use a spoon."

Her green eyes distracted him and for a moment he was deaf and dumb to everything around him, save the look in her eyes. When she continued to stare at him, his brain kicked in. "Sorry. What did you just ask me?"

She laughed. "I said, Isn't that what the biscuits are for?"

He shook his head. "Nope. That's for sopping up what you didn't get with the spoon. Trust me on this one. I've got cousins down South and out West— they've educated their poor Yankee cousins in the ways of biscuits and gravy."

When she sat back, declaring herself to be full, he sighed. "I was going to order pie."

Grace held up one hand. "None for me, thanks. I couldn't eat another bite."

He tucked a strand of hair behind her ear. "I plan to eat mine later," he told her. "After."

The way her eyes showed whatever she was thinking was a plus in his mind. He wouldn't ever have to wonder what was going on. One look at Grace and he'd know whether he was about to catch hell—or head straight to paradise.

They ended up ordering pie to go and picked it up when they paid the cashier. "Thank you, Patrick," Grace said. "I didn't realize I was that hungry."

"You know," he told her, "for someone who doesn't like to use power tools, you sure do your fair share of lifting, hauling, and moving boxes, crates, and stuff around Mulcahys."

He opened the passenger door and waited for her to get in. When he was sitting next to her, she said, "I've never really thought about it before, but now that I have another job to compare it to, I think that's why I've gained weight."

Patrick frowned at her. "I don't follow you."

"I sit behind a desk all day long at my real job," she explained. "I hadn't realized how much moving around and physical work I used to do working for my family."

"It's like being what my ma would call a Gal Friday."

She nodded. "Only with a lot more box moving, lifting, and unpacking."

They arrived at his apartment complex a few minutes later. It was encouraging that she'd been willing to continue as if their conversation from the night before—about New York—never happened. He wished he didn't know that she expected him to tell her what happened, but he did. With that one tiny wrinkle, their relationship was everything he'd envisioned.

"What if my dad thinks he'll be doing me a favor by not letting me come back?"

He closed the door behind her, took her hand, and led her to the living room. Easing her onto the sofa, he sat beside her and wrapped his arm around her. "Decisions and choices that we make are just that. Did you burn any bridges when you made the choice to move to Columbus?"

She seemed to be mulling that over for a moment before she answered. "I don't think so."

"Then it was a choice. Your dad's a smart guy and good judge of character. People are allowed to make changes in their lives. Sometimes they work out and sometimes they don't."

He fell silent, amazed that the words were true for him as well. Although he had said he didn't want to talk about it, he said, "I made the decision to move out here." He wasn't ready to tell her why—wasn't sure if he ever would be. Burying that line of thinking deep, he asked, "So why not just ask your dad for his advice? He might surprise you." He rubbed his hand up and down her arm. "When something isn't working, it's time to do something about it. Change can be good for the soul."

—◊◊◊—

Grace knew by the way Patrick said those last words, softly and almost to himself, that the reason he moved to Ohio, far from his family and those he loved, still troubled him. He appeared gruff and, because of his size, was intimidating at first. Deep down he was a caring man once you got to know him and talked to him.

"Change isn't easy," she offered, wondering if he would accept the statement as it had been meant—as an opening for him to share more of his burden with her.

He shrugged and rose to his feet, leaving Grace to understand that the moment was lost and further discussion of the subject had been carefully avoided. Maybe in time, he would open up and share what was troubling him. She had a feeling that it was either because of his job or something to do with his family—he did have a large one.

"So," he said, drawing her to stand beside him, "about getting you naked…"

She laughed. "God, I'm so stuffed, I'd probably lose dinner if we, uh, did anything physical right now."

He frowned. "OK, so if you were home and this happened, what would you do?"

"Take a long walk. I love the smell of the woods in the summertime, the rambling roses growing along peoples' fences, and the honeysuckle vine by our back door."

"I don't know if I can find any of that here," he said. "But we can take a walk around the neighborhood."

There were a surprising number of people out and about in the warm summer night. "Is it always this busy?"

He chuckled. "You're such a country girl. There are usually more people out—but the guys at the firehouse were talking about a Triple-A game in your neck of the woods."

"Apple Grove?"

He stared at her for a moment before answering, "Columbus—the Clippers."

"My sisters and I used to play baseball, but nothing serious. Just a bunch of us getting together, and we never watched it on TV like Pop does."

"Thought you were soccer fans."

"Well"—she smiled up at him, loving the way he listened to her as if she mattered; she'd missed that with her last boyfriend—"we sort of became interested in soccer once Dan and Meg got married."

After they'd been walking for a while, Patrick turned a corner so that they were working their way back to his apartment. After a few blocks, he said, "So, are you still full?"

She grinned and started walking faster.

He laughed as they power walked the last couple of blocks. When they reached his building, he scooped her up and tossed her over his shoulder.

"You've got to stop doing that!" she protested, hanging upside down.

"Sorry," he said.

He opened the door and closed it, just missing her backside as he did.

"Where are you going?"

He pressed his hand to the backs of her knees to keep her from kicking him as he walked. "My bedroom."

"OK." If she'd been hoping for a prelude to their lovemaking, it obviously wasn't going to happen. "Brace yourself, Bridget," she mumbled, surprised that she was disappointed before they'd even begun.

He set her on her feet and held her at arm's length, staring down at her. "Did you just say 'brace yourself'?"

She lifted her chin and stepped out of his arms, putting her hands on her hips—ready to do verbal battle with him. "So what if I did?"

"Bridget?" he asked.

"Yeah, so?"

"Let's just forget for the moment that it's my mother's

name," he told her, taking one step closer, "and focus on the fact that I wasn't planning to toss you on the bed and have my way with you."

"You weren't?"

He raised his head and looked up at the ceiling. "Please," he said. "I've got mad foreplay skills."

She had to agree with him. The times they'd made love, she'd been gasping for breath and shivering with need. "I suppose that's true."

He grabbed her hand and yanked her close until she lost her balance and tumbled against his chest. "Maybe I'd better remind you."

Grace had no time to think, as, in seconds, she was bombarded with mind-numbing pleasure as he proceeded to do just that.

Later, when they'd exhausted themselves, she shifted so she could lay her head against his heart. "Mad skills," she agreed, closing her eyes and drifting off to sleep.

Chapter 20

"WHAT ARE YOU GOING TO DO WITH THAT?" HE ASKED as Grace paused in the act of pulling a shirt over her head.

"Wear it."

His sigh sounded world-weary. "I thought I explained about keeping you naked."

"You weren't really serious about that," she said. "Were you?"

He eased off the bed and took the shirt from her. Skin to skin, heat to heat felt decadent and delicious, but going without clothes while doing everyday things like cooking and eating was beyond her comprehension.

"I can't."

He brushed her hair out of her eyes and cupped her face in his hands. "You're way too uptight."

She shook her head. "I can't go out into your kitchen and make breakfast."

"Sure you can."

"Not without clothes on."

He let his forehead rest against hers. "I can see this will require a breaking-in period."

She pushed back in his arms. "What does that mean?"

He walked over to the side of the bed and lifted up his T-shirt. "You can borrow one of my shirts."

"But they're too big and slide off my shoulders."

His smile was slow and lethal to her heart. "I know."

She took the shirt when he held it out to her. "What about my underwear?"

He shook his head. "My T-shirt or nothing."

She sighed. "You drive a hard bargain." When he followed her out of the bedroom she stopped. "Aren't you going to put something on?"

He stared at her mouth for the longest time before letting his gaze meet hers. "Not yet."

She had an idea of the direction of his thoughts, but he seemed content to let her make breakfast for them while he made the coffee, distracting her with the bronzed perfection of his body.

She burned the toast because he just had to slip past her, brushing against her until every cell in her body stood at attention—but then again, so did his.

"I'm going to be late if you keep distracting me."

"How am I doing that?"

"Don't try to get around me with that little boy voice and feigned innocence." She frowned. "I promised my dad that I'd be there today. Don't make this so hard for me."

He stood up and heaved another deep sigh. "All right. We'll do it your way." He walked out of the kitchen, leaving her to scrape the blackened edges off the toast.

When he returned, he was wearing a pair of cutoffs. "Better?"

She swallowed the mouthful of coffee and nodded. Words could not begin to describe how yummy he looked wearing those worn out, ragged jeans shorts. She tried to eat without sneaking peaks at him but in the end gave in and openly stared.

"What now?"

She wiped her mouth on the napkin and set it by her plate. "Did anyone ever tell you how beautiful you are?"

His face flushed a deep rosy color. "Guys are handsome," he began.

"You aren't," she told him. When his head shot up and their gazes met, she reached for his hand and said, "Deal with it, Patrick. You're drop-dead gorgeous."

He watched her in silence then slowly shook his head. "That's like saying a guy's pretty," he grumbled.

"Your looks go way beyond mere pretty," she told him as she rose to her feet and kissed the top of his head. "I've got to grab a shower or I'll be late."

"How about if you text your dad and explain that we're running behind? I'll show you just how relaxing sharing a shower can be."

Joe Mulcahy hadn't raised any fools. Grace sent the text and shed his shirt on her way down the hall. Patrick's shorts were by the bathroom door when she wrapped her legs around his waist and he stepped into the shower.

"Now," he rasped, "you let my fingers work their magic and I can promise you an unparalleled relaxation experience."

She nipped his bottom lip and kissed him deeply. "Did anyone ever tell you that you talk too much?"

His response was to turn on the hot water and let it rain down on them while he kissed her long, hard, and deep. When she was writhing against him, he pressed her back against the icy-cold tiles and tormented first one breast and then the other, moving back and forth, licking, nipping, and suckling her until she tensed beneath him and gave a low guttural cry as her release tore through her.

Weak as water, he let her legs slip down until he could brace her with one hand and lather her body with the other—every inch of her until she thought she'd go mad from the sensations zinging beneath her skin and singing from wherever his clever hands and magic mouth touched.

Grace felt like a warm, wet noodle. Her body might be limp, but her brain had started functioning again. "What about relaxing you?"

"Baby," he growled, "I get off watching you come." He kissed her, adding, "My turn comes later tonight."

He turned off the water and stood her in the middle of the bath mat, toweling her dry with infinite care and a tenderness that had her throat constricting and tears welling up in her eyes.

When he looked up, the expression in his eyes instantly changed from sensual to concerned. "What's wrong?"

She shook her head, unable to put what she felt into words. But she could still show him. Her hands linked around his neck, their bodies snug against one another. Heart-to-heart, face-to-face, she lifted her lips to meet his, pouring the love, tenderness, and caring he'd shown her into her kiss.

Without speaking, they watched one another slowly cover bits and pieces of skin that had been kissed and scrubbed and then kissed some more. Dressed, ready to face the outside world, they drove back to Apple Grove.

———

When Patrick dropped her off at the front door to the shop, she asked him if he had plans for his day off. He grinned. "I'll be wrestling with two little rug rats while Dan keeps an eye on Deidre so Meg can finish Mr. Weatherbee's plumbing repair."

"That ought to keep you busy for most of the day."

"I'll be back at lunchtime." He bent to brush her lips with his, marveling at the way the woman had come apart in his arms in his shower. There were so many different ways to make love to a woman and so many different places to explore. He looked forward to each and every one.

She was smiling as he waved and drove down Main Street, turning right onto Elm. A glance at her watch told her she'd better hustle if she was going to accomplish what she'd planned for the day. She was already an hour behind.

Humming to herself, she powered up the computer and listened to the messages on the answering machine. Only a handful of calls—things were going so smoothly since hiring Charlie and Tommy for the summer.

"Maybe they'll find jobs locally and can help us out in a pinch." As soon as she said that, she could have smacked herself in the head. "Now I sound like everyone who wished I'd done the same."

Setting unproductive thoughts aside, she finished deleting the last of the corrupted files, password protecting the templates she'd uploaded. "At least they'll have the templates. I can't do anything about somebody deleting the working files."

Adding the revised templates and files to her memory stick—and her backup memory stick—Grace was surprised when Patrick walked into the office. "Is it lunchtime already?"

"Time flies." He was grinning when he lifted her out of her chair, swung her around, and planted his lips on hers. "Did you talk to your dad today?"

"Not yet, but I will. I don't think I can go back to my routine in Columbus." She kissed him deeply. "I've seen the light and am wondering when we can spend another day naked."

He laughed and hugged her tight. "God, I love you, Grace Mulcahy."

Tears filled her eyes as emotion overwhelmed her. "I'm glad."

He chuckled. "Not the response I was hoping for." He kissed her playfully and urged, "Try again."

She laughed with him. "I love you so much it scares me."

"Good to know I'm not the only one who feels that way."

"I didn't think anything in the world scared you," she said.

"Right now, there are two things that do," he told her, "how much I love you and the thought of losing you."

She smiled. "Then you don't have anything to worry about."

He linked arms with her. "Come on."

She started walking toward the diner when he tugged on her hand. "This way." He led her across the street and down toward the gazebo.

"I thought we were going to have lunch."

"We are."

Instead of stopping at one of the park benches beneath the shade trees, he kept going until they'd crossed the green and were walking down Purity Road. Blackbirds were singing, and in the distance, she heard a hawk.

"So where are we going?"

He drew in a deep breath and answered her question with a question, "Does the air always smell this fresh out here?"

She giggled. "Here, yes. Out by the Parrish and McCormack farms? Not always."

He'd caught on to what she'd been hinting at. "They have cows and chickens?"

"Yes, and a horse or two."

"Ah. Sweet country air."

They were both enjoying the day and one another's company. "Over here," he said, pulling her toward the elementary school and the shade of the oak trees lining the playground.

"Oh!" Hand to her heart, Grace looked down at the plaid blanket spread out under the tree with a picnic basket sitting in the middle of it. "A picnic?"

"I know you like being outside and, hey," he said, "on a day like today, it's a shame to have to be inside."

They lowered themselves to the blanket and Grace couldn't contain her curiosity any longer. "Where did you get the basket?"

"Mary."

"Who made lunch?"

"Everybody."

She opened the lid and exclaimed. "Salads, sandwiches, pickles, and dessert?"

He took out the thermos and poured two cups of iced coffee. "Mary contributed the macaroni and potato salads. Kate made the sandwiches—she swore your favorite was liverwurst and onions, but I didn't believe her, so I asked for ham and cheese on rye and peanut butter and jelly just in case."

"I love liverwurst," she laughed when he made a face at her. "But I'll pick off the onions."

He looked sheepish when he admitted, "I asked her to leave those off. I figured since I wasn't eating them and planned to kiss you until your eyes crossed, then you couldn't have any either."

"Oh really?" She liked the thought of him kissing her until she couldn't see straight. "Hey, these look like Mrs. Winter's bread and butter pickles."

He nodded. "She said you were partial to them."

"And the pie?"

"Peggy made an extra buttermilk pie just because I asked her nicely and remembered to use the magic word."

Grace's heart nearly burst with pleasure at the trouble he'd gone to for her.

Before she could thank him, he leaned close and brushed a featherlight kiss across her lips. "Now unless you plan to just sit here and neck with me, you'd better stop tempting me, woman, and eat your lunch."

While they ate, they chatted about Dan and Meg's boys and baby Deidre, Cait's battle to keep food down. Then they talked about the amazing job Charlie and Tommy were doing for Mulcahys. But there was one subject Patrick hadn't talked about—but she could live with that for now. She'd given her word. He did talk about his current job, but only gave her brief highlights about the last few shifts he'd worked, leaving her to wonder about the details.

"Is it just me, or do you prefer to talk about anything but what you do for a living?"

He looked at her and shrugged. "Some of what I do bothers most people. Not everyone wants to hear the gory details of extracting people from twisted wrecks or burning buildings."

She waved a hand over what was left of the bounty before her. "So this wasn't your idea?"

"It was my idea."

He wasn't quite following where she wanted their

conversation to go. "Then you did it because you wanted to have a picnic?"

He shook his head. "I wanted to do something special for you, Grace. You spend a lot of time worrying about other people."

She looked into his eyes. "Thank you. At first I was worried that your interest wouldn't last."

He frowned. "What the hell is that supposed to mean?"

She started to put the containers away. "You know... a summertime fling?"

He shot to his feet and started to pace back and forth in front of their blanket. "You really think that's how I feel?"

When she reached for another container, he hauled her to her feet and held her by her arms. "Is it?"

"Not after I got to know you better, but you're holding back. I know we agreed not to talk about New York, but I want to hear about your job. I want to be there for you through the highs and lows and ups and downs. I may not have grown up in a family of firefighters, but I know a few—and have grown up in a small town where accidents happen and people are hurt."

She was vibrating with anguish as the past became the present. "I've seen my fair share and held on to my sisters when our father was pacing back in front of the door to the ER, hanging on to the hope that the drunk driver that crashed into our mom head-on hadn't cut her life short."

He shifted his grip so that he was caressing her arms. "Grace..."

"I'm strong, and I've had to grow up living with the result of that tragedy. Loving you includes what you do for a living, Patrick. Why can't you see that I'm strong and can handle your job?"

She wanted to walk away and leave him there with his thoughts, but he pulled her close and rubbed a hand up and down her back, soothing her until she quieted. "You are an amazing woman, Grace Mulcahy. When I saw you standing on the back porch, Deidre in your arms and the sun shining down on your hair, I fell in love with you so hard and so fast, I thought I'd made you up out of a desperate need to find a woman to share my life with."

She couldn't stop the tears, so she didn't try. "Then talk to me. Let me share your burden, as you've shared mine."

"It's not the same."

"Can't you see that it is?"

"Give me time," he asked.

"My vacation's almost over."

"Which is why you're coming home with me after work and I'm bringing you back tomorrow afternoon before I have to go to work—maximizing our time together."

"We can spend even more time together if you let me follow you back to Newark. Then when you have to go to work, I'll drive home."

"I like the way you think," he said. "Let's get you back to the shop."

They cleared up the rest of the containers and Patrick carried the blanket and the basket, refusing to let Grace carry anything. "There you go, making me feel special again."

He linked their hands. "You are."

They were crossing the green by the gazebo when he leaned close and whispered, "Say it again."

She wasn't sure what he meant until her gaze met his. "I love you."

He drew in a deep breath and smiled.

"Well?" She poked him in the side.

He laughed as he moved out of reach of her pointer finger. "What?"

She swung at his shoulder and he grabbed ahold of her hand, pulling her close. "I love you, Grace."

They walked hand-in-hand to Main Street and crossed. When he dropped her off at the shop, he reminded her, "I'll pick you up at five o'clock."

"But we're open until five thirty."

He winked at her. "Not today. I cleared it with your sisters."

"Oh, really?" She wasn't sure how she felt about him doing that but decided they could talk about it later. She had already urged him to open up and tell her more about his job. She didn't want to push too hard too fast. Grace had a gut-deep feeling that there was more about Patrick's job that he internalized than he was aware of.

Maybe she should ask someone with experience handling a similar type of stress. Her brother-in-law, Jack Gannon, was a former navy corpsman. Cait had told her Jack dealt with PTSD as a result of the time he spent patching up wounded marines in the battalion he had been attached to in Iraq.

Feeling better now that she had a plan, Grace changed her mind and her attitude. "Thanks for asking them and not just assuming that we'd close up early just because you want to get back to your place."

He hesitated. "That wasn't the only reason behind my asking them." When she didn't ask him why, he shoved his hands in his front pockets. "You need to spend time with your family and working here in town, but more than that, you need to get away—with me."

"So you think you're just what I need?" When she

started to think about his high-handed way of arranging things, she remembered the trouble he'd gone to getting their picnic together. He was right. She did need him. *But did he need her?*

"I don't think it," he told her. "I know it."

Going with her gut, she moved a step closer until her breasts brushed against his pecs. "You need me too."

"Ah, Gracie," he rasped, pulling his hands out of his pockets and reaching for her. Holding her close to his heart, he whispered, "More than I can say."

He kissed her one last time and shook his head as if to clear it. "If I don't leave now, we'll have to lock the door and draw the blinds."

She knew exactly what he meant. "I'll be ready at five."

"See you then."

Pulling up her to-do list for the day, Grace crossed off what she'd accomplished and worked like a fiend to finish the rest of the items. She was going to leave today knowing that she'd completed the tasks necessary to keep Mulcahys moving in the right direction.

When Patrick returned, she was waiting for him, anticipating the time they would spend together. Praying that he would come to trust that she could handle his job, she ran to the front door and into his arms.

"Let's get out of here."

"That's just one of the many things I love about you, baby," he told her. "Your ability to read minds."

"Really?" She sighed, unsure of just where to begin with the list of reasons she loved him. "Can you tell me what I'm thinking?"

"If I did, we'd both get hauled in for indecent exposure and the corrupting of a minor."

"I'm not a minor," she protested, getting into his truck.

He nodded in the direction of Murphy's Market. "He is."

Grace laughed. The youngest Jones boy was walking into the market with his mother. "We'd better behave then."

A few minutes later, she tapped him on the shoulder. He lifted one eyebrow in silent question, and she asked, "So what am I thinking?"

"You can't wait to get me naked and have your way with me," he said, then added, "and to please drive faster."

Pleased down to her toes, she laughed out loud. "You're a smart man, Patrick Garahan."

His hands tightened on the steering wheel, and he said, "And you love me."

Laying her head on his shoulder, she sighed. "I really do."

When they were nearing their destination, she sat up and asked, "So what's for dinner?"

He turned and slanted a long and meaningful look at her. "You."

She shivered and had to swallow or choke on the drool pooling in her mouth. "I think dinner's ready."

His deep, booming laughter filled the truck cab and her heart. "Maybe I won't be bringing you home to meet my family just yet."

"Oh? Why not?"

"I can't run the risk that my brother Tommy won't try to steal you from me."

"Not a chance," she reassured him. "I've already given away my heart."

He pushed down on the accelerator.

"What's the rush?"

He snickered. "I don't want dinner to get cold."

Chapter 21

THE NEXT FEW DAYS WERE HARD ON GRACE, KNOWING that she wouldn't be able to spend time with Patrick, but the upside was that Cait was feeling better and would be back to work. It was almost as if her sisters sensed that she needed to spend time with both of them, because every time she turned around, they were there, handing her a list of parts or leaving a name and phone number for her to add to the schedule of repair calls. She'd finally talked to her father about quitting her job and working for the family again. He'd been thrilled.

By the time Wednesday afternoon rolled around, Grace was walking around like a zombie. She hadn't slept because she hadn't heard from Patrick. She kept up with the local news and knew there had been a number of fires that the three firehouses in Newark had had to deal with. No casualties—so far. Knowing that the possibility could be in her future, she tried to find ways to keep herself busy and keep from worrying.

He'd warned her that when he was working the night shift, he focused totally on the job and had to let everything else wait. He wasn't a night person, so it took all that he had to get through the night shift. When she'd asked why the twenty-four-hour shift didn't affect him, he had shrugged, unable to explain it.

"Are you all right?" Kate set a cup of coffee in front of Grace, but she didn't move to take it.

"Grace!"

"Hmmm. What?" She sat straighter on the stool by the counter and noticed the cup. "Thanks, I really need the caffeine."

"Since I've seen more of you in the last few days, I have to assume that your handsome fireman is working."

"Yeah, but I was supposed to hear from him this morning."

"He's been good about getting in touch with you so far, hasn't he?" Kate asked.

"Yes. But I can't help but worry that something happened."

"Don't borrow trouble," Kate told her.

"You're right. I guess I'll eventually adjust."

"To?"

Grace smiled. "The life of a firefighter."

"So, you two seem pretty serious," Kate said, leaning her hip against the counter.

"It all happened so quickly, sometimes I find myself wondering if it's a dream or if I've slipped through a portal to a parallel dimension."

"It should scare me," Kate said, "that I can follow your thought process so easily."

Grace chuckled. "Sisters at heart."

Peggy walked toward them with a worried expression on her face. "Have you seen the news?"

Grace felt the bottom drop out of her stomach. "Not since earlier today. Why?"

Peggy pushed her toward the office in the back of the diner. "It's all over the news. There's a three-alarm fire in Newark—and it's bad."

Heart pounding, throat tight, she rushed to the office and sat in front of the monitor, watching the scene in horror. Brave firefighters were rescuing residents from the building's top floors, using the hook and ladder truck Patrick had talked about.

She wished she'd heard from him but, from the look of the fully engaged fire, knew he must have been called in to help. Unable to pull herself away from the screen, she watched as the men battled the blaze and the smoke to get to the residents of the luxury apartment tower.

The reality of what she'd been asking him to talk about had her head pounding and her stomach roiling. He willingly walked toward danger every single time he suited up. She knew that the heat had to be extreme—the flames reminded her of her childhood image of hell.

She quietly prayed that Patrick wouldn't be injured as he worked to save lives and put out that fire.

An hour later, Peggy came back and set another cup of coffee in front of Grace. "I thought you might want another cup. Any updates?"

Grace wondered how she was able to speak. "Twenty-five people have been rescued. Three of whom are in critical condition." Anguish added to the roiling in her gut as she thought of the three that had been so badly burned.

"How can he do it?" she whispered. "Where does he get the strength to walk into hell again and again?"

Kate was standing in the doorway. "I'm guessing his mother prays—a lot. Didn't you say he has three brothers and they're all firemen?"

Kate's question distracted Grace. "Yes. One older and two younger, but they're all at different houses in the city because of the tragedy of 9/11."

"It's like those brothers who were in the navy during World War II and died—all of them on the same ship."

"The Sullivans. The military made changes after that too."

Talking about something—anything—else was a distraction and helped.

———〜〜〜———

Hours later, when she was home watching the news with her father and Mary, she received the text she'd been waiting for, only instead of what she'd expected, she read: Got called in. Am OK, talk tomorrow?

"Everything all right?" Mary asked.

Grace shook her head. "I don't think so. I have this feeling that something's wrong."

Her father was quiet. "When will you see him again?"

"I don't know. He said we'll talk tomorrow."

"Baby girl, the man just fought one of the largest fires of the year. He's got to be exhausted and probably just wants a hot shower and a cold beer."

Grace knew that was probably the case but couldn't help but wonder about the reasons he had left New York. If it had been because of a fire like today, he needed someone to talk to—someone to listen to him as he unburdened what was inside of him.

She finally said, "There were people badly injured."

"But not any of the firemen," Mary added.

"It's not his first fire," her father reminded her.

"I know, but—"

"Give him the space he's asking for tonight. Don't borrow trouble. Talk to him tomorrow."

She knew it was sound advice, but her heart hurt for the man she'd come to love. "I'm going to bed. Thanks, Pop." She kissed his cheek and then hugged Mary.

Emotionally exhausted, she trudged up the stairs.

When she reached her room, she realized she hadn't answered Patrick's text. Her response was short but heartfelt: Worried about you.

As she pressed send, she had second thoughts, wondering if she'd said the wrong thing, confirming his worry that she couldn't handle his job, but it was too late now. She'd just have to buckle down and sort through her emotions so she was ready for his. He had to have some kind of reaction after the adrenaline wore off. For the first time, she started wondering how firefighters dealt with this kind of stress day after day. She'd make a point to talk to Jack tomorrow and pretend the ache in her heart was from something she'd eaten and not because the man she loved didn't want her there when she knew he needed her most.

Patrick stood in the shower, letting the hot water loosen the soot from his face and hands while it eased some of the aches from between his shoulder blades. The last man he'd pulled out of that inferno had weighed over two hundred pounds and had been badly burned.

When the first layer of grime had been rinsed off, he grabbed the bar of soap, ignoring the roiling in his gut and the memory that lay just beneath the surface whenever a fire he fought had victims.

He lathered up, wishing Grace were there with him. She'd rub his shoulders and slide the soap over muscles that burned and a heart that ached from a wound that had never really healed. The little boy's face was a wisp of a memory now. Five years of struggling to bury the slash to his soul when he found out the last victim from that tenement fire had not survived hadn't erased it. The smoke inhalation had been too much for a boy just five years old—his gut clenched thinking of his sisters' children.

Focusing on the number of lives he had saved never really balanced the scales in Patrick's book, because as he rushed out of the building, the boy had opened his eyes and had such a look of trust in them. He remembered telling the boy everything would be all right now, like he'd done so many times with his nephews when they'd gotten hurt. Watching the boy's eyes close, he'd run toward the FDNY paramedic unit and the life-giving oxygen waiting for him.

In his mind's eye, he remembered the boy's mother rushing over to him as he turned the little one over to the paramedics. She'd thanked him over and over, but Patrick hadn't been paying attention to her—he'd been watching the paramedics frantically working to rouse the unconscious boy. While he waited, the boy's face got tangled up in his mind with his nephew Michael's.

Strong arms pulled him out of the way so the mother could get into the back with her son as the unit raced off into the night. The rest of that night would always remain a blur in his mind. He knew that he'd found the boy just after the safe zone for smoke inhalation, but he'd had close calls before. Patrick had beaten the odds before, pushing the limits of his own safety to ensure one more victim would survive because of his actions.

Bracing his hands on the wall, he bowed his head and let the emotions clawing at him free. He'd been twenty-five and invincible—and the boy had died. Haunted by the memory of the little boy's gaze, he'd retreated into a world where nothing and no one could touch him. His girlfriend at the time hadn't known how to deal with what he was going through. Rather than stick around and weather the storm with him, she walked. After that, he tried to drown the hideous pain clawing inside of him.

Two weeks later, he'd requested a leave of absence and left his family, friends, and brothers in fire behind while he tried to outrun the guilt slashing his heart. Time and distance had helped with the nightmares, until the boy's face ceased to be his nephew's and in time blurred completely, until Patrick stopped having them and was finally able to sleep again. He stopped running when he got to Newark, Ohio, and drove past the scene of a fire. Everything he'd been trained to do burst through the deep depression that had him by the throat. The need to be there with the firefighters was strong enough to keep the fading memories at bay.

Five years spent immersed in the work he loved nudged him closer to healing. The final piece to the puzzle was Grace—with her in his life, he felt whole, complete, and everything made sense again. He'd just begun to believe that he'd conquered his guilt and had been able to finally let go of the memory that had kept him company for so long—until today.

His big body shuddered as he held back the tears he refused to shed. The muscles in his forearms tensed until he thought they'd snap. Still he refused to let go of the rigid control that kept his emotions in check and the guilt from eating him alive.

He sank to his knees, head still bowed. When the water ran cold, he crawled out of the shower.

The pounding on the door roused him. He looked up at the television, wondering if the sound had come from there. He shrugged and closed his eyes again, but the pounding kept up.

"We know you're in there, Garahan."

What the hell was Bear doing here?

"Open the damn door!"

Jesus, Sledge too?

"Forget it, guys. I know where he keeps the spare key."

"Fuck me," Patrick ground out. Mike was out there too. They'd never leave until he let them in.

The towel he'd been wearing slipped off, and for a moment, he considered answering the door naked to get the guys to leave. Then he remembered he'd tried that two years ago—the last time they'd nearly lost three victims to a vicious fire—it hadn't worked.

"You've got one minute!" Mike yelled. "Then we're coming in."

Patrick wrapped the towel around him and opened the door as Mike was fitting the key in the lock. "What?"

His friends stood there staring at him. The silence was uncomfortable because he knew each and every one of them could see right through him. They'd fought fires side-by-side for five years. He'd cooked for them, held the bucket in front of more than one of them when the beer had flowed after last year's victory at the firefighter's Olympics.

"You look like hell," Bear told him as the three men pushed past him into the kitchen.

"You fall asleep in the shower again?" Sledge wanted to know.

"You should have called Grace," Mike bit out.

Grace. He'd forgotten to call her again. If she was like his ex, she wouldn't be speaking to him right now—or maybe she'd already decided to cut her losses.

"Somebody grab his clothes. We're taking his sorry ass out for breakfast."

He only struggled to hold out against the three until he started to think about Grace again. She wanted to talk to him about his job, but he hadn't opened up to her. *Maybe she was different. Maybe she'd pass the Garahan sticking test.*

Ten minutes later, he was dressed, and they'd walked down to the diner by the firehouse. "Why the hell couldn't you let me sleep?" he grumbled.

The waitress shot a worried look his way, but Bear just smiled and said, "This man needs the special—can you make it a double?"

"Yeah," Sledge added. "He didn't eat much yesterday."

"I can speak for myself," Patrick ground out, glaring first at Bear and then Sledge.

Mike snorted. "Yeah, but we're going to keep feeding you until your nice side starts to show. Better bring three pots of coffee, Linda."

She took the rest of their order and hustled to the back, reappearing with one pot in her hand and two pots and eight glasses—four with orange juice and four with water—on a tray. "I saw the news." She set one pot of coffee by Bear and the other by Patrick while she started pouring mugs of fragrant coffee. "You four are heroes."

Patrick's stomach rumbled and she looked over at him. "Aren't you the firefighter who pulled the last man out?"

He didn't want to talk about it, but Linda didn't seem to be paying attention to what he wanted; she was too wrapped up in what she was saying. "He and two other victims are still in the ICU, but they're going to make it thanks to you."

Bear nodded and gently reminded Linda that they were hungry. "Oh, sorry. Be right back," she promised, hustling toward the kitchen doors.

"She had her eye on you, Garahan," Sledge ribbed him.

"Our man here isn't interested in just any blonde," Bear rumbled. "There's a sweet little woman just waiting to hear the sound of his voice," he said, "if the asshole would just give her a call."

"Don't hold back, Bear," Mike snickered. Looking at Patrick, he said, "Dan called yesterday."

Why hadn't Grace called him? Patrick had a feeling that he only added fuel to the fire by not calling her. She'd probably blow everything out of proportion—like his ex had.

"Don't you want to know why?" Mike asked.

"Why what?"

"Why Dan called," Mike grumbled.

Patrick didn't really want to know, but he asked anyway, "Why did he call?"

"He saw the news and was checking up on you."

Thoughts of Grace filled him, twisting the ache inside of him. Why hadn't she called him? "That's it?"

Mike shrugged.

Linda brought their food and smiled. "I'll keep it coming. You just holler for me."

"Thanks," Sledge said for the group.

When she'd gone again, Patrick shifted in his seat, knowing everyone was staring at him. "What?"

Bear shrugged. "We like Grace."

"You only met her once," Patrick said, setting down his coffee.

"Only took that one time for you to fall ass over eyebrows in love with the girl," Mike reminded him.

And it was true, he was—but there was more going on that he couldn't sort out yet. "I thought you weren't sure about her?"

Mike stared at him and then shoveled in another forkful of pancakes.

Sledge poked Patrick in the shoulder with his beefy forefinger. "What are you afraid of?"

Afraid?

"I'm not afraid of anything," he grumbled, draining his mug.

No one argued with him, but they were suspiciously silent. He looked up and wished he hadn't. Every one of them was staring at him with that look—the one that said they weren't buying it.

Hell, he'd already admitted to Grace that he was afraid of losing her and afraid that he'd mess things up with her. His friends had gotten to the root of Patrick's problem by catching him off guard. He was afraid that Grace wouldn't be able to handle the life of a firefighter and would walk. He was so far gone over the woman, he was pushing her away so she couldn't tell him to his face that she was leaving him.

"Give it up, Garahan," Mike said. "Talk to her."

"She won't walk," Bear predicted.

"She's a Mulcahy," Sledge reminded him. "That counts for a whole lot in my book."

Patrick knew that it did, but how did it matter to Sledge? "What do you know about the Mulcahys?"

"Everything you've told us since the night Meg and Dan shadowed you when you and that sweet little Honey B. had dinner a few years back."

"Yeah," Bear said. "And what we read on the Internet about the Love Locks cut-a-thon in Apple Grove."

They filled him in on how it started, and just when he thought they'd stop harassing him, Sledge asked, "What are you waiting for?"

"I—" He paused and shook his head. Looking at his friends he shrugged. "Don't know."

"Come on, guys," Mike said. "We're supposed to meet Muldoon in an hour."

Patrick left the tip—a big one—and followed his friends. "Where are we meeting him?"

Bear shook his head at him. "We are; you aren't."

"I don't get it," Patrick said. "He specifically asked for you three and not me?"

"That's right," Sledge said.

Mike took pity on Patrick and said, "Muldoon wants you to settle things with Grace first and then come to the firehouse for a meeting."

Patrick couldn't believe it. "Big Jim said that?"

Three heads nodded in unison, but they ended up stopping in at the firehouse because Patrick didn't believe them.

Confronting his lieutenant was the hardest thing Patrick had to do, but he needed to know if his friends weren't just trying to force his hand where Grace was concerned. Big Jim placed a hand on Patrick's shoulder. "You worked overtime when that three-alarm call came in. Your buddies didn't. So get going and you can come back after you sort things out with Grace."

"But—"

"The love of a good woman is hard to come by in our line of work, Garahan. Go fix things with her," Muldoon said. "You can thank me later."

Patrick didn't move. He had two choices: do what everyone seemed to think was the right thing, or be the coward and just let the most amazing woman he'd ever met slip through his fingers.

"I'm no coward."

"Good to know, Garahan." Muldoon slapped him on the back and pushed him toward the door. "Now get out of here."

Chapter 22

PATRICK LEFT HIS FRIENDS AT THE FIREHOUSE AND walked home, using the time alone to try to figure out just where to start when he talked to Grace. He was walking up the stairs to his apartment when he muttered to himself, "An apology?"

"It's a good place to start."

"Grace?" She was standing in the hallway, waiting for him.

His gaze raked her from head to toe and then back to her eyes. The sparkle wasn't there, and her face was devoid of color. Patrick knew without a doubt why she was here: she'd come to break things off with him because she couldn't handle his job. She wouldn't stick.

She was staring at him as if she wanted to say something but couldn't bring herself to. Finally, she said, "Hi."

He'd already spent last night reliving hell. He wasn't ready for another visit so soon. Grace leaving him would tear his guts out. "What are you doing here?" he asked, his voice harsher than he intended.

If possible, her face grew whiter. He hated hurting her—needed to hold her. Maybe he should just make it easy for her. "I know I said I'd call, but right now I just want to be alone."

The flicker of light in her eyes went out as she swept past him and walked out of his life.

He fumbled with the lock and opened the door,

slammed it behind him, and hit his knees, praying, "God, don't let her leave me."

After a while, he sat back on his heels and struggled to his feet, drawing the hurt and heartache inside of him. His phone buzzed. Drawing it out of his pocket, he held on to the hope that maybe she wasn't leaving after all.

The text message was from Dan and it read: Eat shit.

He pulled out a chair and slumped into it.

His phone buzzed again.

Obviously this text message was connected to the first one: Get sick.

He set the phone on the table to rub his hand over his heart. When his phone buzzed a third time, he almost didn't pick it up, but figured Dan might show up and beat the crap out of him. He'd need to be ready.

And die.

Hell, he felt as if he had. The longer he sat there, the more he realized he should have let her say whatever it was that brought her to his door. No matter how much it would have hurt, she deserved the chance to say her piece.

He'd said his, and she never said a word. *Aw, Grace,* he thought. He should have begged her to stay.

Dragging himself to his feet, he shuffled over to the cabinet above the fridge and opened it. The bottle of Jameson was the one thing he'd fought not to sink into again after he'd left New York. It was there to remind him of the part of his life that he fought daily to put behind him. It wasn't meant for drinking.

"Fuck that." He reached for the bottle and a glass, opened it, poured three fingers, and tossed it back. It burned through the block of ice that had settled in his throat. He drew in a breath, let it out, poured another glass, and carried the bottle with him to the living room.

While the sun moved through the sky and headed toward the horizon, he emptied the bottle of whiskey. For every drop he swallowed, he felt the razor-sharp pain of regret, guilt, and loss welling up inside of him.

Her name was on his lips as he passed out.

———

"What do you mean, you didn't say anything?" Kate McCormack stood with her hands on her hips and glared at her friend. "That's not the Grace Mulcahy that I know and love."

Grace shrugged—even that tiny movement added to the raw pain she'd carried home with her from Newark.

"Grace!" Kate grabbed her friend by the arms and gave her a shake.

"I don't want to talk about it."

"Tough, crap," Kate shot back. "You're hurting inside and you need to get rid of the hurt."

"I feel like punching someone."

Kate shook her head. "I'd be happy to drive you back over there so you can punch him."

Just the thought of it roused her out of the stupor she'd sunk into on the drive back from Patrick's apartment. "Maybe tomorrow."

"You aren't going back to Columbus early, are you?"

Grace didn't want to have to think anymore. She'd spent the last few days thinking, worrying, and wondering what had happened to the man who'd turned her world inside out and upside down by loving her...and now that same man was pushing her away, shoving her out of his life.

"Maybe."

"What about Sunday dinner?"

Grace thought back to the meals she'd shared with Patrick, the conversations, and the lovemaking that had been such a vital part of who and what they'd been together. "I thought we had something special, damn it!"

Kate nodded. "You do."

"Then why did he dump me when I could tell he really needs me?"

Kate sighed. "Come on."

Grace tried to shrug out of her friend's grip but couldn't. "Where?"

Kate started dragging her down the street toward Doc Gannon's office, but Grace resisted. "I'm not sick."

Her friend's answer surprised her. "You are inside."

Drained from the non-argument she'd had with Patrick, she gave in and let herself be led. She'd planned to talk to her brother-in-law but hadn't had the chance, and now Kate was dragging her there. She sighed and let herself be led.

Jack was waiting for them when they arrived. "So, Grace," he said, walking over and taking her by the hand, "come on back and tell me what's going on."

Kate waved and left Grace alone with her brother-in-law.

"I'm not sick," she protested.

Jack's concerned look warmed the ice forming in her belly. "Sometimes we just need to talk to get to the root of what's ailing us. It's not always physical to start with, but if what's in here," he said, pointing to her heart, "is left to fester, then you'll be back complaining of very real pain."

She sat down while he closed his office door behind

him. "Now," he said, leaning a hip against his desk, "what's going on with Patrick?"

"I didn't say—"

"Grace, you don't have to. I've been in Patrick's shoes."

She frowned up at him. "When did you fight fires?"

He frowned down at her before reminding her of the IED that had broken his leg and ended the life of a marine Jack had respected but could not save.

"But that's not the same."

"Think about what Patrick does for a living and the extraordinary circumstances he has to deal with, wading through fire to save people before putting that fire out. The men and women in the military have to lay their lives on the line on a daily basis for our country. Some come home suffering from PTSD—some aren't that lucky."

He grew quiet until Grace reached out and touched the back of his hand. "Maybe I am beginning to see the comparison, but how can I get through to him? I know he needs me, but he pushed me away and I didn't even have a chance to say anything."

"Talk to him, Grace," Jack advised. "Even if he doesn't want to hear what you have to say, you'll have planted the seeds. It might take some time, but if you love the man and let him know, eventually, he'll realize that he needs to open up and share what's crippling him on the inside."

She got up and hugged her brother-in-law. "Thanks, Doc." Pressing a kiss on his cheek, she said, "My sister is one lucky woman."

"You've got that all wrong, Grace. I'm the lucky one." She smiled as he opened the door for her. "Talk to Patrick."

"I think I'll sleep on it before I do."

He waited until she'd left his office before picking up the phone. "Joe, it's me, Jack. I'm going to need your help tonight."

"Sure, what do you need?"

"Backup on a mission to save Garahan from himself."

Joe muttered something beneath his breath about daughters and the stubborn men they loved, which had Jack chuckling. "Exactly. Patrick loves Grace. He needs her right now, but he's being proud and stubborn. He needs you to talk to him."

"And then you'll tell him about your PTSD and how it almost cost you the love of your life?"

Jack didn't hesitate. "Absolutely."

"When do you want to leave?"

"Grace just left here. I'm going to call Cait and have her drive over to stay with Grace while we're gone."

"Sounds like it'll be a long night."

"Dan just got a 911 text from Patrick's friend Bear. They just tossed him in a cold shower. He should be sober by the time we get there."

"I always did love a challenge."

"Thanks, Joe."

"I'd do anything for my girls."

"Maybe I'll get lucky and our baby will be a girl—just like Cait."

Joe laughed. "Be careful what you wish for, Jack."

—◦◦◦—

Joe and Jack arrived in time to see Bear making coffee while Sledge and Mike took turns walking Patrick around the apartment.

"Jesus," Joe muttered. "It's worse than I thought."

Bear shook his head. "From what we could get out of him, he's ruined things between him and Grace—permanently."

Joe snorted. "My daughter's stronger than Patrick realizes."

"He said she never said a word when he broke things off with her."

Jack spoke up. "I talked to her before coming here. She's going to sleep on it, but she loves him—she's not giving up on him, but she's hurting right now and needs to think about it."

Mike's face lit up. "Can we tell him?"

Sledge reached around Patrick and smacked Mike in the back of the head. "No. He needs to grovel first to realize just how important it is to have a strong and beautiful woman like Grace in his life."

"She'll be his anchor," Joe agreed. "But if he messes this up, I will personally dump him in the middle of the Atlantic." When the men just stared at him he shrugged. "It pays to have friends in the coast guard in high places."

Bear handed Sledge a cup. "Bottoms up."

They roused Patrick enough to have him swallow most of the coffee.

Jack and Joe took over for Sledge and Mike, who were headed to the firehouse for the evening shift.

Bear stayed and filled them in on the sketchy details he knew about five years ago. "Garahan never told any of us the whole story, but each one of us held his head over a bucket a time or two after we helped him empty a bottle, and we got each got a different piece to the story."

While the men sobered Patrick up, they got the bare

bones of the tragedy pieced together. "He's got to let go of the guilt," Jack ground out. "Take it from me, I know."

When Patrick's stomach started to heave, Bear tossed him over his shoulder in a fireman's carry and ran for the bathroom.

The pitiful sound of a man puking his guts up carried down the hallway. "Glad I gave up tying one on in my youth," Joe murmured. "I'm way too old for that shit."

Jack grinned at his father-in-law. "You're the salt of the earth, Joseph Mulcahy, even if you served as a puddle pirate."

Joe smiled back. "I could still whup your ass, navy boy."

Jack nodded. "Don't doubt it."

Joe harrumphed. "Watch what you say about the coast guard, then."

"Aye, aye, Captain Bligh."

They were laughing when Bear walked back into the room with Patrick tucked under one arm. "I think he's ready to listen to reason."

"Am I still having a nightmare?" Patrick swayed as Bear eased up his hold on his friend.

Joe stood up and glared at Patrick. "For making my baby girl cry, I should be your worst nightmare."

Patrick agreed. "It's your right, sir."

"Don't call me sir," Joe grumbled. "Makes me feel old."

"Hell, sir, um, Joe, you are old!" Patrick wasn't quite steady on his pins yet, so Bear led him to the sofa and shoved him on it.

"You might not want to insult Grace's father, Garahan," Bear said. "I'm told the Irish have really long memories."

Jack and Joe readily agreed. "Now," Joe said, crossing

his arms in front of him, "you're going to sit and listen to what my son-in-law has to say and then you're going to be civil to my baby girl when she comes back to talk to you."

Patrick's wobbly legs held when he shot to his feet. "She's coming here?"

When he swayed, Joe put a hand to the middle of his chest and shoved him back down. "Not tonight, you thickheaded Irishman. You're going to listen," Joe warned him. "And then it'll be your turn to talk."

Patrick looked as if he was going to contradict Joe, but in the end, Grace's father got his way. Jack took Patrick back in time to relive the horrors Jack faced as a medic—the guilt at not being able to save his friend.

Patrick listened as Jack described the private hell he lived in after he'd come home to have a series of surgeries on his leg.

Then it was Patrick's turn to unburden his soul. When he finished, it was after midnight.

"You two should head on back to Apple Grove," Bear said, getting to his feet. "I'm on night shift again tomorrow, so I'll be up surfing the channels if our friend here wakes up and needs anything."

"Have a bottle of aspirin and glass of water ready," Jack advised.

Bear chuckled. "I've had hangovers before, Doc, don't you worry. I'll take care of lover boy for Grace. They need each other."

"Yeah," Joe said, looking down at the man who, if he played his cards right and owned up to his stupidity and then bared his soul to Joe's baby girl, would be his son-in-law before summer's end. Joe had put money down on that fact and intended to collect.

"Come on," Jack said, tugging on his arm. "I'll drive home."

"It's my truck," Joe protested.

"Yeah," Jack said. "And I've always wanted to get behind the wheel of your F1. Come on, Joe. Please?"

"Hell." Joe handed him the keys.

Chapter 23

JOE STARED DOWN AT HIS YOUNGEST DAUGHTER AND asked her again, "Are you sure you don't want me to drive you?"

Grace stopped midstride and looked at her father. That he'd been gone half the night and wouldn't say where and now asked to tag along when she drove over to talk to Patrick had her Spidey-sense on full alert. "No thanks, Pop," she said, pushing the screen door open. "I'll be fine."

"Gracie?"

She paused and looked over her shoulder. "Yeah?"

"After you have your say, listen to the man—really listen."

"I promise. Don't wait up."

"It's eight o'clock in the morning!" her father grumbled.

"Gotcha! Be back in a little while."

When she shut the door, he chuckled to himself. "Not if Patrick has anything to say about it."

As Grace drove, she thought about everything that Jack had told her yesterday. She'd wrestled with what she wanted to say to Patrick for most of the night after her sister and Jack went home.

She knew without being told that her father and Jack had paid Patrick a late-night visit. What she didn't know was why or what had been said. But she intended to find out.

The hurt was still there, but alongside that was hope. Jack had given her hope that the man she loved wasn't pushing her out of his life because he'd grown tired of her. He had done it to protect her from the grim realities he faced every time the fire alarm sounded—realities that had forced him to run away from everyone and everything he loved in New York.

He'd run to Ohio and fate had brought them together. Grace believed in fate, destiny, and that karma could be a stone bitch, but if you lived your life to the best of your ability, treating others with kindness as a rule, then life could be feckin' awesome.

The short time she'd spent with Patrick had opened her eyes to what could be, and she wasn't going toss that aside because her man was too proud to ask for help, too guilty to share the heavy burden—whatever it was—that he carried.

She raced up the steps to his apartment and pounded on the door. When a sleepy Bear opened the door, she stared up at him. "What's wrong?" she rasped. "Where is he? What's happened to him?"

It took Bear a few minutes to process the fact that Grace was here and pushing her way inside Patrick's apartment. When it finally registered, along with her mounting panic, he held up a hand and pointed toward the living room. "He's on the sofa."

When she tried to step around him, he caught her hand in his. "Go easy on him, Grace," he pleaded. "The guy loves you and was only trying to protect you."

"From what?" she asked, although she was pretty sure she already knew the answer.

"Himself."

"I promise," she reassured the big man. "Thank you for being his friend."

Bear shook his head and told her he was going back to bed.

Grace watched him stumble in the direction of Patrick's bedroom. When she heard the door close, she walked to the living room. Patrick lay sprawled out on the sofa facedown with a bucket on the floor within reach.

She knelt beside him and gently stroked his brow. When he began to stir, she pressed her lips where her fingertips had been. But he didn't wake up, so she decided to go with a different approach. She had things to say to the man, and this time, he was going to listen to her. She walked back to the kitchen, poured a glass of water, and approached the sofa.

Leaning close to his ear, she called him name again, but he didn't move. "Time for Pop's water torture." She flicked water in his face. He grimaced but didn't wake up.

She spent half the night sorting out what she wanted and what she was willing to put up with in her head—and now he wouldn't wake up? She was starting to get steamed. "We've got things to talk about, and I'm tired of waiting," she grumbled. He didn't move, so she tossed the rest of the glass in his face.

Patrick roared and shot to his feet. "What the hell—Grace?"

Bear came running down the hall. "What's wrong? What happened?"

Grace had her hands on her hips. "I wanted Patrick to wake up so I could talk to him and he wouldn't," she explained. "So I used Pop's patented method of waking us up as kids—Mulcahy's water torture." She crossed her arms in front of her. "It usually only takes a few flicks of water to the face, but you were more difficult and I got tired of waiting."

Bear shook his head and laughed. "She's all yours, Garahan. Since I'm awake, I'll head on over to the firehouse and see if I can catch breakfast." He paused in the doorway and frowned at them. "Fix this. You two belong together."

"He's right, Grace. I'm sorry about yesterday. I should have listened." Patrick reached for her hand and tugged her toward the sofa.

"I was just so shocked that you were ready to push me out of your life. It took me a while to work around to being mad at you."

"We'll come back to that, but I need to tell you that I was afraid."

"Of what?"

"That you wouldn't be able to handle the pressures of my job. My ex walked out when I was hanging on by a thread—that night, the last fire I fought in the Projects."

She squeezed his hand and waited.

"Watching them work on that little boy to revive him, it hit me that he was the same age and size as my nephew Michael. My gut scraped raw at the thought of not being able to save that boy, but my head got it all mixed up a few hours later, and all I could see in my mind's eye was Michael—lying so small and still. That night, the nightmares started and every damned night, the boy's face would morph into Michael's. It was tearing me apart; sometimes I'd dream that it was two of them—and I was never able to save either of them."

Grace didn't bother to wipe the tears from her face; she didn't want to let go of Patrick. Her grip like iron, she asked, "Did you ever tell anyone that part of your dreams?"

He shook his head. "I didn't want them to think I was crazy."

She sighed. "My grandmother used to hear voices in her head—but she wrote short stories and my grandfather said she had so many to tell, her characters used to wake her up nights until she wrote them down." She smiled. "We never thought she was crazy."

He tugged until she scooted closer. He pulled her onto his lap. "For a long time I wondered if I'd gone over that line from sanity to madness, but then the nightmares would ease up, and I'd be fine until the stress built up again."

"Do you think you'd be able to try something different—like talking to me about your day? Maybe it would be as easy as that to deflect some of the stress before it builds up and starts to snowball."

He rested his chin on the top of her head. "It's a hard existence, Grace, but it's what I'm meant to do."

"I know."

"Old habits die hard," he warned, "but I'm willing to give it a try if it means that you'll still be in my life—even if we have to start over."

"No do-overs," she grumbled, pushing back in his arms.

"But—I thought?"

"Life's kind of like the street I grew up on—smooth in some sections, potholes in others. But if you want something badly enough, you learn to navigate around those pesky potholes. You don't need to start over."

"So I'm like a hole in the road?" His baffled expression was endearing.

"Better to be a pothole than a sinkhole," she warned.

"Hell.".

"We've all got our private hells, Patrick. Mine is the image of my mom in that hospital bed—broken beyond repair and dying." Her voice broke. "Yours is that nightmare with both little faces haunting you. But if we never experienced hell, how would we know to recognize heaven?"

"So I'm a heavenly pothole?"

She chuckled and they both started to laugh, easing the tension in the room. "Something like that."

His expression grew serious again. "So what changed your mind? Why did you come back today?"

"Not what. Who. After what you said, I thought I'd been wrong and maybe you really did want me to go— and I started to believe that you did."

"Who changed your mind?" he asked.

"Kate, Doc, and my dad." She cupped the side of his face. "You acted like an idiot," she told him, "and I still don't know why I love you so much."

"I'm an idi—" His grip tightened on her hands. "You still love me?"

Grace knew then that Jack had been right. Patrick pushed her away to protect her. "Don't you want me to?"

"I don't deserve you," he said, pulling her against his heart.

"No," she agreed. "You don't, but you're stuck with me."

"Jesus, Grace," he rasped. "I thought I'd lost you for good. That's why I tried to drown myself in a bottle of Jameson."

"Ah," she said, nudging the bucket with the toe of her sneaker. "Is that was this is for?"

"Bear likes to be prepared."

"Drinking isn't an answer. It just numbs the pain."

His gaze locked with hers. "I know."

"I knew it was a possibility—and wasn't sure if I could handle it if you got lost in a bottle."

"It's a hell of an existence," Patrick whispered. "I'm so sorry," he added. "I didn't want to drag you down into that black hole with me."

"It took me a while to decide whether or not I wanted to go down there with you and drag your amazing backside back up here with me."

His eyes widened.

"Come on, Garahan, you've got to know that you have an excellent butt."

"I, uh—"

It is going to be all right, she thought. They would work through this and move forward. "I came back because after talking to Doc and spending the night worrying about you, I couldn't stay away—even if it meant having to deal with you falling off the wagon when the pressures of your job get to be too much."

"I'm not an alcoholic, Grace—but sometimes when the nightmares won't leave, I drink too much."

"I'm glad you told me."

"I am too—and maybe your idea will work. Are you really willing to hang in there with me?"

"I wouldn't have come back if I wasn't."

He rested his chin on the top of her head again and sighed. "I didn't think I was ready to talk to anyone about the reasons I left New York, but things changed after you left me."

"Hey," she said, pushing against his chest until he loosened his hold on her. "Let's get that one point clear: I didn't leave you—you gave me the boot."

He pulled her back against him. "After I made the

biggest mistake of my life and told you to leave, I realized how badly I needed you to stay. If it wasn't for Bear and the guys, and Jack and your father, I might have ended up in the ER with alcohol poisoning."

She knew it cost him to admit it, so she didn't say anything, but she did put her arms around his waist and squeeze him.

"Grace." He paused. "I need to tell you the rest of it—why I left New York. It was more than just the fire."

For the next half hour, he took her through his life in Brooklyn and his work at the firehouse. That he loved every minute came through clearly. The heart-wrenching details of the last fire he fought in the Projects had tears welling up in her eyes for a second time that morning.

He was beyond brave—that he'd carried such an incredible burden for so long without telling anyone was a testament to how strong a person he was. The fact that his ex dumped him when he needed her support most was criminal—but then, fate couldn't have intervened and sent Patrick to Ohio. "Your mom and sisters must pray for you every day."

He shrugged. "I guess."

"You're a lot like my father and brothers-in-law. Kate dragged me over to talk to Jack yesterday. She said I was sick on the inside—and I guess I was, sick at heart that I'd lost you." She pressed her lips to his forehead. "Jack told me about his PTSD and one of the main reasons he suffers from it." She thought about how much Jack and Cait loved one another and knew she wanted the same with Patrick. "The guilt was eating him alive."

"I know. He talked about it last night."

"So? Are we OK?" she asked. "Are you ready to let go of the guilt and try things my way?"

He was quiet for so long she wondered if she'd pushed him too far too fast. She eased back so she could cup his face in her hands. Pressing a kiss to the end of his freckled nose, she said, "First, you have to forgive yourself. You put your life at risk when the tank was running out of air but didn't give up until you found that boy."

"But—"

"Patrick, none of us is God and we can't wave a magic wand and make life work out the way we want it to. We have to accept the things we can't change and work like hell to change the things we can."

"Jeez, now you really sound like my ma."

"So when am I going to meet her?"

"I'm flying out for her birthday on Labor Day, but I've got this other idea."

"Oh yeah? What?"

He tugged and she fell back into his arms. "I could transfer to the fire department in Columbus; we'd be able to spend more time together."

She shook her head.

He drew back and stared down at her. "You don't want to spend more time with me?"

She slowly smiled. "I do, but it's a long drive from Apple Grove to Columbus every day, and I was just getting used to the forty-five-minute trip."

He shot to his feet and whirled her around in a circle before pressing his lips to hers. Around and around they went as the kiss deepened and her heart cried with joy. "You talked to your dad? You're moving back to Apple Grove?"

"Yes," she told him. "I realized that my dream wasn't exactly what I'd thought it would be, but I gave it a shot and am ready to go back and do what I do best."

"Oh? And what's that?"

"Drive my sisters crazy while I keep them organized in my own color-coded way."

"I'm crazy about you, Grace Mulcahy."

"You're crazy period!" she teased.

"Not exactly what I was hoping to hear," he grumbled.

"So how about it?" she asked.

He speared his hands into her hair and tilted her head back. When his lips were a breath away from hers, he paused. "How about what?"

Need for this man was making her insane. If he wasn't going to ask her, she'd ask him. "Want to get married and have babies with me?"

He was quiet for so long Grace thought that she'd made a mistake and rushed things.

He lowered his mouth to hers and rasped, "Can we start now?"

Chapter 24

"I'M GLAD YOU DECIDED TO WAIT UNTIL ALL OF THE families could be here," Mrs. Garahan said to Grace, helping her into the lace and tulle confection she'd wear to say her vows.

"Once we started writing down everyone's name, I realized that we needed a spreadsheet to coordinate everyone. Ranchers, firefighters, U.S. Marshals—we realized that it was more than just getting time off from work." Grace stood still while Patrick's mother fastened the row of tiny pearl buttons up her back.

"There. Oh, you look lovely," Patrick's mother told her.

Grace felt like a fairy princess—not that she'd ever aspired to be one, but the dress made her think of all of the times she'd watched Cinderella when she couldn't sleep after her mother died. She'd felt a connection because Cinderella didn't have a mother either, but that's where the similarities ended.

"You're going to knock him dead," Kate said with a grin.

She shook her head at her friend. "Oh my God, please don't say stuff like that today. I can't believe he spent hours in the ER last night and no one called me."

"He was with his brothers and his cousins, dear," Mrs. Garahan reminded her. "If it had been just a cut, either one of his Texas cousins could have stitched him back together—they've had to do that once or twice out on their ranch, the Circle G. Would have saved him the trip. But a break…"

"Besides," Meg said, "you needed your beauty sleep, so you could be extra gorgeous today."

"If I had known he'd fallen—"

"You would have rushed to Newark to the hospital and ended up getting zero sleep, instead of spending the time relaxing with us and having a fabulous spa-treatment party," Peggy reminded her.

"But my place was with Patrick," Grace grumbled. "We're supposed to be there for one another."

Mary walked over, took ahold of Grace's hand, and patted it. "Grace, dear," she said, "life is too short to worry about something that you cannot change."

"If you're going to survive being married to my Patrick," Mrs. Garahan told her, "you'll need to learn to be more flexible."

Meg and Caitlin started to laugh. "Grace, the queen of the spreadsheets? Flexible?"

Grace was starting to get annoyed.

"Now don't tease the bride, girls," Mary warned them. "This is Grace's day, and she just needs to get past this tiny little hiccup. The rest of the day will be just beautiful."

Grace hugged Mary before turning to Caitlin and asking for the hundredth time, "Are you sure he's going to be all right?"

"Doc's never wrong," Cait said. "He reassured me, Patrick will be fine."

"My brood was blessed with strong constitutions and bones," Mrs. Garahan added, stepping back to clap her hands together. "You're going to knock his socks off."

Grace rolled her eyes. "He'll only be wearing one sock today with that cast."

Mary handed Grace her flowers. "A little thing like a broken ankle won't hamper your honeymoon, dear. Now stop worrying."

Meg laughed softly. "Honey B. just texted. Mitch promised the charges would be dropped, so no worries about not being able to leave town for your honeymoon."

Grace sighed. "Tell me again what Patrick and his cousins were doing trespassing on the water tower?"

"I think there was beer and a lot of machismo involved," Kate said as she straightened Grace's veil.

Mrs. Garahan laughed. "Those boys have always been trying to outdo one another every time they get together. The only ones who ever hesitated were Matt and Ben Justiss, their Colorado cousins. Lord were they a handful the last time they all came to Brooklyn to visit."

A knock sounded on the door. "You ready, baby girl?"

"Ready, Pop!"

Joe Mulcahy opened the door and smiled at his youngest. "You're beautiful." He held out his arm for Grace to hold on to. "One look at you, and he'll forget all about his ankle and the hangover."

Grace squeezed her father's arm. "Hangover?"

~~~

Patrick stood beneath swags of honeysuckle, morning glories, and wild roses waiting for his bride. "What if she changes her mind when she finds out about last night?"

His older brother, Tommy, leaned toward him and said, "She already passed the Garahan sticking test. A little thing like a run-in with the law won't change her mind."

Patrick wasn't worried so much about Mitch. Apple

Grove's sheriff had been there for Grace and Kate. Patrick was prepared to let the late-night trip to the sheriff's office—and then the lecture Mitch had delivered on the way to the ER—be forgotten.

His cousin Tyler chuckled and helped Patrick to stand up. "Broken ribs didn't stop me from making love to Emily—you just have to be a little more creative."

Dan snickered. "You mean flexible? Take my advice, and just pretend it doesn't hurt and she'll never know."

Patrick shook his head. "She'll be pissed."

Jack shrugged. "She'll get over it. Grace is more forgiving than Cait—and Cait came around once I bared my soul to her."

Patrick's head began to pound. "Tell me again why I let you guys talk me into rappelling off the water tower?"

"Son, that was the Shiner talking," Dylan told him.

Jesse handed him his crutches. "Glad we shipped a couple cases of the best brew in Texas out here for the bachelor party."

Ben frowned at him. "Why couldn't we just have kept drinking? Who was it that dared him to do it?"

Dylan cleared his throat. "Might have been me. A couple beers go to my head these days. I don't drink as much as I used to."

"Family man," Tyler quipped.

"If our boss gets wind of last night—" Ben began.

"Hell," Matt interrupted, "he'll just add that to the list of infractions. Good thing our stellar performance on the job still outweighs the trouble we get into from time to time."

The pain in Patrick's ankle eased once he leaned on the crutches.

Reverend Smith walked up to the men. "Are you ready?"

One of Patrick's cousins hollered, "Hell yeah!"

Patrick grinned. "Let's do this."

———

Grace smiled as she walked toward the arbor in her backyard and the broad-shouldered man leaning on crutches. If not for that one glitch, it would have been the wedding of her dreams. The sun was bright, and the sky, clear blue. Kate and Peggy had outdone themselves decorating the cake—deep purple icing with pale yellow and lavender pansies swirled from the tiny top layer all the way around to the bottom. Rumor had it that it was a red velvet cake underneath all of that purple.

Mary, with the help of Mrs. Garahan and Grace's sisters, had decorated with yards and yards of tulle and deep purple satin ribbon. Her brothers-in-law and Patrick's cousins had helped her father set up the rows of chairs and tables where the food would be served.

Neither she nor Patrick had been allowed to lift a finger, which, considering his injury last night, was the least they could do.

Miss Trudi and Mrs. Winter were seated next to Mr. Weatherbee. Honey B., Mitch, and their kids were in the row in front of them. Rhonda was videoing the wedding and reception as her gift to the bride and groom. Everyone who mattered in Grace's life was here to share in her day.

Halfway to the arbor, the realization struck that she should have known she was getting in over her head when Patrick's cousins arrived from both coasts, bringing with them the tools of their trade: lassos, spurs, handcuffs, and a fireman's hat with her name on it as a wedding present. What she hadn't counted on was those same men trying to get her fiancé killed last night. The fall from the top of the water tower could have broken his neck.

Seeing Patrick all in one piece—even though he was in a cast and on crutches—eased most of her worry. When her father put her hand in Patrick's, she felt his warm, firm grip and knew she was ready for the wild ride that would be the rest of their lives.

Her father brushed a finger along her cheek and nodded to Patrick. "You take better care of my baby girl than you have yourself," he whispered, frowning down at Patrick's cast. "I still have that contact in the coast guard and a rowboat with your name on it—in the Aleutian Islands."

Patrick's face grayed.

"Pop, what—"

"Man talk, Grace."

Reverend Smith cleared his throat and beamed at the couple before winking at her. "You think you'll stay awake through the ceremony, Grace?"

Her father's rumbling chuckle sounded in harmony with Reverend Smith's before the clergyman drew in a breath and began, "Dearly beloved—"

Grace looked up into the handsome face of the man she was going to love for the rest of her life and repeated the vows they'd written together. "I, Grace Mulcahy, promise to love you, honor you, and keep you on your toes for the rest of your life."

As family, friends, and neighbors chuckled, Patrick repeated his. "I, Patrick Garahan, vow to love you, honor you, and give you those six children we talked about."

While his brothers and cousins burst into laughter, he added, "Or die trying."

"I now pronounce you man and wife. You may kiss—"

The hooting and hollering grew to a crescendo as the groom tossed his crutches to his brothers, dipped his bride, and kissed her.

Gram's Boston Cream Pie

The first time I baked this cake was to impress my then-boyfriend DJ. He loved it so much he hung around to see what I'd bake next. FYI, he's still hanging around our kitchen to see what I'm baking. ~ C.H.

¼ cup butter (or margarine)
1 cup sugar
1 teaspoon pure vanilla extract
2 eggs, well beaten
1¾ cup sifted cake flour
¼ teaspoon salt
2 teaspoons baking powder
½ cup milk

Cream the butter, adding the sugar gradually. Add vanilla and eggs, beat well. Sift the dry ingredients and add to the creamed mixture alternately with the milk, beating after each addition. Line two layer cake pans with wax paper. Pour mixture into the cake pans and bake in a moderate oven at 350 degrees for 30 minutes. When cool, put together with cream filling—recipe follows—top with confectioner's sugar.

Cream or Custard Filling

¾ cup sugar
5 tablespoons flour or 2½ tablespoons cornstarch
¼ teaspoon salt
2 cups scalding milk
2 eggs, well beaten, or 4 egg yolks
1 teaspoon pure vanilla extract

Mix sugar, flour, and salt together in a double boiler, add hot milk gradually, stirring constantly. Cook until mixture thickens. Pour a small amount over the eggs and mix thoroughly. Add to the first mixture and cook for two minutes. Remove from heat and cool. Add vanilla.

Acknowledgments

A special thank you to Sean McGoldrick, firefighter with the FDNY, for taking the time out of his busy schedule to be interviewed. His insight—and promise not to laugh when I asked dozens of questions—helped with the characterization of the hero, Patrick Garahan. Any mistakes or misinterpretations are my own.